WRO

VIRAGO
MODERN CLASSICS
444

Nina Bawden

Born in 1925, Nina Bawden CBE, was one of Britain's most distinguished and best-loved novelists, author of forty-eight books for children and adults. *Carrie's War*, her famous children's book, was based on her childhood evacuation to Wales during the war. Her novel, *Circles of Deceit* was shortlisted for the 1987 Booker Prize. In 2004 she received the Golden Pen Award for a Lifetime's Contribution to Literature. *Dear Austen* (2005) followed the terrible train accident at Potter's Bar in 2002 in which her husband, Austen Kark died and which left Nina Bawden badly injured. In 2010 her 1970 novel *The Birds on the Trees* was shortlisted for the Lost Man Booker Award. She died in 2012 at the age of eighty-seven.

THE WORKS OF NINA BAWDEN

NOVELS

Who Calls the Tune (1953)
The Odd Flamingo (1954)
Change Here for Babylon (1955)
The Solitary Child (1956)
Devil by the Sea (1958)
Just Like a Lady (1960)
In Honour Bound (1961)
Tortoise by Candlelight (1963)
Under the Skin (1964)
A Little Love, A Little Learning (1965)
A Woman of My Age (1967)
The Grain of Truth (1969)
The Birds on the Trees (1970)
Anna Apparent (1972)
George Beneath a Paper Moon (1974)
Afternoon of a Good Woman (1976)
Familiar Passions (1979)
Walking Naked (1981)
The Ice House (1983)
Circles of Deceit (1987)
Family Money (1991)
A Nice Change (1997)
Afternoon of a Good Woman (1998)
Ruffian on the Stair (2001)

CHILDREN'S BOOKS

The Secret Passage (1963)
On the Run (1964)
The White Horse Gang (1966)
The Witch's Daughter (1966)
A Handful of Thieves (1967)
The Runaway Summer (1969)
Squib (1971)
Carrie's War (1973)
The Peppermint Pig (1975)
Rebel on a Rock (1978)
The Robbers (1979)
Kept in the Dark (1982)
The Finding (1985)
Keeping Henry (1988)
The Outside Child (1989)
Humbug (1992)
The Real Plato Jones (1994)
Granny the Pag (1995)

PICTURE BOOKS

Princess Alice (1986)

NON-FICTION

In My Own Time (1995)
Dear Austen (2005)

CIRCLES OF DEICEIT

Nina Bawden

VIRAGO

Published by Virago Press in 1997

Reprinted 1999, 2000, 2006, 2012

First published in Great Britain by Macmillan Ltd in 1987

'Musée des Beaux Arts' is reprinted by kind permission of Faber and Faber Ltd from *The Collected Poems* by W. H. Auden

A CIP catalogue record for this book is available from the British Library.

ISBN 978-1-84408-370-1

Typeset in Goudy by M Rules
Printed and bound in Great Britain by
Clays Ltd, St Ives plc

Papers used by Virago are from well-managed forests and other responsible sources.

MIX
Paper from responsible sources
FSC® C104740

Virago Press
An imprint of
Little, Brown Book Group
100 Victoria Embankment
London EC4Y 0DY

An Hachette UK Company
www.hachette.co.uk

www.virago.co.uk

for Cathy, Robert, Terry and Perdita

and with grateful thanks to Tom Espley,
for his patient instruction and painterly advice

CARTOON

About suffering they were never wrong,
The Old Masters: how well they understood
Its human position; how it takes place
While someone else is eating or opening a window or just walking
dully along;
How, when the aged are reverently, passionately waiting
For the miraculous birth, there always must be
Children who did not specially want it to happen, skating
On a pond at the edge of a wood:
They never forgot
That even the dreadful martyrdom must run its course
Anyhow in a corner, some untidy spot
Where the dogs go on with their doggy life and the torturer's horse
Scratches its innocent behind on a tree.

In Brueghel's Icarus, *for instance: how everything turns away*
Quite leisurely from the disaster; the ploughman may
Have heard the splash, the forsaken cry,
But for him it was not an important failure; the sun shone
As it had to on the white legs disappearing into the green
Water; and the expensive delicate ship that must have seen
Something amazing, a boy falling out of the sky,
Had somewhere to get to and sailed calmly on.

'Musée des Beaux Arts' by W.H. Auden

The key is the torturer's horse; the apparent irrelevance to what is, in fact, the main theme. I think this is the point of the poem but I cannot be certain. I distrust poetry. It has always seemed to me the most deceitful art, full of attention-seeking tricks, like a child showing off. *Look at me, how clever, bet you can't guess what I mean.* But I like this particular poem.

Clio used to read poetry to me. She read from Auden and Yeats and other, more modern, poets, sitting in the corner of my work room (I dislike the alien romanticism of *studio*), long, straight hair, glossy as butter, falling forward over her shining, earnest, bespectacled face, long, flexible legs twisted around the sturdier legs of the stool. She was not trying to open my philistine mind to the wonders of literature. She was hoping that the dead passion of other men's words would revive my love for her. And, more slyly, using them as a means of reproaching me. *About suffering they were never wrong, The Old Masters*! It was *her* suffering she meant me to listen to!

There was a brief period when she could have read out a laundry list and I would have listened with pleasure to her soft, slightly nasal voice, touched by the knowledge that its sexy huskiness arose from a permanent catarrhal condition. Later, it drove me mad. As she read aloud to me all I could think of was the dripping mucus from her infected sinuses, the used balls of Kleenex in the waste-paper basket.

My poor Clio! At the time of these readings I was still deeply ashamed of the pain I had caused her. If only she had not demanded what I could no longer deliver, we might have settled for a comfortable existence together, an agreeable friendship. I understood the sense of insult she felt, the loss of self-esteem, the unresolved anger, but all these things (as to mitigate my offence, ease my guilt, I once foolishly tried to explain to her) arose from a form of self-regarding vanity. If she truly loved me, as she maintained, she would swallow her pride and accept what I was still able and happy to offer; my concern, my affection, my genuine sorrow that I could not be all that she wanted. (What claptrap, I think now. What codswallop! Some people stammer under stress. I become pompous.)

Looked at one way, it could be said that Clio's suffering is as irrelevant to this story as the torturer's horse in the picture. Certainly neither are central to the main drama. And yet, looked at differently, nothing could have happened without them. Both are the products of vanity.

To explain. I am a painter. I paint portraits and townscapes – views of the inner city, of shabby streets, small, dusty parks, crumbling tenements. That is my art, my reason for living. Unhappily, it is not productive in the crude sense. In spite of kindly reviews of my occasional exhibitions and the loyal response of old friends who attend the private views, drink the mock champagne and buy the smaller paintings, my work only brings in a pittance. The trade that I live by, that pays the rates and the mortgage, the bill for Clio's athletic activities, her Health Club, her yoga classes; that sends Helen (my first wife, my darling) a small monthly sum that she neither wants nor needs but is kind enough to accept to satisfy my pride, and my mother the necessary allowance to keep her in reasonable comfort in her small house in Bow, is that of a copyist.

I am (I must make this clear) an honest craftsman; not a cheat, not a forger. I am no Tom Keating, ageing a picture with a spoonful of Nescafé, spraying on fly specks with a mixture of asphalt and turpentine, pretending to have come upon an unknown Old Master in a junk shop or attic. I paint copies of famous paintings, sometimes for private persons or institutions, but mostly for the directors of companies who want an impressive decoration to hang in their board rooms. Deception of an innocent kind is their intention; asked if the picture is genuine, few of them, I imagine, would lie. Nor would they be wise to. Whether they know it or not (and in some cases I am sure that they do know, collaborating with me in a further, minor deception out of pleasure in their treasured British sense of humour) my copies are never exact.

That is where vanity comes in. One wants to leave one's mark on the world. (Clio wants to leave her mark too, I suppose, which is why she has tried to elevate her girl's romantic disappointment in a middle-aged husband to the level of tragedy.) Like many another craftsman, like an apprentice stone cutter carving a gargoyle on a cathedral, I want to make my individual contribution to the grand design. I copy the painting with all the skill at my disposal, all the tricks; squaring up, measuring with calipers, using photographs, a projector, a light box for transparencies to get as near as I can to the true colour. I try to match the pigments used by the artist, grinding my own Naples yellow, or buying it in a tube from Budapest where it is still legal to sell it ready made with lead and antimony. But instead of adding my signature, I change some insignificant feature. I alter the expression of a man in a crowd, add a tiny animal face in a dim corner, a mouse or a weasel, replace the diamond on a woman's hand with a ruby, paint a watch on a wrist in an eighteenth-century portrait. Which is why that poem about the torturer's horse has an appeal for me that is unconnected with its literary value. I think that I might change it to a mule or a donkey. How many casual observers would notice? Or care if they did? Most people chortle to see experts confounded.

All art, of course, is full of deception. Nature, too, and human behaviour, but more of that later. Remember the story of Zeuxis? No? Then I'll tell you. (Bear with me. The tale will develop, I hope, when I can find my way into it, but I am only a painter, unused to the art of narrative flow.)

This Zeuxis lived in Athens in the fourth century BC. He painted a picture of grapes with such skill that sparrows flew in and tried to peck at the fruit. Amused, Zeuxis invited another painter to witness a repeat performance. A rival, whose name was Parrhasius. He affected to be unimpressed. To cheat sparrows was nothing extraordinary. 'Bird-brained' was his buzz word. The birth of a cliché?

Parrhasius went home and brooded. His turn to ask his friend Zeuxis to inspect a painting. It was concealed behind a curtain. Zeuxis tried to unveil it and failed; the draperies had been painted. Zeuxis, who was either a fool, or a very nice man, or simply somewhat short-sighted, was generous with praise. 'I was only able to deceive a few sparrows, but you have deceived me, a man and an artist.'

Like the Auden poem, this hoary old legend has its quirky, private significance. Ever since I first heard it, at school, it has made me think of my father.

I cannot remember him. I have no idea what he looks like. No photographs. Nothing. My mother left him before my fourth birthday. She rarely spoke of him and when she did it was always as 'your father', as if his connection with me were some kind of biological accident that had nothing to do with her. All I know is this story that her sister, my Aunt Maud, has told me.

He met my mother in 1942, at a dance hall in London. He was a captain in the Free French Forces, she was a cockney from Bow, a skinny, pretty, lively girl, working in a munitions' factory. Her parents ran a public house called The Snared Bird.

My father had a little English but not enough (according to Maud) to make the nice judgements about accent that English people use as naturally as they breathe to place each other socially, nor to discover that my mother, who had left school at fourteen, had no intellectual resources or conversation. 'Maisie was bright enough, it was just that she never needed to bother,' Maud said. 'She was what they used to call in those days a Glamour Puss. Only had to walk into the Palais on a Saturday night to have all the men after her.'

There is no evidence to support this typically Maudish suggestion that if my father had understood that my mother was 'common' – I put quotes round the word because it isn't one that even Maud would use now, in the eighties – he wouldn't have married her. My mother took him home to meet her family, they were married in Bow parish church and held the reception at the Snared Bird. My grandparents were merry old souls, given to much lifting of the elbow, immoderate laughter, and, in my grandfather's case, to the public removal of ill-fitting dentures when he wished to masticate comfortably. (After the war, when he could have had better teeth provided free by the National Health Service, he refused on the grounds that he was a life-long Conservative voter and didn't intend to encourage the profligate ways of the new Labour Government.) A fine, sturdy man, salt of the earth, but one evening spent in his company and my father could have had no illusions about what sort of people he was marrying into. Uneducated, ungentrified, and cheerfully content with their station.

Except for Aunt Maud, of course. Maud the clever one, the natural mimic, is a prime example of upward mobility. The war that had sent my mother into the munitions' factory had evacuated my thirteen-year-old aunt from her home in the East End, billeted her on a pair of intelligent spinsters (one a history teacher, the other a headmistress) who refined her vowels and her manners and set her ambitious feet on the educational ladder; a good country grammar school, a women's college at Oxford. But my father's French ear would hardly have caught Maud's fledgling attempts at a 'superior' accent. At the time of the marriage she was still a schoolgirl; a plain, younger sister.

My father had what Maud would call 'background'. His father had been a Rear-Admiral, hydrographer to the French Navy. There was a house in Paris, estates in the country. By the time the war was over the Rear-Admiral was dead, and all that was left of the rural estates was a small vineyard in Provence. It had always produced a good wine but it was not a great name, not a château, and when my father returned in 1945 it was clear that the financial return was hardly enough to support my mother and me, his old mother, a widowed aunt, and a couple of unmarried sisters who, in the French manner, expected to be provided with dowries.

My father shouldered his responsibilities. (I have a fellow feeling with him there.) He got a bank loan, bought up the harvest of a larger but inferior vineyard and sent, to a wide selection of hotels and restaurants, two bottles of wine, one his own excellent vintage, the other rough peasant stuff, thin and vinegary. A covering letter invited the recipients to open one bottle and taste it. If they wished to place an order (at an exceptionally low price) they must pay in advance; if they preferred to wait for delivery the cost would be trebled. This was an unrepeatable offer, a loss on my father's part, his only concern the establishment of a name and a reputation for what was as yet an unrecognised Grand Vin Du Pays. He suggested that in their own interests his customers should keep the second bottle unopened as a check of quality against the consignment which would be sent as soon as he received payment.

Ingenious. Foolproof in its simplicity. About half of those who sampled the good wine sent their cheques with their order and when it arrived found it to be the same undrinkable filth as the bottle they had kept in reserve. No redress. The French police did their best to prosecute my father for what was to them a fearsomely criminal act but could find no one who had kept the good bottle. Everyone who had opened the bad bottle first had thrown the other away in disgust without tasting it. 'I expect they got him for something else in the end,' Maudie said, rather regretfully. In spite of her irreproachable respectability – political biographer, lecturer, magistrate and attentive member of a vast number of worthy committees and quangos and Government Think Tanks – my good aunt has a sentimental liking for rogues.

My mother, who had married one, obviously felt differently. When she understood what my father had done, she packed up and left him – and perhaps was grateful for the excuse. Forty years ago, and she has not been out of England since. 'No thank you, dear, I wouldn't want to go anywhere I can't speak the language,' she says, whenever I offer to take her, or send her, abroad on a holiday. Once, when I persisted, tried to persuade her, she flared up in a rare, panicky, outburst of temper. 'Might as well be deaf and dumb if you can't speak or be spoken to. Or an idiot to be sniggered at.'

'Were the family very unpleasant to her?' I asked Maud. 'Why on earth didn't she try to learn French?'

'Provincial France must have seemed like the back of beyond to her, a girl who'd never been out of London, so why should she take the trouble? And Maisie has always been intellectually lazy. But you know what the French are like, I daresay they were pretty unwelcoming. Not that she said much, she wouldn't. But she refused to ask for a penny from your father, that shows you how she felt.' Maud rolled her navy blue eyes – her most striking feature – and gave a snort of dismay. 'If it wasn't for me, you'd have been brought up above the pub.'

I could imagine worse fates. I had always been happy to visit my grandparents; my jolly little grandfather, five foot four and round as a ball, my tall grandmother, skeleton thin, fierce-eyed as an eagle, known to the regulars of the Snared Bird as Razor Annie – no rough drunks in her bar – but, all the same, quick with a joke, gales of surprisingly girlish, high-pitched, cackling laughter. They were indulgent to me; I liked the warm, yeasty smell of the pub; was excited above all by the life of the streets, the crowded markets, the bustle, the colour, the faces of the people, nobbly, wise, scarred and tuckered by life. More good faces in the East End, I told Maud, than anywhere else you can think of.

But Maud was conscious of her own narrow escape. If it hadn't been for Hitler, she'd have been stuck there. Awful thought to contemplate, all that suffering, so that she could rise up in the world, but dishonest not to admit it. 'Mind you, I'm not saying that I wouldn't have been a good barmaid, just that I was lucky to be given the chance not to be!'

For my mother, uneducated, divorced, and landed with me, the choices were fewer. Maud, in her first job, teaching history at London University, had just finished her first book. She plonked down the publisher's advance of five hundred pounds, whipped round the family, parents, uncles and aunts, bullied a bank manager, and produced enough to buy and furnish a boarding house in Southend for my mother to manage. Not much of a step up from a pub it might seem from the grander heights of society, but for Maud, only twenty-three, it was an achievement. A nice little business, independence for sister Maisie, good fresh air for the boy.

We took lodgers; a couple of single men as permanent residents and, in the summer, families on their annual jaunt to the seaside. (This was before the package deal boom, before working-class people went abroad for their holidays.) It must have been a grind for my mother sometimes but she never complained and she never seemed busy to me; I remember long, golden days on the shore, picking up pebbles of different colours and sizes, eating gritty sandwiches in the shelter of a breakwater, poking my finger into the iridescent, velvety slime on the rotting piles, watching the sun flash gold and silver spears into the rucked, rolling sea. I won't run on about my childhood as I have noticed some novelists do, meandering idly about in the past instead of getting on with the present, except to say that it seemed to me then that the whole world had been arranged for my comfort and pleasure. I cannot remember any unhappiness; I never heard a voice raised in anger. I loved my mother, I knew she was pretty, I saw the men watching her, but I was only proud, never jealous. To say that I was close to her would be an understatement. She was an extension of myself; I could not imagine that she had any existence apart from me.

I was, of course, deceived.

'He's not academic.' That was Aunt Maud, snorting her disappointment over a school report. But she was not a woman to accept defeat. Gathering up my drawings of pebbles, flowers, insects (all the small things that delighted me) she marched me off for an interview at a private boarding school that had, she said, a good art department. Neither my mother nor I protested. Aunt Maud was the man in our family.

If the art lessons did me no harm (the teacher was a sensible man who taught us a few art-school dodges but mostly encouraged us to look around and use our own eyes) that isn't true of the main thing I learned there which was a cheap and vulgar snobbery. I began to recognise that my mother spoke 'badly', that running a boarding house was a rather low way of earning a living, and that there was something pretty peculiar in not having a father. The only thing to be said for me is that I suffered these painful discoveries silently; glowering and rolling my eyes, I daresay, whenever my mother opened her mouth at school occasions, but that was the conventional response to the presence of parents and, so, unremarkable.

There came a time when I feared my mother remarked it, however. She was shy with me, apparently nervous, and I was miserably convinced that she had sensed my disloyalty. When, at the end of my fourth term, she produced the Galloping Major, my overwhelming feeling was one of relief. She had let me down, not I her! To get married behind a son's back was a fearful offence in a mother. Any sensitive boy would be emotionally crippled! Grave with hidden suffering, heavy with virtue, I said I was glad she would no longer be lonely without me and hoped she'd be happy.

I basked in the credit I got from this blatant hypocrisy. My mother was tearfully grateful and Eric Major took me aside, thanked me for 'taking it well' and gave me ten pounds.

He was a large, puce-faced, sweaty man with a crown of thin, curly hair and an affable manner. He wasn't an army man, nor as dashing as the nickname I gave him when I went back to school. The 'galloping' prefix referred to his motor car, a pre-war Delage saloon with a beautiful, long, gleaming body and a Cotal electric gear box that 'only a superb mathematician', so I told my friends, would be able to put right when it went wrong.

The car made him an immediately acceptable surrogate father. He drove me to and from school, allowed me to ask other boys out for what he called a 'spin', lunched us at the best local hotel, was generous with money. He had a used-car business that was successful enough to make my life (as well as my mother's) more comfortable. No more lodgers, no more summer visitors. By the time I returned for the next holidays the house had been re-decorated, rearranged to be suddenly spacious; a large room on the second floor that had once held five beds (for a couple with children) had been made ready for me; the old dining room on the right of the hall furnished as a sitting room for my mother.

'Eric says it's time I had a chance to put my feet up,' she said, with a sly wink at me and a bit of a giggle, but she obviously enjoyed his solicitude, the fuss that he made of her, settling her in a chair with cushions at her back, closing windows in case she should feel a draught on her shoulders. 'As if Maisie were an invalid,' Aunt Maud grumbled as we went for a walk on Easter Sunday. 'Making a fool of her. Do you like him?'

I said that I liked him very much. I thought that Aunt Maud was jealous. Eric had deprived her of her masculine role as protector. At lunch, my mother had teased her: *Eric says, Eric thinks, I must ask Eric*. 'Does Maisie love him, do you think?' Aunt Maud asked, in a different, almost beseeching tone, and I saw the blood rise in her already high-coloured face, her navy eyes darken. Love, romantic love, was a reverent matter to Maud. Though this seemed absurdly embarrassing to me in a woman her age (I was fourteen, Maud in her thirties) I should have made some sensibly anodyne answer. But at that (precise) moment, walking in the back streets of Southend, I was too seized with the discovery that colours were brighter this lowering spring day than under bright sunlight, that a clump of daffodils glowed with an almost shocking brilliance and that the pale trunk of the tree they were planted around had suddenly become incandescent, appearing to float in the air, to concern myself with love and its related, complex, adult emotions. I said, boorishly, boyishly, 'I don't know, it depends what you mean,' and she sighed. She said, 'Oh, I do hope so. It would be dreadful to think she'd made use of him.'

A remark that had echoes. I don't know if my mother loved Eric or was merely grateful for his doting affection, his dependable, husbandly presence that enabled her to play the married woman in front of her spinster sister. When he died of a cerebral haemorrhage three years after their marriage she wept, though not inconsolably. The first night of her widowhood she drank several glasses of Bristol Cream sherry, her favourite tipple, and told me that before he died Eric had taken out an insurance that would provide an annuity for her of eight hundred pounds a year. With her widow's pension, that was a reasonable sum in those days. She said, 'Poor Eric, he was so kind to me,' and not understanding how high a value she might place on kindness, on being cared for, and remembering what Aunt Maud had said, I was shocked by what seemed a casual dismissal. I said angrily, 'He was a good provider, if that's what you mean, why don't you have it carved on his tombstone?' And felt guilty at once, because that was really all he had been to *me*, and then a kind of shamed awe. Eric Major had come into my life and gone out of it and left nothing of himself behind.

My mother looked, simply, surprised. I said I was sorry. She said, 'I know the money isn't important, dear. I could always let rooms again. I'm not frightened of work, you know that.' She looked into her glass, frowning a little, and then suddenly smiled. 'I can't help being a tiny bit pleased, all the same. Fancy me with a *private income*! It's a bit of a poke in the eye for Maud, isn't it?'

And she laughed like a mischievous girl.

*

I daresay I was shocked again. If so, I was wrong to be. My mother is innocent, honest, straightforward. (In most matters, that is, not in all, who could be?) Although the fact that she still speaks with a sharp, cockney twang is in part an act of defiance against what she calls 'Maud's airs and graces', it is also a simple dislike of pretence. *I am what I am*, she is saying when she drops her aitches, *take it or leave it*. Nowadays, her lack of affectation is fashionable. It delights me to see her at my exhibitions, pretty, lined, rosy face beaming, courted by everyone; my splendid old Ma in awful, elaborate hats that she buys (I suspect to annoy sister Maud) at charity shops, who knows what she likes and says, within limits of an innate, natural courtesy, what she thinks. It is Aunt Maud with her received pronunciation, matching handbag and gloves and general ladylike air, who is out of date, quaintly mannered.

You could write, around my Aunt Maud and my mother, a crisp little monograph on the British class system. But if I want to write a novel I suppose I must resist that sort of didactic digression and learn to put things in some sort of order; a tidy sequence of events, a strong plot. The trouble is that this approach strikes me as a plodding business, lacking the raucous, rumbustious confusion of life. My instinct is to present everything happening at once, simultaneously, separate but related, as in a painting. In my mind's eye I see a number of circles, or watery bubbles, changing shape, shifting in and out of focus, wavering from light to dark, cloudy to clear, connecting, contiguous, but each with its own independent and busy life, private passions and secrets. I am there, dimly seen, somewhere in the picture; a workaday painter, bothered by bills and artistic conscience in about equal measure, physically short and rotund like my merry, dead grandfather, but unlike him (I hope for his sake) susceptible to, bullied and badgered by women.

My women. Currently first but sequentially last, Clio; my sulky child bride, teenage mother, whose bastard boy holds us together, a bond she is too young to take seriously and I am too old to ignore, whom I have treated abominably and deserve to be punished by, if in not quite the exemplary fashion she has in store for me, who reads (or likes to be seen reading) poetry, and who runs for miles every evening, an exercise that she claims 'keeps her in tune with her body'. She runs to escape, I imagine, but I would think that, wouldn't I? Portly, middle-aged, lazy, creaking here and there at the joints, I treat my body like a dear old friend, respectfully, tenderly. I wince for Clio's arches, her ankles, her knee, thigh and pelvic bones, her small, bouncing breasts, as she runs, pale hair flying, through the dusky park, through the dark city.

My ex-wife; Helen, in her surgery, bending over the open mouth of a handsome male patient, green eyes intent on her task, lower lip caught between her own uneven but excellent teeth, the slight flush on her stretched, shapely neck touchingly exposed to the man in the chair as it was exposed to me in a like circumstance, years ago, our first meeting. Stirred by this memory, my ludicrous jealousy that can turn drilling a cavity in a back molar into an erotic activity, makes me wonder if this patient is already in love with her. Already her lover.

Maisie, my mother; innocently happy in Bow, busy with God to whom she turned after Eric died (rather as she might have turned to a kindly third husband), with her weekly visits to the public library for a fresh supply of 'nice' novels, and with her voluntary work for old people which now sadly includes regular visits to Razor Annie in a private home for the senile. Part of the cost of this (I am irritated by novels in which who pays for what is left unexplained) is borne by the Department of Social Security, the rest by Maud and me. Maud would be happy to carry this burden alone, reckoning (rightly) that I have more than enough on my plate, but my mother's pride makes this impossible. I must 'pay her share' for her mother, since she is unable to. 'I'd rather starve than take a penny from Maud,' she says, apparently forgetting a time when she took, or was given, much more than that. But her pride keeps her perky. When Maud comes to take her out, driving from Chelsea in her silver Porsche, her sporty pleasure, my mother dresses up, puts on her most annoying, most flamboyant hat.

My aunt; Maud in her Chelsea house, Maud in her silver Porsche, Maud the (almost) public figure, the literary busy body with a gruff manner and a shy, girlish heart, who looks as she grows older more and more like a barmaid; broad, florid face surrounded by hair stiff as hay sprayed with varnish, thickening, corseted body, stalky legs, skirts always too short. (A barmaid caught in a time warp, that is; the girls behind the bar in my local pub wear tight jeans and frilly Victorian blouses.) My Aunt Maud whom I laugh at and boast about, who is generous and clever and silly, who is a sucker for titles and what she calls 'old families', and whose admirable eagerness to advance my career has got me into my present trouble.

There are many other characters on this mental canvas. Friends and relations and friends of relations. My ex-brother-in-law; Henry, the civil servant, oozing his way along the corridors of power, doctoring the advice that he gives his Minister, heart (charitably assuming that he has one) divided between his rich, jolly wife who runs a market garden in Norfolk, and his charming young mistress, who is Clio's close friend and the daughter of *my* old friend George, the art dealer. And, of course, supporting the leading actors there is a huge cast playing minor, even unseen, but not insignificant roles; daily helps and child minders; dustmen and window cleaners and postmen; my West Indian neighbours; the man with the barking dog down the street; the punk squatters in the house opposite whose lengthy, painstaking preparations for appearing in public (the shaving, the curling tongs, the application of hair gel) I can observe from my window.

And so on. Ad infinitum. A scene from one of the Brueghels.

What comes to mind, as I write, is a scene of men working in fields. There is a distant view of a harbour. In the corner, a faint splash. *The Fall Of Icarus* by Pieter Brueghel the Elder.

MAUD

Once, in the days of unsigned reviews in the *Times Literary Supplement*, an unkind piece dismissed my Aunt Maud as 'the most boring biographer since Habakkuk'. Rage, always her response to pain, mottled her forehead. 'Underhand, anonymous *creep*,' she bawled. 'Some jealous hack,' I suggested, to soothe her, and her expression grew distant. 'Hack isn't an absolute term of abuse, in my view. If he'd called me a competent hack, I wouldn't have minded.'

Maybe true, maybe not. If Maud nursed grander ambitions, she would never say so; a combination of pride and humility makes her too vulnerable. And her talent for industry has not served her badly. Beavering away with scissors and paste she has become, in her own field, a bit of a monument. Nowadays most reviews are respectful; her fat books are usually Book Club Selections, always go into paperback, and are prominently displayed as meaty travel companions at airports. She works at her success; travelling, lecturing, appearing on radio and television book programmes; known in her trade (to use an old theatrical term) as a Reliable; someone who will not be offended by being called upon at the last moment and can be trusted to give a decent performance.

There are other sides to her, naturally. She likes good food, malt whisky, classical music (chiefly Beethoven, played very loud) and fast cars. (She bought her first, a second-hand MG from Eric Major, who acknowledged their shared interest when he died by leaving her his Delage.) More unexpectedly, she shares an allotment on the south side of the river with a retired postman called Prime. I called in one day after I had been to the Tate, to the Stubbs exhibition, and found an elderly man with a pleasant, baggy face, having tea in her kitchen. 'Mr Prime has brought me some beautiful runner beans,' she said, *all* she said then, explaining later, when he had finished his tea and departed, about the allotment to which she drove her Porsche twice a week to sow, weed and harvest. 'No room for vegetables in my little garden, and a bit of digging keeps the arthritis at bay. Before he retired, Mr Prime used to deliver my mail; he's got more land than he wants, now his children are grown, and he's been a good friend to me.'

Surprising, I thought, that I had not heard about him before. On the other hand, Maud is a name dropper and Mr Prime, presumably, was not a name worth the dropping. If he had been anyone of significance she would not have titled him 'Mr'. She would have used his Christian name, flattered by the intimacy this implied. Michael, or Ted, or Iris, or Norman. Occasionally this innocent boastfulness is puzzling but I can usually work it out, given the context. Literature, or politics.

'Ned' is Lord Orwell. This is not his real name for reasons which will become apparent, just the most unlikely one for a peer that I can think of. As the Hon Edward Orwell, he married one of Maud's Oxford friends, her dearest friend, Jenny, with whom she set up house for a while when they were both in their twenties, both teaching in London. As I remember her from school holiday visits (arranged by Maud as a strenuously educational programme of art galleries and museums) Jenny was a sweet-faced, milk-and-roses blonde in long, swirling skirts and romantic lace blouses whose natural languor (or laziness) Maud encouraged, pandered to, doing the cooking, the cleaning and shopping, insisting that Jenny should 'put her feet up' before she went out in the evening, while Maud ironed her dress for her, ran her bath; making, in fact, the same kind of solicitous fuss that Eric, several years later, was to make of my mother. *As if Maisie were an invalid*, Maud had said to me then. And *It would be dreadful to think she'd made use of him*.

Had she been remembering Jenny? Seeing in Eric's foolish devotion a parallel with her own loving folly? Regretting it, feeling that *she* had been used? No, of course not – or not consciously. If Maud had been hurt at the time she would have stamped on her pain, locked it away out of sight. When Jenny married, Maud would have thought only of her happiness, rejoiced for her, told herself that she was lucky now to have two friends instead of one. And in the way that this kind of simple virtue is sometimes rewarded, so it turned out to be.

There were interruptions to friendship, shifts and changes. For several years Maud was a frequent visitor to the large, draughty house in north Norfolk that had been built by Ned's grandfather, the art collector, with the profits from the family brewery. Although Maud was impressed by its aristocratic connection, its mock Palladian grandeur, she found it 'cold hell' in the winter and only endured its unheated rigour to comfort Jenny who was trying, and failing, to have a baby. After she had miscarried for the fourth time, in the eighth month of her pregnancy, Ned took her to Greece for the summer. Maud had expected them back in early November. When she telephoned at the end of October to check the date with the housekeeper, she was surprised to find that they had been at home for a fortnight already. Ned explained that Jenny had been meaning to ring her, but that she was still very low in her spirits and easily tired. Her doctor had said that she needed a period of rest before 'facing too many people'.

Naturally, Maud would have none of that nonsense! She knew exactly how Jenny was suffering. She had given up her teaching career to marry Ned, have a family; now it was obvious she would never bear a live child she must feel a terrible failure. Ned had probably made things worse by taking her travelling; as if he thought she needed to hide her shame from the world! To make her 'rest' now, cut her off from other people, was not to protect her; it might even deepen her sense of inadequacy. And she, Maud, was not 'people'! She was Jenny's *friend*, who was suffering *with* her and *for* her.

'Not too much, I trust,' Ned said bracingly. And then, 'I hope you won't tell Jenny you think she's inadequate.'

He laughed, to take the sting out of this. But why say it if he didn't mean it? So cruel, so unnecessary! Before Maud could speak her indignant mind he fetched Jenny. And, of course, Maud had been right. The poor darling was longing to see her! 'Dear Ned' had been 'fussing like an old mother hen'. He had expected miracles from their lovely, long holiday so that he was a bit disappointed that she was still a bit under the weather. Not that Jenny was ill, she just felt a bit *dull*, not very good company . . .

As if Maud minded that! Surely Jenny didn't think she needed amusing? If Jenny wanted to talk, fine; if not, Maud would sit quiet as a mouse. She didn't need fancy meals, either. If Jenny did, she would cook for her. Otherwise a hunk of bread and cheese and an apple was all that she wanted. 'Darling Maud, I think we can manage to feed you,' Jenny said, sounding rather faint and faraway suddenly.

Preparing for a peaceful weekend, Maud piled books into the back of Eric Major's Delage – still on the road, but not for very much longer. It broke down twice on the way up to Norfolk and when Maud arrived, five hours late, Jenny was on the steps of the house, watching for her. She ran to Maud, hugging her fiercely. 'I thought something dreadful had happened. Why didn't you ring? I was *terrified*.'

She was shaking. She felt very frail in Maud's arms. Disengaging herself a little self-consciously (she rarely embraced other women in case, being unmarried, she should be suspected of lesbian tendencies) Maud saw that Jenny's face, brown from months of Greek sun, was lined with anxiety.

Maud said, 'Oh, my dear duck, I'm sorry. Abysmally thoughtless. I had trouble with Alice. That doesn't excuse me.'

'Alice?' Jenny wrinkled her forehead. Too much sun, Maud thought. It's made her look older.

'My poor old car,' she explained, surprised that Jenny should have forgotten. 'She's had her chips, I'm afraid. Just about ready for the great *garagiste* in the sky. It's the welded body. Alice has got metal fatigue, like an aeroplane.'

Jenny squeezed her hand. 'Poor Alice. I'm sorry to have been so silly. I get in such a stupid fuss nowadays. If Ned is just ten minutes late coming home, I start to imagine disaster. He gets quite cross with me.'

'He ought to know better,' Maud said. 'He knows what you've been through. Not that any man can ever understand, really, what it means to a woman, losing a baby, how deeply it's bound to affect you.'

'It was Ned's baby too,' Jenny said. 'And it's worse for him in a way. Doubly painful. He minds about the baby and he minds about me.' She looked at Maud gravely. 'So don't be hard on him, will you?'

Maud felt hurt, but she laughed. 'I'm not such a bull in a china shop, am I?'

Jenny blushed, and smiled. 'Oh, Maud, it is *lovely* to see you, I've missed you so much.'

'A lot to catch up on,' Maud said. 'I want to hear all about Greece; we'll have a good, long, cosy talk as soon as I've cleaned myself up a bit.'

She was a little taken aback to find that other people had been invited for dinner that evening. 'We thought it would be more fun for you than just Ned and me,' Jenny said. Maud protested that she would have been perfectly happy to spend a quiet evening, but she was touched and pleased, all the same. It was true, she *did* like a party, even if, when it came to it, the other guests were not her sort, really; nor, she would have thought, calling to mind other occasions chez Orwell, Ned and Jenny's sort, either. No one even mildly bookish or interested in the arts; just a couple of rich local farmers with plain, horsey wives, and a manager from the brewery who said to Maud, 'Dear Lord, if old Ned had warned me I was going to meet a real writer, I'd have done a bit of homework this last week, got my secretary to look you up in the library.'

He roared with delight at this neatly turned variant of a joke Maud was used to; a cheerful, confident, funny man, good looking in a healthy middle-aged way that produced in Maud an agreeable sexual flutter. She was sorry, when they went into dinner, to find herself seated between the two farmers who talked across her a lot of the time, boasting about the number of birds they had bagged in the first shoot of the season. On the other hand she was glad to hear Jenny's light, happy laugh from the other end of the table; coaxed by the brewery manager, she became her old, sweet, smiling self for most of the evening, her anxious look only returning when the guests had gone and Maud was helping her and Ned stack the dishwasher.

In the clinical light of the kitchen, Maud was shocked to see that in spite of her tan she looked ill; her lovely face drawn, her pretty arms scrawny. 'You look thin, my duck,' she said as she kissed her good night. She would have said more, enquired if Jenny had had any tummy trouble in Greece, always her weak spot when she and Maud had travelled abroad together before Jenny's marriage, but the frowning look on Ned's face somehow stopped her.

Later, brushing her strong, wiry hair before bed, seeing her own ugly mug in the mirror, weary and pouchy, she decided that the evening had been a strain on them all. Ungrateful of her to admit it, perhaps, since it had been arranged for her pleasure, and presumably these dreary folk had been the only ones available for a last-minute party. But no denying the fact that, apart from the jolly man, they had all been heavy going; both farmers bone-headed backwoods Tories – one of them, when the conversation turned to the recent street riots in Birmingham, seriously prophesying the collapse of society and talking about 'arming his beaters'. And their wives, though less objectionable politically, had no wider interest than the domestic; deep freezes and microwave ovens were the liveliest topics they touched on. Well, that was the only thing about country living that Jenny had ever complained about. Although there were soul mates around, there were rather too many bores, worthy neighbours that Ned felt they must invite sometimes; taking on, now that his parents had retreated from the main house to warmer and more comfortable quarters in the converted old stable block, the role of local lord of the manor.

It wasn't until she was in bed, tentatively extending her

cold feet into even chillier regions, and wishing she had thought to ask for a hot-water bottle, that it struck her that this evening had in fact been one of those duty occasions. How stupid she'd been! Even if she hadn't caught on when the brewery man made his double-edged little joke about 'doing his homework' she should have known that duty guests were not the kind to be asked at short notice. It was she, Maud, who had forced herself on the company, who was the odd one out, the unexpected intruder. Unwelcome, too; since the others had been invited already, it was *she* Ned had meant when he had said that Jenny wasn't ready yet to 'face' people. He feared that she might make Jenny feel inadequate. He had more or less said so. It followed that Jenny must have suggested something of the sort to him.

Maud wasn't cold now. Boiling, she threw back the covers. It was as clear as day now and she must face up to it. Jenny's unusually passionate greeting, her desperate concern for Maud's safety, had been prompted by guilt. She had betrayed her old friend by not wanting to see her. That was how good, sweet Jenny would feel, how she would try to make amends, force herself to be loving. Oh, the poor creature. Impossible to blame her, be angry.

Maud lay awake all night, blaming herself, racked with pain. It was determination to spare Jenny the knowledge of how much she had hurt her that carried her through the weekend. She popped into the stable block to visit Ned's crippled father. She pretended she had an urgent piece of work to finish and retreated for hours to her icy bedroom. She said she really must 'have a good blow of sea air', and drove to Holkham Bay where she marched, weeping, along the sands in a high, salty gale. She played Scrabble with Ned on Saturday evening and left Sunday morning. The days were drawing in and as Alice was 'clearly a bit of an invalid' Maud felt she ought to drive her home before dark. When Jenny begged her to come again 'very soon', Maud said she would love to, but not for a month or so; her publishers had asked her to do a book on Kenyatta, she hadn't made up her mind yet; before she did, she ought, perhaps, to spend a few weeks in Africa. 'Lucky Maud,' Jenny said, 'how nice to be so busy and sought after.' Then, blushing (as if she feared that this sounded envious), she threw her arms around Maud and kissed her.

Maud sold Alice through the *Exchange and Mart* to a vintage car enthusiast, a teacher of mathematics who claimed to understand the Cotal electric gear box, stroked Alice's scarred, welded flanks tenderly and enquired when she was 'born'. Maud hadn't the heart to replace her, nor for anything much; she turned down the book on Kenyatta. Then Jenny rang, chattered away merrily as if there was nothing at all wrong between them. She had to see a consultant at a London hospital; nothing wrong, just a few routine tests, could she and Ned please stay in Chelsea, with Maud?

Cheered, Maud bought her first Porsche. After the visit, Jenny pressed her to come up to Norfolk. Maud accepted the third invitation and everything was almost as it had always been; she almost felt easy. Perhaps she had been over-sensitive. Seeing slights where none was intended was a spinsterish failing. But trust had been broken, innocence lost. When Ned asked her if she would like to be appointed to the Council of the Royal Society of British Art and Literature that had been founded by his grandfather and of which Ned was currently Chairman, she suspected that this was meant as a placatory gesture. All the same, she accepted; no point in cutting off her nose to spite her face, and she was certainly flattered.

The work was not arduous. The Council met in London six

times a year to arrange a programme of lectures and art exhibitions and to administer a number of charitable trusts, one of which had been set up by Ned's family, for the benefit of impoverished elderly artists and writers, and to provide occasional grants to struggling young ones.

Maud began to see more of Ned than of Jenny who rarely came down to London. Before the Society's meetings Maud and Ned usually lunched together; sometimes, after an evening lecture, he stayed the night with her in Chelsea. When Maud wrote her biography of Ned's great-grandfather who had been a friend of Disraeli and ennobled for pioneering various agricultural improvements, Ned helped her sort out family papers, letters and diaries. He took her to visit an ancient, mad great-aunt whose senility had not affected her long-term memory and whose spicy tales about the old man's robust sexual appetites enlivened what would have otherwise been, in spite of the Disraeli connection, a conscientious but pedestrian account of fen drainage and crop rotation.

In the portrait by Daniel Maclise reproduced on the front cover, the first Lord Orwell looks more farmer than aristocrat; a modest country gent with a rough, lumpy face, somewhat resembling a Jerusalem artichoke, with small, deep-set, simian eyes. Ned is this portrait come to life; eyes twinkling with a shrewd kindness, speech slow and precise. The first time we met (at the publisher's launch for Maud's book) his concern and affection for her were apparent. 'I hope the book's a success. Maud's idea, of course, and once she sets her mind on something there is no stopping her, but I can't help feeling a bit responsible. He was a dullish sort of chap.'

I said I didn't think he need feel responsible for the dullness of his ancestor, and, anyway, Maud was skilled enough to make him seem interesting; she knew all the tricks of her trade. I had intended a compliment but he frowned as if he thought it faint praise.

'She's a remarkable woman. All she's done, without help from anyone, and success hasn't changed her. Still the same good-hearted girl. That's pretty rare you know.' I said I knew that and admired her for it. He seemed mollified. He said, 'I can't stand seeing hard-working people put down. Bitchy critics, that sort of thing. It takes a lot to write a book. Or paint a picture, come to that.' He grinned at me, showing surprisingly uncared-for teeth. 'Maud gave Jenny one of your pictures, you know. Your *Vision of London*.'

I hadn't known. It had been the largest (and therefore the most expensive) picture in my last exhibition; the first in a series of post-industrial landscapes, a scene of derelict Victorian factories on the banks of the Grand Union canal. 'I thought it had gone to a dealer. I wish Maud had told me.' But of course she wouldn't have done. She would have wanted to pay the full price. I said, 'It's a bleak sort of vision.'

'We like it very much. I'd like you to see how we've hung it. My poor Jenny is a bit under the weather just now but later on, when she's better, you might get Maud to bring you to see us. If you're brave enough to be driven by her. I'm not. Too old. Though I don't think I was ever brave enough to be one of Maud's passengers. Never mind. You come. Jenny remembers you. Soon as she's over this bad patch we'll fix something.'

They had hung my *Vision* next to a Stubbs of similar size; a harvest scene, oil on canvas, of uncertain provenance but probably an early finished study for his romantic enamels exhibited at the Royal Academy in the 1780s. England before and after the Fall, had been Jenny's idea, so Ned told me, but by that time she was dead.

She never got over the 'bad patch'. She put up a good fight; she was in her fifties when the cancer finally killed her. She died at home; Maud helped Ned to nurse her through the last months and it was natural that he should turn to Maud for comfort when the ordeal was over. They shared the same grief. That was how Maud saw it, anyway. She 'devoted' herself to Ned and when his old father died, several months after Jenny, and he inherited the title, she decided that the proper diversion for him, ease for his double sorrow, was to encourage him to take his seat in the House of Lords. Ned's total lack of interest in politics did not deter her. As energetic in what she conceived to be his interest as she had always been in her own, she entertained for him, gave dinner parties at which the other guests, Members of Parliament, journalists, academics, were carefully chosen to rouse up his interest in this or that 'issue'; economics, racial equality, housing, penal reform. The idea that Ned might feel his social duty adequately fulfilled by his Chairmanship of the Royal Society of British Art and Literature (a chore that he had almost certainly undertaken out of family piety) did not cross her mind, and Ned was too polite and too kind and, perhaps, too genuinely at a loss without Jenny, to try and enlighten her.

Meek as a lamb, he came to her dinner parties. He took her to the theatre. People began to invite them as a couple, together. My aunt could never be other than plain, but during this period her strong-featured face appeared to soften, grow younger; she began to wear high-heeled shoes, ruffled blouses; she spoke about Ned with a shy, girlish playfulness, little involuntary smirks, archly significant glances, that made her both absurd and touching.

At this time I was still married to Helen. She said, as we were walking home late one Saturday night, 'It's nice to see old Maud so happy. I hope his Lordship doesn't let her down.'

Maud's name hadn't been mentioned all evening. But I thought I saw the connection. We had been dining with George and his daughter Elaine; an exceptionally pretty girl with a charming habit of catching one's eye in a bold, amused way, and then lowering her gaze, lashes sweeping her slightly flushed cheeks, as if overcome with modest confusion. George, who spoke of their joint ménage as a 'one parent family' – a quaint conceit this, since Elaine had been nineteen when her mother ran away with one of George's rich South American customers – doted upon her, and she appeared to adore him; dropping the odd kiss on his bronzed, bald head as she passed the back of his chair, sitting on the floor at his feet, soft white arm draped over his knee, laughing delightedly at his jokes, flatteringly serious when he made a solemn pronouncement. This was a general procedure guaranteed to inflame any other middle-aged man in the vicinity without seeming calculated to do so which made it all the more enviable but was not, perhaps, quite so attractive to women. About halfway through this enchanting performance I had thought that Helen had fallen unusually silent.

It occurred to me now (as I assumed it had occurred to her then) that Elaine was only free to play the dutiful daughter at weekends because Helen's brother was busily occupied playing the dutiful husband in Norfolk. Helen and I had often wondered if George knew about Henry (and if so, if he knew that *we* knew) and during these cosy but fairly uninteresting speculations Helen had not appeared noticeably disapproving of her brother's behaviour. The fact that he had confided in her, even though he had been more or less forced to, after we had bumped into them at the National Theatre one evening, had given her a sense of complicity with him. He had, of course, sworn her to secrecy, and although she was fond of her sister-in-law, she recognised that while Joyce was happy in the country with her children and her market garden, Henry was lonely in London. But perhaps Elaine's provocative display of youth and beauty this evening had reminded Helen that she had just celebrated her fortieth birthday, thus triggering off a spot of straight female jealousy leading to a more general feeling of female solidarity with other older women, and thence to severe thoughts about the perfidy of men. From Joyce she had moved on to Maud of whom she was more than fond; indeed, dearly loved in much the same way that I did, with a mixture of amusement and deep, loyal affection.

I said teasingly, proud of my imaginative leaps, 'I wonder what made you think about Maud, all of a sudden?'

'I had to think of something, didn't I? Watching you gawping at that silly girl pawing her father. No wonder Lily left him. She must have been sickened.'

'I don't remember that sort of thing going on when Lily was there. And I didn't think it was sickening. Just, lucky old George!'

I squeezed her hand and added, in case this was really what was upsetting her, 'Though as far as I'm concerned she's just a lovely *child*. Out of my age group! Though, of course, Henry is older than I am. Poor old Joyce. Do you think she knows what he's up to?'

Helen didn't answer. This wasn't particularly odd since we were turning into our street where the sound of loud, crashing music assailed us. The location was almost immediately obvious. Not the squat, which was dark, but another house, several doors further down, where the young barrister son was taking advantage of his widowed mother's absence (we had seen her drive off that morning, car loaded up) to give a roistering party. Lights were turned low but through the long, uncurtained windows of the first-floor drawing room massed bodies could be dimly seen, close-packed as a football scrum, swaying and stamping and from time to time letting out wild, jungle cries as a counterpoint to the music. Our West Indian neighbour – a senior civil servant and a family man of respectable habits – was standing on his doorstep, fully dressed in dark suit, white shirt and MCC tie, glumly observing the frolic. 'Half-past one in the morning,' he said, when we greeted him. 'Up to twelve o'clock, fair enough, I was young myself once. After that, decent people consider the street.'

'Well, it is the weekend,' I said, cravenly hoping that he wouldn't suggest that I rang the police as he had asked me to do once before when the punks in the squat opposite had held a dawn to dusk love-in, and then, at once, feeling guilty on several counts; one, because I wondered if he believed that the policeman would pay more attention to me than he would to a black man; two, that he might be right about that; three, because the reason we had moved our bedroom from the front to the back of the house a couple of years ago had been the nightly din from the squat which before the punks took it over had sheltered what had sounded like at least fifty West Indian trumpeters.

These layers of guilt silenced me. Helen said, 'I know it's awful, the noise, keeping us all awake, but what really worries me is the numbers. All those people in that one room, all of them stamping! What if the floor should give way?'

'Please God, I pray not,' he said earnestly. But Helen's diversionary tactic had calmed him. She was good at that sort of thing. They started chatting cheerfully about the structure of our terrace, the pitch-pine joists, thick, load-bearing walls, developing the comforting theory that houses that had stood for well over a hundred years were unlikely to collapse under the weight of a party.

I left them to it and went into the house, running downstairs to switch off the burglar alarm that the insurance company had made us put in to safeguard the sometimes quite valuable paintings I kept in my work room while I painted a copy, and to drink several mugs of cold water. By the time I came up from the basement, Helen was in the hall. She said, 'Tim's not home.'

'Well, no. The alarm was on.'

She was chewing her bottom lip. I said, 'He was going with Mike, wasn't he? Mike's fairly reliable. For God's sake, don't start to worry.'

'I'm not,' she said. 'Actually, I was thinking perhaps I should ring over the road, ask if the sound could be turned down a bit. I expect he will. He's quite a nice young man, really.'

I should have thought of that. But Helen would do it more diplomatically. I said, 'Good luck,' and started up the stairs, thinking of Tim on his motorbike, roaring along, weaving between thundering container trucks and articulated lorries, at risk from madmen in Jaguars, from the crazed drivers of overnight coaches. While I cleaned my teeth (conscientiously massaging my gums as Helen had taught me) I saw him lying untended and bleeding in some muddy gutter. By the time I was settled in bed, vaguely selecting and rejecting various paperback thrillers, I had managed to persuade myself (or at least had prepared myself to persuade Helen) that it was, on the whole, fairly improbable that he had been involved in an accident.

Helen was still on the telephone. The instrument by the bed was emitting a tinny, incomprehensible quacking. I said, when it finally stopped and she appeared in the doorway, 'That was quite a lengthy chat you managed to have with our rising young barrister.'

'You weren't *listening*?'

'Of course not!'

She grinned in a shame-faced apology. I concluded that she had in fact been ringing Mike's mother to see if her boy was safe home, if our boy was with him. If that had been the case she would already have told me. If not, she would be embarrassed to admit that she had woken the poor woman up to no purpose. And worried sick, naturally. But to go into *that*, plug on with the usual painful and fruitless discussion of Tim's whereabouts, his mental state, his present companions, would keep us from sleep for the rest of the night, of which there wasn't very much left anyway. So I said, speaking slowly and judiciously, as if I had been thinking about nothing else all this time, 'I suppose if Joyce does know Henry is having an affair – and if she loves him she must know, don't you think? – she may simply have decided to lie low and wait till it's over. If that's the way of it, then it isn't so bad.'

Helen was taking her clothes off. Her slip crackled as she stepped out of it. I said, 'Lots of static there. If the light was off, you'd see the sparks fly. I suppose the sad thing would be if she didn't know just *because* she loved him and trusted him.'

Helen said nothing. This was slightly surprising; a sympathetic contemplation of other people's woes was a pleasure that I could normally rely upon to distract her. Perhaps her lack of response – and her sudden, sad, brilliant look – should have warned me. I must have registered her expression in some part of my mind because I was able later to recall it exactly. But after a second of standing there naked, she dived into bed, cuddled up, hid her face on my shoulder.

She muttered, 'Do stop going on about Henry and Joyce, you old gossip,' and seemed to fall asleep, almost instantly.

I heard Tim come in just after seven. Helen was sleeping. I put my mouth to her ear and said, 'He's back,' and she smiled in her sleep. About half an hour later she woke and said, 'Was he very late?' I wondered about the nice distinction between late, just a bit late, pretty late, very late, applied to the time a nineteen year old came home from a party. I said, 'Early hours, not unreasonable, really. All the same I think we can reckon on having breakfast without him.'

We went down to the kitchen together; Helen boiled eggs and squeezed oranges; I made coffee and toast. We ate, read the papers, in what I thought was companionable silence. Helen's hair caught fire in a shaft of sun from the window, her eyes, reflecting colour from the kimono I had bought for her birthday, were greener than usual, and there were a couple of lines I had not noticed before running from her nose to her mouth. She had a thin nose, a sharp chin. I said, fondly, 'Foxy-haired witch.'

She didn't look at me. She had finished her egg and was crushing the shell in its cup with her thumb. She sighed. She said, 'I'm terribly sorry.'

She had a lover. The affair had been going on over a year. Fourteen, fifteen months; she couldn't remember exactly. The man's wife had found out. Helen was afraid she would tell me. 'She's a vindictive woman,' she said; disapprovingly.

I laughed. Apart from a curious, tingling sensation, a little like drunkenness, I seemed to feel nothing. Helen went on mashing her egg shell. I said, 'That's a nursery habit. My mother used to say, crush an egg shell, save a sailor from drowning.'

Helen said, 'She had a miscarriage last week. That's why he

told her, though you'd have thought it would have been a good reason not to. Silly fool, I suppose it made him feel guilty. I'd no idea she was pregnant. He'd told me they didn't have sex any longer.'

'Did you tell him *we* didn't?'

Her chin quivered. She glowered at me like a reproachful, woebegone child. A kind husband wouldn't ask such a crude question. She was hurt! I should comfort her! I said, 'Do I know him?'

The telephone rang. She looked at me – pleadingly now. I shook my head. She said, with ordinary, everyday irritation, 'You lazy bastard!'

The kitchen telephone is on the wall by the door. Helen stood with her back to me. The painted dragon on the back of her kimono dived between her shoulder blades. She said, 'Oh, Maud. Hallo. No, you haven't woken us, we've just about finished breakfast.' She listened. She said, 'How awful, what a shock for you, oh, Maud, I'm terribly sorry . . . yes . . . yes . . . he's here, hang on a minute.'

She whirled round, her face swollen and dark, bursting like a ripe plum with hysterical laughter. She held the receiver against her breasts. 'Ned's getting married, he told her last night, it's all *fixed*, the date, everything, she wants to talk to you. Oh, God, this is ludicrous timing. I'm terribly sorry.'

I said, 'There seems to be a lot of terrible sorrow flying about at the moment.'

She hissed at me, 'Don't you dare tell her.'

I raised my eyebrows. Her face fractured, like a cracked plate. 'Please,' she said. I stood up, walked round the table, took the telephone from her. She made a hoarse, whooping sound and fled from the kitchen.

I put on a comic voice. 'Maud, what's all this then?' I felt a disgraceful elation. A silly sentence came into my mind. *If betrayal was on the menu today, at least I wasn't dining alone.* I cleared my throat, wiped the silly grin off my face. I said, 'Maud, I really am terribly sorry.'

She didn't want sympathy. She was growling with anger. 'Poor Ned, he's been caught good and proper, it's a monstrous conspiracy between the girl's parents and his wicked old mother. They're rich and she's greedy; buying and selling a title is the name of the game. Not that they'll fork out enough to get old Ned out of the financial mess his Dad left behind, Estate Duty, Capital Transfer, whatever they call it; if there was a chance of that, there might be some sense to it, but I'm afraid that's pie in the sky.'

She gave one of her vigorous, throaty snorts. I said, 'Oh, come on, Maud, you're not living in a nineteenth-century novel. And Ned's neither venal nor stupid. Do you know the girl?'

'I've met her a couple of times I suppose. Her family only moved to Norfolk quite recently, her father made a packet out of property companies, bought a house in the country, and is busy splashing his money about, spending his way into local society. Last time I spent a weekend with Ned we went to a great fancy party. Champagne, barrels of oysters, barbecue by the swimming pool. It rained, of course, so we all went inside. It's a nice old Queen Anne house but they've made it suburban, full of over-stuffed, self-satisfied furniture, not a book in sight, naturally. The mother collects *teapots*. I asked her why and she said, well you have to buy *something*, don't you?'

I said, 'It sounds a harmless activity. What's the girl like?'

'Ordinary. Quite pretty, quite pleasant, but no intellect, no conversation, what on earth will she and Ned talk about? I imagine he hopes to breed from her but that pleasure's soon over and Ned's a damn sight too old to be a good father.

Besides, it's an insult to Jenny. I've written to tell him so, just posted the letter, but I don't expect him to answer. He'll be too ashamed and quite right to be. No fool like an old fool, as I told him.'

I said that this was not perhaps the most tactful way of discouraging him if that was what she hoped to do, and she snorted again. 'No point in being mealy mouthed at this stage. What's there to lose? Only thing is to march into battle, all guns firing. Operation Rescue Ned. You could help there. You ought to talk to him anyway. I expect he'll have to sell some of the pictures to pay off the tax man. I don't know if he wants any of them copied or not but it wouldn't do any harm to suggest it.'

I said incredulously, 'You mean you want me to get hold of Ned, tick him off about the girl, point out his folly, and *at the same time* offer to fill up the blank spaces on the walls of the old home, tout for his *custom*?'

'What's the matter with that? Kill two birds with one stone, and you could do with the work, couldn't you? If it embarrasses you, then forget it. How's Helen? I thought she looked a bit peaky the last time I saw her.'

'Did she?'

'Oh, men never notice. You ought to fuss over her a bit more. She's a lovely girl but she has all the worry with Tim. I know you have, too, but they say it's always worse for the mother.'

I said, 'Helen's all right, Maud. A bit tired, perhaps. Her partner's been sick, so she's had to take some of his patients.'

Until I repeated this excuse I had believed it. Helen, coming home late, flushed, beaming, bright-eyed. *Tired*? Bloody hell. I said, 'I can't think it'll do any good, Maud. But I'll try and see Ned.'

*

In fact, Ned rang me two days later and asked me to lunch. We met at his club and ate in a gravy-brown dining room, served by ancient waiters with faint, creaking voices, all apparently paralysed in one limb or another. Ned said, 'Sorry, not very nice here, dreadful food, I'd forgotten. These last few years I've usually put up with Maudie. Or, rather, she's put up with me. Suppose that's at an end now, more's the pity. You know all about it, I gather; she said when she wrote she was going to tell you. Never thought she'd take it like this. I suppose I was stupid.'

He touched one of the fleshy excrescences on the side of his nose with a tentative finger as if wondering if it had grown, or was sprouting, a hair. He said, 'I'm very much afraid that I've hurt her.'

I said, bracingly, that 'hurt' was the last thing she seemed to be and he nodded. 'It's like her to put up a bold front. But I imagine you know that.' He looked at me keenly; bright, clever eyes, unexpectedly young in that weather-beaten, vegetable face. He said, 'I promise you that I never knowingly gave her cause to think that there was any feeling other than friendship on my part. Nor thought there was on hers, until now.'

I said that as an old friend she was naturally concerned for him, and he sighed. 'It seems a bit more than that. A bit more over the top. She wrote me an angry letter. I expected that. But there was something else after.' He sighed again, very deeply. 'That's why I wanted to see you. It's a touch delicate. Betraying a confidence. One doesn't care to do that. On the other hand, one is anxious on her behalf. I would like to feel she had someone to turn to. There's nothing I can do, in the circumstances. And I know she is fond of you.'

He was hesitating, hand in his inside breast pocket. I said, with suitable gravity, 'I think you can trust me.'

He passed me a folded sheet. Opened out, it was a birthday greetings telegram with spring lambs cavorting around the edges. He said, 'Apparently the Post Office, in their wisdom, have discontinued the ordinary telegram.'

> NED MY DARLING I KNOW YOU ARE LONELY BUT THIS MARRIAGE IS MADNESS I WOULD DO ANYTHING TO SAVE YOU FROM IT MARRY YOU MYSELF IF YOU WISH IT I CANT BEAR YOU CHILDREN BUT YOU WOULD HAVE MY UNDYING DEVOTION I WOULD FOLLOW YOU TO THE ENDS OF THE EARTH.

Ned cleared his throat. 'Please understand that I think this is a very fine gesture. Typical of Maud's generous spirit. I feel very honoured. I would like her to know that. But as I said, it's a delicate matter. If one were to write or to telephone oneself she might misunderstand.'

Scared stiff, poor bugger! 'You mean she might go on pestering you?'

He frowned at this explicit vulgarity. 'I don't want to cause her any further distress. Later on I hope we will be able to pick up the threads again. Once she has accepted that I am committed.' He gave a short, rueful laugh. 'As Maud would say, an old fool in love.'

'I'll try and soften the blow,' I said, wondering how he thought I was going to do this and if what he really feared was that Maud would show up at the wedding.

'Thank you, I would be more than grateful.'

He was pushing his food around his plate. He had barely eaten a mouthful. This abstinence may have been due to the dubious provenance and general disgustingness of whatever it was he had ordered as much as to his sensitivity about my aunt's feelings, but his voice, when he next spoke, was certainly troubled. 'I do care for her very deeply. In fact, if I'd known how she felt – well, never mind that. But to be honest I've always been rather in awe of her. She's a formidable woman.'

'It's her manner. She gives the impression that she ought to be running the country. Prime Minister. Or a great General. I think she might be more diffident in personal matters.'

'Yes,' he said. 'I'm afraid so. A pity.' He picked up a gobbet of some unidentifiable meat, put it in his mouth, and chewed thoughtfully. Then he looked at me and smiled, visibly recalling his hostly duty, and asked me what I was working on at the moment. I told him a rather busy nineteenth-century portrait, not all that distinguished, but worth enough at present day prices, in an inflated art market, for the owners to have decided to sell it.'

'How do you mean, *busy*?'

'A lot of background detail, very exact. But that's simply fiddly. It's the face that I'm having trouble with. It's not defined very clearly. A bit wishy washily pretty. Very Victorian.'

'I suppose that must make it difficult. It must be a temptation to update, paint a more fashionable face.'

I don't know why I should have been surprised that he understood this. I said, 'As long as you're aware of it you try to avoid it, of course. That's easier if you're making a straight copy with the picture in front of you than if you have to work from photographs. There's always some degree of distortion when you project the photograph on to the canvas. But if you aren't copying an actual painting but trying to paint – like Van Meegeren – say, in the style of a couple of centuries earlier, then a modern idiom is more likely to creep in.'

'You mean, Vermeer's seventeenth-century beauties all turned out looking like Greta Garbo? Heavy lidded. I remember reading that somewhere. Or Jenny told me, more likely.

And no one picked it up till much later because Garbo was everyone's ideal of beauty at that time. Very comic, made everyone look pretty silly. Hard to be disapproving, though I suppose one should be. Jenny used to say that what intrigued her was how one would react if a forged painting was better than the original. If Van Meegeren's technique had been superior to Vermeer's. Well, one knows that it wasn't. But just for example.'

'Technique isn't the point. You can't forge technique unless you have it and if you have it there's no need to forge it. Vermeer discovered how to paint light like no one else. That was what Van Meegeren forged. Stole. The original, creative discovery. That's always the important thing.'

'All right. Suppose Rembrandt had copied a painting by some inferior but better known artist.'

'Rembrandt's would be a better picture.'

'How would you tell, if he'd copied exactly?'

'By looking at it, I hope.'

I was beginning to be bored with this conversation and feared that I sounded it. I said, in apology, 'I think one would know, though I can't tell you how. Some sort of straight connection between the eye and the brain. There has to be more in a good painting than you can put into words, though less of the sort of thing a writer might deal with.'

He nodded. He pushed his plate away finally and said, 'I think we'll have the Stilton, safest choice, unless you fancy a pudding? No? Wise man.' When the waiter had crept away with the plates he grinned at me and I saw he had had his teeth tidied up, the front four neatly capped. He said, 'Jenny said something along those lines once. We've got three nice Stubbs. My grandfather bought them because he liked horses. We had a man come just before Jenny died to value the whole lot for insurance, though we didn't take him up on it, actually, damn sight too expensive. Anyway, there was this man, rabbiting on about what a brilliant recorder Stubbs was, not only horses but people, rich and poor living together in a vanished rustic stability, a marvellous social historian, really, and Jenny said that might explain why Stubbs was an interesting painter but not why he was a genius. Only your eyes could do that.'

I said, 'Good for her.'

'Of course, she was in a wheelchair by then.' He closed his eyes briefly and said, 'Oh, God, I do miss her. Tell Maudie that, will you? And that I was touched by her telegram. No. That I honour her for it.'

Walking across St James's Park, I contemplated conveying this somewhat condescendingly sentimental disclosure to Maud and decided against it. If I had sent that telegram I would prefer to forget it, even though, on reflection, there had been an amplitude about its ridiculous message that I found rather enviable. I thought – I could send Helen a telegram! I LOVE YOU MY DARLING AS LONG AS YOU STAY WITH ME NOTHING ELSE MATTERS. A simple statement to clear the muddy waters in which we seemed to be floundering, thrashing wildly about, stirring up ancient resentments and grudges from the mire at the bottom, some of which, surfacing, had displayed a shockingly immediate relevance.

Like the house we had nearly bought eighteen months ago; the rambling old rectory that we had come upon quite by chance one weekend, on our way to stay with Henry and Joyce in the country.

Helen wails, 'If only we had moved to Norfolk this would never have happened.'

'It was your fault we didn't. Oh, I know you went on about how lovely it would be to escape from the city, the rubbish, the dog shit, but it was just a velleity. Willing the end without being prepared to expend any effort.'

'I know what the word means. And I fell in love with the house, you know that. But I had to think of the practice. You can paint anywhere.'

'I'd have thought that even people who live in the country need their teeth fixed occasionally. And I thought we'd worked that out anyway. You didn't mind commuting, you *said*, until Ted got a new partner. Spending the odd night in town.'

She says quickly, 'Yes, I know. But the house was too big for us, really.'

'I don't see why. I could have used the whole of the attic to work in. We could have converted the stable block, sold it, or let it. And we would have had room for my mother. I know she's okay on her own at the moment but she may get ill or old. Or lonely. She and Razor Annie were quite merry together before the poor old bat lost her marbles. And I think the expense of the house worries her sometimes.'

'Worries *you*, you mean, don't you? I know how your mind works, my lad. There you were, fancying yourself lord of the manor in this lovely old house, totting up the cost of making it habitable, and you thought, well, if Maisie sells up and moves in, she can help pay to convert it. Nice for her, nice for us, why didn't you say so?'

'You have just demonstrated why. You would have assumed that my natural concern for my mother was bound to be connected to a financial advantage.'

'Oh, stuff that. I know that you love your Mum.' She says this sweetly, affectionately, not a trace of daughter-in-law-ish resentment. Then, reproachfully, 'If I'd known you were thinking about Maisie, I'd have felt differently.'

'That would have been twisting your arm, wouldn't it? Once you'd decided you didn't really want to leave London.'

'Oh, you are *stupid*.'

There is a funny look in her eye. Sly? Guilty? Regretful, perhaps – after all, she does love my mother. 'Do you think she would really have liked to move in with us?' she asks, but a split second too late. The truth has already hit me with the shock of an unexpected physical blow; my stomach contracts, my balls freeze and harden. I say, 'You're dead right I'm stupid! You didn't want to leave that convenient flat!'

At the time she and Ted bought the lease of the surgeries in Kentish Town, the two rooms, kitchen and bathroom at the top of the house had been occupied by a charming old queer who made jewellery. Since he died just over a year ago they had done it up, furnished it, been on the look out for a suitable tenant. Meanwhile Ted Frobish, married and living in Sussex, used it occasionally when he, or he and his wife, had a late night in London. How often had that been, I wondered.

'Oh, very convenient,' I snarl. 'My God, I've heard about porno videos, fantasies about the milkman, the window cleaner, the man from the clothing club. Dentists make quite a new slant! Any patient you fancy. A quick fuck between fillings.'

'Don't be disgusting.' Her face darkens. A thin glaze of rose madder.

'I can't help being interested. I hadn't considered the erotic possibilities of your profession before. Do you do it before, or after? Is it the drilling that turns you on? Or plugging the cavity?'

She says nothing. She is breathing fast, visibly; I can see her breasts rising and falling.

'Pain, I suppose,' I say, almost gleefully. 'The infliction of pain. I'm sorry I didn't know. Though I can't promise that I would have obliged you.'

She screams at me, 'Oh, you are cheap, that's a cheap, filthy crack, you think what I do is a *joke*, it's always been a joke to you, hasn't it? I've heard you say, *my wife is a dentist*, putting on one of your silly voices, a kind of leering *apology*, as if it wasn't somehow respectable, not like being a *doctor*.'

And she launches herself at me, hard as a bullet, hitting my chest and my throat with bunched, flailing fists, her face twisted, a fixed mask of pure anger as if, incredibly, this foolish nonsense is more important to her than what we are really quarrelling over. If there was a knife handy, she would have used it.

I catch her flying fists with some difficulty; she is a strong woman. 'Listen, you idiot, that's what *you* think, not what I think, nothing to do with me,' I shout, not quite truthfully, because, yes, there is something in her accusation; I have never understood why anyone should choose to spend their working lives peering into other people's mouths, and may have laughed sometimes, a teasing joke between close, loving friends and I had thought that was how she had taken it; after all, it was how we had *met* for God's sake, when I staggered into the London Hospital one pain-wracked Sunday morning to be rescued from agony by a beautiful dental student, a beautiful, red-headed, angel of mercy. All this goes through my head as she hurls herself backwards and forwards, struggling to get free, making feral, low, growling noises. And then the real reason for her unexpectedly violent attack is suddenly clear to me. I say, 'It's Ted, isn't it?'

She stops fighting. I let her fists go. She steps back and stands still.

I wait for her to deny it. She doesn't. I say, 'Well, I suppose that is convenient, too.'

She says, 'You've always sneered at him. You once introduced him as *my wife's partner, the Australian dentist.*'

I affect bewilderment. 'I'm sorry? Which of those words do you object to, exactly?'

She says, impatiently, 'You know what I mean. As if it were intrinsically *comic*.'

'Accurate, though. He comes from Australia. He is a dentist.'

What else to be said for him? Nothing much in my book. He is tall, lean, I suppose handsome if you go for a clean and square-jawed and healthy appearance. He has more hair than I have but then he is younger. Younger than Helen, too. Must be ten years between them. Is that the attraction?

I say, 'Well, now if you prefer it I can say *my wife's lover*. It certainly gives him a more solid identity. And at long last he and I have something in common apart from my root canals and dry sockets.'

This is in every way a sore point. I crack jokes about dentists because I am frightened. (As Helen knows, must know, surely?) The memory of Ted, not so long ago, shoving his hideous instruments, needles and probes, into my parched, gaping mouth, adds a further exquisite humiliation. Helen had said, 'Let him do it, darling, it's an awkward job and I'll be scared I might hurt you.' Pah! Clearly, the truth is, the state of my shabby old fangs has always disgusted her. I say, unforgivably, 'Is it his lovely strong teeth that you go for?'

And so on, and so forth. This elevated exchange is a fair example of the intellectual level on which we ended our marriage. No point in repetition; rows, recriminations, reproaches between most married couples in a similar plight must run the same boringly predictable course. The real wound being deeper than you care to admit to, you squabble over minor cuts and abrasions. 'Another shirt with no buttons,' I roar, hurling this evidence of her lack of affection on to the floor from which she, equally angered by my petty and unjust complaint (I have always sewn on my own buttons), declines to retrieve it. We have run out of lavatory paper and other toiletries. 'Not even basic needs are attended to,' I thunder, intending (or half intending) a joke, but she leaves, weeping, and when she returns the remorse with which her tears briefly filled me flies out of the window. The soap she has bought is not the simple, unscented kind that we have always used in our household. I suppose that what she has substituted, a more expensive, perfumed variety, is what Ted prefers and so what she prefers, too. It matches the aftershave she explains, holding out a cut glass spray bottle, a peace-making present. 'I don't want to smell like your lover,' I shout, 'I'm a painter, remember, not a poncey dentist; my God, I always wondered why his surgery stank like an aged tart's boudoir.'

Enough of that! As I have said, not very edifying. My only excuse is that I was obsessed not only by natural pain and resentment, but by fear of a kind that was not amenable to reason. I was terrified that she was going to leave me and yet, perversely, everything that I said and did seemed fuelled by an uncontrollably lunatic impulse to drive her away, face the worst, get it over with. I took to picking her up at the surgery, arriving early and waiting outside in the car, timing the interval between the last patient's departure and her appearance. On one of these evenings she told me that Ted was leaving the practice as soon as she could find a new partner. I said, 'I hope his wife will be pleased.' And, when she groaned, 'I'm not quite sure what line you expect me to take. It's not much of a compliment to you that he should give up so easily. Should I, perhaps, be offended?'

It was my own behaviour I couldn't bear finally; the inescapable evidence of spite, silliness, lack of generosity and plain common sense. When she left (the surprise, looking back, is that she hung on as long as she did) I felt the relief of a criminal at the departure of a key witness against him. Now I could begin to modify and edit my guilt, admit to some lesser charge like stupidity, something I might hope she would come to forgive after she had spent some time alone in the pokey flat over the surgery. A temporary refuge for her, a time of healing for me. We both needed to 'think things over'. I needed to 'recover my self respect'. That was the jargon!

I was working hard on the busy Victorian painting, a slow, niggling job that I had already spent too long over for the fee that George had agreed upon. As usual, the more I fussed over it, the less I liked the result, but although that was frustrating for me I was fairly sure no one else would notice much wrong. And at the same time I was doing a portrait of Tim for his grandmother's birthday; a traditional painting because that is what she likes, plenty of rich colour with a nice glow to it. Like a Goya.

He sat very patiently. He is fond of his grandmother. He didn't talk much, but then he never did, or not to me, anyway. He only spoke once about what had happened. He said, turning in the chair where I'd placed him, rolling his eyes shyly (or slyly) towards me, 'Is it my fault, Dad? I'm sorry, I mean I'm sorry to ask, but I need to know, honestly.' Although the question seemed childishly put, egocentric, I saw the muscle twitch in his cheek and knew what it cost him. I said, not quite honestly, because of course his illness had affected us, our life together, 'No, Tim, not hers or mine really, either, or not absolutely, but not yours at all,' and he frowned for a second, rightly suspecting this answer, and then accepting it, or accepting the loving intention behind it, smiled at me gratefully.

The portrait that hangs in my mother's sitting room, pride of place over the flickering electric coals in the fireplace, is not a bad likeness if a little romanticised; a reddy ground giving a warmer and healthier tone to his pallor and a gleam to the black of his sweater; dark hair trimmed and glossed up a bit to please his grandmother; curving mouth sweetly set. The picture I see in my mind, the shadowy image behind the finished portrait, is paler and thinner; skin taut over nervous bones, tense with the effort to contain the chaos within him, but much more alive, much more vibrant. In the image that I hold in my heart from this time he is smiling.

As his mother is weeping. Helen's face is stubborn as stone when I answer the door bell (although she still has her keys she wishes to demonstrate that she has only come as a visitor, to pick up warmer clothes for the winter) but some time, perhaps half an hour later, turning from the closet, arms bundled with garments, this valiant stone face is dissolving, deliquescent, liquid with grief. The room, our bedroom, is filled with the gold light of autumn. The words of that unsent telegram sing gladly inside me as I hold out my hands, move towards her. I LOVE YOU MY DARLING . . .

But she isn't grieving for us, for our lost happiness. She is grieving for her dentist lover. Ted's wife rushed out of the house yesterday, after a quarrel; crashed the car, injured her spinal cord. 'Poor Ted,' Helen says, her tears gushing, 'I can't forgive myself for what we have done to him.'

Can't forgive *me* she means, naturally. I had made life impossible, forced her to leave home, made Ted feel responsible, divided his loyalties. She is blaming me as if I were not a betrayed husband but some powerful, Olympian figure – her father, maybe – and the injustice outrages me. And so we part, finally, both reduced by pain to hurt children.

I wrote to my mother. A dignified letter. 'I am sorry to have to send this bad news. Please don't let it make any difference to your affection for Helen. I know she is deeply fond of you as you are of her, and in spite of everything we are still fond of each other. There is no bitterness between us, only resignation and sorrow. At least we have had, until now, a good marriage, good years to remember.'

I made several drafts. They became increasingly lying and righteous. I should go and see her. I totted up the excuses. I had the Victorian painting to finish; the house was filthy; I had to cook for Tim, wash his clothes and mine; find someone who would clean for us; our daily help, usually so reliable, had been away sick the last couple of weeks; Helen had chosen a fine time to leave, hadn't she?

My mother would be sympathetic to that. She had always held to the view that keeping house was a woman's work; had always slightly disapproved of Helen having a full-time job. I thought I might telephone. But my mother is a little deaf. Besides, she would almost certainly say something like, *Oh dear have you thought about it?* Or, *I can't believe it, you've always seemed so happy together.*

Thinking about the foolish things my mother might say made me angry. I wanted to hear her say them so that I could refute them. But it is undignified to quarrel with a deaf woman on the telephone.

I rang Maud. I barked at her. 'Helen's left me.'

'Is this some sort of joke?'

'No. Helen and I have decided to separate.'

'You must be out of your mind. You've always been so happy together.'

I gave a sardonic laugh. 'Not now. Evidently.'

'I can't believe it. Have you *thought* what you're doing? Have you told Maisie?'

This was very satisfactory. I said, with a patient sigh, 'Yes and no, Maud. Yes, I *have* thought about it. And no, my mother doesn't know yet. I'm writing to her.'

'Have you posted it?'

'Not yet. It's not easy, she's fond of Helen, you know, deeply fond, and I don't want to spoil that, upset that apple cart, I have to think what to say very carefully.'

'Whatever are you *talking* about? Whatever you say will upset Maisie terribly.'

'I can't help that, can I? I know you've always tried to protect her, I've never quite understood why because she's very tough, really, not some kind of weak, feminine, incompetent creature. In fact, your attitude towards her has always seemed to me rather patronising.'

'Rubbish. That's absolute rubbish. All I mean is, don't rush into it . . .'

'She'll have to know some time.'

'Not if you change your mind. If you and Helen have just had some sort of lovers' tiff. Great Scott, you're *married*, you've been married for *years*, you can't just break it up casually because of some stupid quarrel. You don't know how lucky you are, having a nice girl like Helen. Of course marriage is difficult, you have to work at it. I suppose your generation doesn't understand that, you come to a bumpy patch, a rough bit of road, and you decide to bale out. I suppose the truth is you've found someone else, some silly, pretty young thing, well, that's an old story.'

'Not mine, though.'

'I must say, I'm shocked. I thought better of you. Who is she?'

'There isn't anyone, Maud. Though I suppose I ought to be flattered that it's the natural conclusion you jump to.' Better to be thought a heartless philanderer than a cuckolded husband! Absurdly, I found myself chuckling.

Maud said, 'How can you *laugh*? You don't mean to tell me that Helen . . .'

'No, I don't. Why should you assume it's so simple?'

She was silent. Had I not sounded convincing? I said, hastily assuming a loftier, more impersonal tone, 'Honestly, dear, people drift apart without always realising what's happening. It can go on for years. There may be an actual *event* in the *end* but it's rarely important. You just wake up one morning and find you have been muddling on to no purpose, that there's nothing more to be said, no true common interest, that you're going nowhere together. It can be a painful and difficult thing to admit to . . .'

'Are you talking about yourself and Helen, or about two other people? Has Helen actually *gone*?'

It seemed almost a philosophical point. Could she be said to have 'gone' when I hoped she'd come back? My hope was not her intention. Did I still hope? What did she intend? And so on. How many angels can you get on the head of a pin? I said, 'She has left the house. She's living in the flat over the surgery. Neither of us has started divorce proceedings. That is, I haven't. If she had, I think she'd have told me.'

'Has she taken her *clothes*?'

'Yes. Well, not all of them, I think there are a few things left in the cupboard.' I knew precisely what was there; a black wool coat, a couple of silk shirts and a skirt, none of which she had ever liked, and three pairs of shoes; a pair of low-heeled patents scuffed at the toes, a pair of silver evening shoes that had always pinched badly but that she had been unwilling to throw away because they had cost so much money, and a pair of fraying, rope-soled beach sandals. 'Old things,' I admitted. 'Nothing I've seen her wear lately.'

'Oh, God,' Maud said. 'Then she really has left you!'

I answered with heroic restraint. 'I told you she had left *me*. Are her clothes so much more important?'

'It's simply a matter of what defines people. You'd know I'd left home if I'd taken my books and my compact disc player.'

'That's a bit different. You've made Helen sound vain and trivial.'

'Not at all. Her clothes are a creative pleasure to her.'

'Like my mother's hats?'

'Helen has *taste*! Her pretty things are part of the way she expresses herself, not just a frivolous vanity. If you don't understand that, then I'm not surprised she has left you.'

'Thank you, Maud.'

'Oh, I'm sorry, my duck, I shouldn't have said that, I'm upset, that's the truth of it.' A pause. A sigh. 'I know you're upset too, this is horrible for you, I really am sorry.' A deeper sigh and a longer pause to formally indicate sorrow, a moment of mourning. Then, briskly, 'No point in wallowing. You get back to work again, that's the best medicine. Pick up the traces. Have you heard from George yet? Ned and I saw him yesterday evening. That nice lass of his – what's her name? – cooks a jolly good dinner. Ned ate like a horse.'

'Elaine. George's daughter is called Elaine. No, I haven't

spoken to George today. I thought you weren't talking to Ned.'

'Oh, for goodness' sake, why shouldn't I be? He gets off the leash sometimes. Needs to, poor fellow, with Polly having a baby and making a great to-do over it. Big healthy girl like that, you'd have thought she'd take it in her stride.'

'Polly?'

'Ned's *wife*. You knew he was getting married.'

'I seem to remember. You weren't best pleased about it.'

'Wasn't I? Well, that's water under the bridge now. The silly chump had got the girl pregnant so it was a case of Hobson's choice for a man of Ned's kind of old-fashioned integrity. Surely I told you? Maybe I didn't, or you weren't listening. I can't remember when Ned told me, to be honest, he wasn't exactly proud of himself, pretty sheepish, though it's working out better than one might have expected, I'm glad to say. I get on quite well with Polly, she needs a bit of support in that household, a bit of stiffening to cope with the Dowager. Ned can't give it, he's too scared of his fearful old mother, she's one of his troubles as I've always told him, why he's always been frightened of women.'

I felt like Rip Van Winkle. In the five months or so I had been locked away from the world, quarrelling with Helen, breaking our lives apart, other people's lives had moved on, been shaken as in a kaleidoscope into new patterns, exposing new angles, different details emerging. Aunt Maud had ploughed on with her work, her 'best medicine', dug her allotment, attended her meetings, been reconciled with her dear old chum Ned, adjusted her sights in that quarter; established her position as the third partner in the new marriage, the husband's best friend and adviser, comforter to the new wife.

Not really much change there; one new member of the caste, that was all. Would Polly knuckle under like Jenny? Unlikely that Ned would stand firm; a man who was 'frightened' of women had little chance against Maud. He'd broken away long enough to get a girl pregnant but it seemed that he was now back in harness. Which was what he wanted, most probably. A victim can often be a conspirator and Maud had always given his life a needed extra dimension; a busy emotional bustle of intrigue and drama. I wondered (not for the first time) if he and my aunt had ever been lovers.

Maud was saying, '. . . reckoning on selling five or six pictures to settle the tax bill. The National Gallery's interested and Ned wants them to have first crack, anyway, but George said last night that he thinks they'd do best in New York. Of course they'll have to be referred to the National before they can get export licences. It'll all take a fearsome time, of course. Isn't Helen's brother at the Board of Trade? I told Ned he'd be a useful man to get on to. Though I suppose it might be a bit awkward now you and Helen . . .'

I said, 'George knows the ropes. I shouldn't worry about pulling strings, Maud.'

She didn't worry. Playing puppet master was her amusement, her pleasure.

Her life blood.

She said, 'It's not just the tax, Ned's pretty strapped in other directions, it takes a lot to keep that huge, windy barracks just about ticking over, and it's got to the point when a vast amount has to be spent; structural things, the roof, the main staircase up to the gallery. Dry rot, wet rot, death-watch beetle, you name it, they've got it, and God knows what they'll uncover once they get started. Ned looks quite *grey* sometimes.'

'Poor old Ned. Perhaps he ought to apply for Social Security.'

'Don't be smart. I know poverty's relative. I daresay you think he should just hand the whole thing over to the National Trust and be done with it. But he happens to think it's his duty to keep the bulk of the Orwell collection together, not just out of family piety, though of course that comes into it, but for everyone, for you and for me, for *posterity*. I happen to think that's an honourable and responsible attitude.'

'A bit out of the way for most of posterity, isn't it? A private house in north Norfolk?'

'They're open two days a week. People come from all over. If the pictures were divided up, shunted around to the public galleries, most of them would end up in store half the time, you know that as well as I do. It's a wrench that some of them have got to go but at least they can be copied and the copies hung in the collection as a matter of record. You ought to be interested for that reason, not just for the money. Though of course there are millions involved. It's ironical, really. Ned's grandfather bought his pictures because he liked them, to look at, not to make money. One man's taste – it gives the collection a certain individual *slant*. I thought you'd approve of that, you do, don't you? Ned says he wasn't sure how you felt when he put it to you.'

'When did he do that?'

'You had lunch with him, didn't you?'

'That was months ago. As far as I can recall it, he mentioned the paintings but he didn't "put" anything to me. We talked, well, about other things, mostly.'

Had she really forgotten what those 'other things' could have been?

'Ned is a deeply shy man,' she said, reprovingly. 'And perhaps, at that time, he wasn't quite sure of his ground. But he was pleased last night when I told him I thought you'd be delighted to do this job for him. And George approved too. It would be good for your reputation to have examples of your copying work hung in a distinguished collection, attributed to you in the catalogue.'

'The artist as competent hack?'

She laughed. 'Oh, you remember that affair, do you? I got my own back in that quarter, I'll tell you how some time. But surely you're not ashamed of your technical competence? And if Ned were to hang some of your own paintings as well, it might make for some useful publicity. The gallery will have to be closed while the repair work is done but when it re-opens it should be possible to drum up some interest and along the way focus a bit of attention on you. The skilled copyist who has also produced some fine original work. The difference between a good copy and a reproduction. That sort of thing. It shouldn't be difficult to get hold of some art critic who will write a sensible article. There's that very intelligent man on the *Guardian*. Forward planning, I know, but one can't start too soon. Meanwhile it would be good for you to take this on, steady work, no time to brood, take you out of yourself. Go up to Norfolk, look at the pictures, get a good blow of sea air.'

My aunt is unstoppable; a natural, elemental force, like the wind. Nothing to be done except to duck down and let it blow over you. I murmured submissively that of course I was interested but I would have to discuss it with George, who would have to discuss it with Ned, that there were a lot of things to consider, other possible commissions in the pipe line, among them an enquiry that had come through the American Embassy from an historical society in Boston. They wanted copies of portraits of George the Third and William Pitt. I had said I would think about it.

Maud said, 'Well, when you have thought, let me know. If

Helen has taken the car, I can always take off a bit of time to drive you to Norfolk.'

In my mind I hold a conversation with Helen. 'Maud's making use of me, isn't that typical? Oh, not consciously, I daresay she truly believes that she has only my interests at heart, but Ned has escaped her, or partly escaped her, and she has seized on this way of forging a new link between them. Something she can ring Ned up about, an excuse for a visit, something that has nothing to do with his wife, that Polly can't really object to. I'm to be a kind of entrance fee! Oh, she is *devious*! Plotting and planning! I wonder how she got even with that poor reviewer who was brave enough to say she was *boring*? That was years ago, how many years did it take her to get her own back, I wonder? Oh, she's a dreadful woman, a kind of succubus, really . . .'

'I don't think you quite mean that, my lad,' Helen says, with a giggle. 'Look it up in the dictionary. It should be *succuba*, anyway. Why are you so angry? Huffing and puffing. Maud likes to fix things for people, it's the way she shows love. It's quite sad when you think of it that she feels it isn't enough just to love them, as if, on its own, her love was worth *nothing*.'

'She likes to have a hold over people. Put them in her debt. I want to run my own life.'

'That's childish. Do you know how childish you sound? Ned wants his pictures copied. You need the work. If Maud gets a bit of fun out of making arrangements, what's wrong with that? She gets precious little else from either of you. Ned's treated her badly. And you didn't bother to thank her, I bet. As far as you're concerned, she gives and you take. It's the same with your mother. Both those women have spoiled you, the only boy, little princeling, and that's how you like it. What you expect from all women.'

'Is that why you left me? Because I'm a spoiled, selfish brat? Thank you for telling me. How do you mean, Ned's treated Maud badly? She wormed herself into his life, tried to take him over. He can't help it, not loving her.'

'He must have known how she felt, he isn't so stupid. But he took what she had to give while it suited him. So in that sort of way, out of a cruel kind of weakness, he cheated her.'

'You're a fine one to talk about cheating!'

She says, with a wispy sigh, 'You're not angry with Maud, you're angry with me.'

And is instantly gone. As always, when I attack her directly, she won't stay to answer, she slips away silently, fading like a pale colour in sunlight; I can't visualise her, let alone hear her. Even fantasy has to have some probability, and the only words I want to hear are ones that I cannot hope she will speak. I *love you, I want to come home to you . . .*

Tim puts his head around the door of my work room. 'Why are you talking to yourself, Dad?'

'First sign of madness,' I mutter.

Madness, sadness. Death must be like this, bereavement; I conjure up Helen's ghost out of an aching void, an empty hollow of grief.

'It's hard work being mad,' Tim says. And then, quickly, as if he fears I may think he means to reproach me, 'Can I get you something? A coffee? A beer?'

He wants, needs, to do something. He gets up late, does the crossword, walks to the corner shop for his cigarettes. Sometimes he conquers his terror of strangers and goes to the supermarket for me. I cannot imagine his terror. I say, 'Look up a word for me, will you? Succubus.'

He withdraws his head. I am finishing his portrait, glazing the background with umber and black. I wipe out the light area behind the hair with a cloth. His face and his throat are too pale and I use my finger to rub rose madder into his cheeks and below his jaw line.

He has come in without my hearing him. He stands behind me, regarding his likeness. I say, 'What do you think? Will Gran like it?'

He nods. 'A succubus is a female demon who has intercourse with sleeping men. That's all it says in the Concise Oxford Dictionary. In the Shorter Oxford it says that it was used in the seventeenth century to mean a strumpet or whore. Who were you thinking of, Dad?'

He is watching me warily. He adores his mother. Little Oedipus we used to call him when he was small. Now I don't find this so funny. I say, 'No one, Tim. It was just a word that was banging about in my head. I realised that I didn't really know what it meant, that was all.'

'Ah,' he says. 'That's okay then. It's hardly a term one would apply to any lady of one's acquaintance except as a form of enraged hyperbole.'

I laugh heartily. 'Good,' I say. 'Oh, *very* good, Tim.' And am moved almost to tears by his quick, lopsided grin, his evident pleasure at the success of his little joke.

CLIO

It is sequence that I find difficult; the exact timing of events, the crucial moment of change. At some point that winter Tim began to drift between me and his mother and various friends; a few days here, a night there. But I cannot remember when he finally left home to move in with Patsy. Maud's definition of 'leaving' isn't much use in this case. Tim travelled light; a bed roll and a plastic bag of books dumped in the hall marked his passage.

There must be a trick to ordering memory. There are tricks in all trades. Copying a picture, colour is the main thing to go for; the combination, the range. Is it the mixture that makes a particular colour – Prussian blue and burnt umber? Or the underpainting? Glazes stain and darken; a highlight of white thinly applied over brown looks blue without being blue. Or relativity; what is next to the colour, or what surrounds it.

Perhaps professional writers keep notebooks. I have never even kept a diary. All I can do is summon up images, thumb through a mental photograph album. I know Tim came with me to Norfolk that time from a single, fixed picture. Tim in the Orwells' house; standing at the bottom of the handsome, wide staircase that leads to the main gallery, his tousled hair looking greenish and dusty in the light from the glass dome above him, his chin tucked shyly into his lifted shoulder as he turns to Ned's young wife, Polly. Gawky, flat-featured (as if she had spent her life with her face pressed to a window) she is only beautiful because of her pregnancy; long, straight back complementing the smooth, ripening pear that she carries before her. She is wearing a scarlet shift that follows this sweet curve of her body and several heavy gold chains. Her small, squashed nose is tinted vermilion around the nostrils, her wide-set, speckled eyes, pale as pebbles, and cold.

Anxiety mixed with irritation is the emotion that goes with this picture. Perhaps I had just heard her ask Tim a question that he hadn't answered, or was struggling to answer, petrified by this cold-eyed, clipped-voiced young woman, or, more simply, numbed by the arctic chill inside this grand house. Only Ned's mother seemed suitably dressed for it, in ski pants and high boots; a small wizened witch whose clawed, bony fingers occasionally emerged from the long sleeves of her huge, heavy, cable-knit sweater to indicate a painting that my ignorant eyes might have missed, or at least undervalued, without her instruction. Ned had introduced me, Maud's nephew, the painter, but I remained a nameless peasant to her. 'Mr Er,' she called me. 'I'm afraid I don't know your work, Mr Er.' I think she may have just said this, which was why I had turned away at that moment, to avoid the embarrassment of listening to poor, patient Ned speaking kindly of my *Vision of London* as he pointed it out to his mother, and to check on Tim who might be feeling agitated, left behind, unprotected.

In fact, of course, Joyce must have been there. She was fond of Tim and would have been unobtrusively watching, ready to leap to his rescue. We had stayed the night with her; she had driven us over. I have a smudged memory – a faded, blurred, sepia picture – of her chattering away to me in the car afterwards, and presumably Tim was silently sitting behind us. We would hardly have left him behind with Ned and his wife and his quite dreadful old mother. (Maud had been right about her; one meeting was enough to convince me. 'Mr Er – if your copies are really so good, how will one be able to tell the difference? After all, there is a lot of money at stake.' I answered that she would be able to tell the original by the frame, and she responded, triumphantly, 'Exactly, Mr Er, you see why we have to be careful.')

Joyce said, in the car, 'Oh, that is a poisonously ignorant woman. She knows nothing and she thinks she knows everything. Or maybe she knows she knows nothing and has decided that anything *she* doesn't know can't be worth knowing. I don't know how you managed to be so bland and polite, I just wanted to *hit* her. I don't think they make women like her any longer. If they do, thank God I don't meet them. It isn't just old age with her, either. My grandmother remembers her when she was young, they used to meet at hunt balls, vast coming-out parties – extraordinary to think that sort of life made up the *life* of some girls in, when was it, the early 'twenties? My grandmother says she was amazingly pretty and just as amazingly stupid, pleased as punch with herself and rude to anyone she thought was her social inferior, which in her view was just about the rest of the world, more or less, all those people who didn't have *titles*. Just the sort of brainless aristocrat you'd set up as Aunt Sally if you were a Communist! Not that her family were aristocrats, just rich, *solid* with land, farming money, and determined that their daughter should marry into the county gentry. That sort of thing goes on, though less *openly* nowadays, naturally. I only met Ned's father a couple of times, he went to visit my grandmother when she was ill a couple of years ago and we met in the hospital, he and Gran were good friends, in fact a bit *more* than that once I think, years ago, which is maybe why she's always been a bit over the top vitriolic about Hermione Orwell, but that's by the by. What I was going to say was that I thought that he was a lovely man, even though he was crippled, poor darling, sort of twinkly and quiet and kind, just like old Ned, and that I only hope *he* hasn't been caught by his Polly in the same way as his Dad with Hermione, though she just seemed a bit dull, I thought today – Polly, I mean – not enough character to be *nasty*. Did you know Ned's first wife? Jenny was such a darling even though she wasn't very well, really, when Henry and I first moved back to Norfolk – that is, *back* to Norfolk for me, Henry had never lived anywhere other than London – and your nice Aunt Maud introduced us. But she was so sweet and friendly, both she and Ned were, having us over to meet all the locals . . .'

I cannot honestly say that I have reported this monologue with absolute accuracy. If I had done it would have been very much longer. But this is enough to give a fair indication of Joyce's usual conversation, thinking aloud rather than taking part in a dialogue, which is the kind of style, I suppose, that women who spend too much time alone, or (Joyce has three teenage children) without adult company, may be forced into. Although I think that I got the general drift, I wandered off from time to time down various byways; wondering if the van Dyck, hung in the entrance hall, was really a Lely; visualising the pictures that Ned had suggested I might copy for him; calculating the amount of time I would have to spend in that freezing house in the preparatory stages, and how much I could do at home after; hoping that my West Indian neighbour would be able to manage the burglar alarm when he went into the house to feed my old cat, and trying to remember if I had left the tin opener beside the tinned food I had left on the kitchen table.

At some moment towards the end of this journey (an hour, more or less, across the frozen flat lands of Norfolk, a dark landscape turning black and silver as the moon rose) I must have absented myself for longer than was polite. I heard her say, '. . . sorry, I'm *boring* you, aren't I? You should shut me up! Henry says, it's like sitting under a waterfall.'

'That sounds rather peaceful,' I said. 'He's a lucky man if that's all he's got to complain about.'

She laughed. She has a charming laugh, light and girlish. It removed any sympathy her torrent of disconnected information might have made me feel, very briefly, with Henry. Although Joyce is essentially a minor character in this story (if I were an eighteenth-century painter I would employ an assistant to paint her into the background) I like and admire her. No great skill would be required to depict her; only a certain amount of respect and affection for a nice, ordinary woman, salt of the earth, with a compact, sturdy body and a round, slightly hairy face – a lot of fine, peachy down on her cheeks and her throat. (I had never been disposed to make sexual advances to Joyce, but I had often wanted to stroke her.) What else is important about her? She is kind to old people; her parents, her ancient grandmother, Henry and Helen's quite difficult father, are always either being visited or invited to stay with her, and she is an excellent mother to her three children who are good mannered, intelligent, and healthy as apples.

Peaches, apples – there would be a glowing bowl of fruit somewhere in her portrait, and not just because she keeps a market garden. For my assistant, filling in the details of that visit to Joyce would be a pleasant task, romantic in a wholesome way, sketching in the comfort of the converted farmhouse;

sprigged cotton curtains, faded carpets on polished wood floors, good, thick, homemade soup and fresh bread, a crackling log fire. Joyce saying, curled up in front of it, on a large, sagging sofa (after we had eaten and Tim had disappeared to play some game with the children) that she was sorry about what had happened between me and Helen, pausing long enough for me to talk if I wanted to but not long enough for me to feel that I had to. Saying that Tim seemed a bit better than when she'd last seen him, a bit more outgoing, that if he ever wanted to come and stay she would be delighted, and not just for his sake; she could always do with extra help in the garden, and of course she would pay him, a proper rate by the hour, and deduct the cost of his board so he wouldn't feel it was in any way charity. Asking how I was managing at home, had I got someone coming in (I must have told her our daily had given us up), and if not, she knew a woman in Norwich who ran a good agency, providing sensible country girls, carefully vetted, not foreign au pairs who so often spelt trouble; language difficulties, homesickness, social problems . . .

All this, of course, at much greater length than I have set down, embellished with asides of different lengths, anecdotes about people I didn't know, comments on the local television news (nothing further afield interested her) and several horror stories about employing girls from abroad, the only one of which I remember was about a friend who was having a baby, who met her Swedish mother's help at the airport and was horrified to see an even more pregnant woman emerging from Customs and advancing, beaming and fecund, towards her. 'Worse than you might think,' Joyce said. 'Of course my friend couldn't send her back, I forget why, exactly, the Swedish girl had some long, tragic story, but *that* part was all right, they both had their babies and it was really working out very nicely, but then the girl ran off with the husband who was going off for six months to Australia, he's with one of the international oil companies, and she actually *left* her *baby* behind her . . .'

I expect that I shook my head, gave a little sigh, then a rueful laugh; generally aiming to strike the appropriate balance between sympathy for Joyce's friend, disapproval of the husband's behaviour, and a mildly amused amazement at the silly games people play. But since I was bored by now with the servant problem, I said that I was fixed up, hoped that I was about to be, anyway. George, or rather his daughter, had a friend who might be prepared to move in for a bit and take care of things. I was so busy reminding myself not to tell Joyce that this friend of Elaine's had a four-year-old child in case it produced a deluge of further storm warnings that I had momentarily forgotten that she probably didn't know who George was, nor, more importantly, who his daughter was, what she was up to with Henry.

I remembered as soon as I'd spoken. As if on cue, a large log toppled out of the fire, yellow flames spurted, and the whole of this dimly lit scene, this casual detail at the edge of the picture, sprang into sharp focus. I bent to replace the fallen log, banged at it to make it settle, and to see the sparks fly up the black chimney; then sat back on my heels, watching the molten caves at the base of the fire while I explained that George was my dealer and agent and one of my oldest friends; we had been at art college together. I wondered, aloud, if Henry had ever met him. I thought that he must have done, at some point or another, but then again he might not. I simply couldn't remember! Trouble was, I was getting to the age when the old mind was beginning to leak a bit, when you begin to discover the truth in commonplace phrases. Memory like a sieve. That sort of thing . . .

I thought she was regarding me rather oddly. Not with

suspicion, exactly, but something pretty close to it. Wary. Perhaps it was only surprise that I had managed several consecutive sentences without her butting in, but for safety's sake I thought that I had better employ a more certain diversionary tactic. I said, 'Another example. Marriages made in Heaven. When Helen went off with her dentist I realised for the first time what that really meant! The truth behind that particular cliché is that Heaven makes a botch up of most things!'

After that we were safe. Oh, how *dreadful*, why hadn't I told her before, she was so *dreadfully* sorry. There was quite a lot of that, enough to make me feel conscience-stricken, before she got off the sofa and stumbled across to me, tripping over a ruck in the hearth rug and collapsing, half on the low chair I had removed myself to after I had dealt with the fire, and half on my lap, putting her arms around me and holding me fiercely tight as if I were a child to be comforted. Then she was kissing me; little motherly or sisterly kisses, on my eyes, on my mouth. The hairs on her upper lip were stiff, a bit prickly; I wondered if she cut them, or shaved them, and this, combined with her general clumsiness made her seem sweetly vulnerable. I began kissing her back in a way that quickly became less fatherly or brotherly than I had intended. She nestled into this phase with considerable enthusiasm, nestling warmly against me with eager, soft grunts and sighs; when she finally murmured, 'Oh, no, we *mustn't*,' it struck me that if I had inadvertently let out the truth about Henry, she would not have protested at all, even for form's sake, but simply got on with what she obviously very much wanted to do. To let it out now was out of the question. Besides being unkind and disreputable it would only lead to talk and tears rather than action. And getting on with it couldn't in any case be exactly so simple – where, anyway? on the rug? on the sofa? – with my son and her son and two daughters occupied somewhere in the house at the moment but not necessarily for long enough, indeed more than likely to blunder in any second. I was astonished that she hadn't, apparently, thought of this probability. So much for Joyce, the careful, concerned, considerate mother! I kissed her kindly but firmly and shifted our relative positions so that I could look into her damp, furry, flushed face. I said, 'No, you're right, bless you, I'm sorry.'

She slid off my knees, fairly neatly and gracefully, and sat at my feet, looking up at me. I smiled. She smiled back, a bit shyly and shakily. I said, 'I suddenly thought of the children.'

She said, 'Oh, my goodness, yes! I don't know what . . . oh, never mind. I'm sorry, I shouldn't have *dashed* at you. It was just . . . I mean, I had no idea about Helen. I suppose I thought. I mean, you seemed so calm. I just thought you had *both* decided, in a sort of very *modern* way . . .'

'I suppose it was a bit like that, really.'

'Do you want to tell me about it?'

'There's nothing much to tell.'

Nothing, that is, that I wanted to tell her. I outlined what had happened. I said, 'She didn't *go off* with him. In the end, it was my fault. I've been stupid.'

She said, 'Yes, I suppose it must feel like that now.'

She was quiet for a little, looking into the fire. Then she said, 'You know, in a way, it's all *Henry's* fault.' This seemed a bit tangential, even for Joyce, and even she must have realised it, because she went on at once, very quickly, 'What I mean is, she wouldn't have thought of being a dentist if Henry hadn't had such a ghastly time with his teeth. He had to have a simply vast amount of fancy bridge work when he was thirteen or so, it had been put off longer than it should have been because he was such a coward – he says that himself, so it's all right to tell you – and when it was done at last, he simply *hated* the whole, dreadful business, got himself into a frightful state, pain and fear, and in between visits to the surgery he used to work it off, playing with Helen's dolls, poking sharp things into their mouths. Of course she caught him at it and asked him what he was doing, and he couldn't really explain, poor child, so he said he was practising being a dentist, he wanted to be a dentist when he grew up. So Helen said she wanted to be a dentist too, and Henry said that she couldn't be, girls couldn't be dentists, only boys. He was only teasing, trying to hide what was really upsetting him, but it made her *furious*. She flew at him, Henry says, kicked and punched him in the face, right in his poor *mouth*, which is, of course, why he remembers all this so clearly. She screamed that she'd *show* him, she'd *teach* him to be rude about girls. If Henry was thirteen, she'd be eleven, the sort of age people get fixed on something and, anyway, she's always been enormously stubborn; Henry says, when she made up her mind to a thing nothing could stop her. I think, to be honest, he's always been a bit scared of her, determined women alarm him, though of course he adores her . . . I'm afraid if he knew she'd been off with someone he'd be dreadfully shocked, he's such a loyal person himself.'

I was intrigued by this picture of Henry as a gentle soul with a delicate conscience. I said, in that case she had better not tell him, that in fact I would rather she didn't, and not only for his sake and Helen's, but for my sake as well; the last thing I wanted was to be looked upon as an injured party. She nodded wisely and said that was very *fine*, very *brave*, and of course if that was how I felt she would respect my confidence, say nothing to Henry, even though they always told each other everything, it was one of the most important things about a good marriage . . .

*

I helped myself liberally to Henry's Glenfiddich, patiently enduring this sad little comedy. *Innocence Betrayed*, a sentimental Edwardian painting, I thought, watching her earnest, flushed face in the firelight. It wasn't until I was in bed, vaguely wondering if she might come padding along to me (hoping that she would and that she wouldn't just about equally to begin with, and finally coming down on the side of feeling quite strongly that I would prefer that she didn't for reasons that had nothing to do with any kind of moral scruple, only with comfort, convenience, and general avoidance of emotional complications on her part) that I began to see a quite different picture. Looking, as it were, through a Claude Glass that reflects a view in miniature, eliminating detail so that the pattern is clearer; eliminating, in this case, the actual words that were spoken and showing the panic behind them, a torrent of speech tumbling out as if she were running fast over soft, marshy ground, terrified of standing still, of sinking into the mire, of losing her innocence . . .

And yet, in the morning, she was calm and rosy and smiling. I kissed her downy cheek. She said, 'Come any time, you and Tim, either or both of you. During the week would be best, perhaps, Henry's so tired at weekends that he just wants to *flop*, though of course if you needed to come then, he'd understand, and I'm sure he'd be pleased, because you wouldn't want *entertaining*, you'd be part of the *family*, it's having to be what he calls *on parade* that exhausts him, poor lamb . . .'

In the car, going home, Tim said, 'She's pretty wound up, isn't she, Dad? Has anything happened to make her unhappy?'

I remember that remark, though not how he looked as he made it. He was sitting in the back seat as he usually did on long journeys so that he could chain smoke without my complaining. Apart from Tim in Ned's house with Polly, the only other clear image I have of him from that period is in the kitchen with Clio; of both of them sitting at the table, mugs of instant coffee in front of them, both of them turning to look at me with mildly guilty expressions because it is some time since breakfast, or perhaps lunch, and the remains of whichever meal it was are still not cleared away; there is a clutter of greasy pots and pans on every available surface. And I, coming in through the door (coming home unexpectedly?) am irritated by this slovenly muddle, by the sticky brown rings their coffee mugs have left all over the table, and thinking with something close to despair that I have acquired, not the domestic freedom that George had hoped Clio would give me, but an additional responsibility. Three children instead of one.

Although, to begin with, I was happy to play the father to Clio. Twenty years between us restored me to adult dignity, allowed me to put aside the miserable memory of my humiliating failure with Helen.

I said, when she came to see me, 'George will have told you what's happened, of course. Why I need someone. My wife's left me. It's been a dreary business but that part is over now, we're quite adequately friendly, so that need not bother you.' I smiled, crinkling my eyes up. Wise. Sad. Avuncular.

Clio blushed. At first sight, she was a gawky, pudding-faced, bespectacled child who blushed easily. Her spectacles were tinted blue. She wore a fluffy pink sweater and faded jeans and scarlet leg warmers. Her little boy, Barnaby, watching me gravely, seemed in some ways older than she was. More composed, certainly. I said, 'Do you think you'd like to come and live with me, Barnaby?' and he answered cautiously, sensibly, husky-voiced like his mother, 'I might. I don't know yet.'

'He won't be a nuisance,' George had promised. 'Nice little chap, what I've seen of him, very quick, very quiet. Had to be, poor little rat, any trouble and the grandparents would have had them out on the doorstep. Never darken my doors again. A bit of an odd attitude in this day and age. Anger and disappointment, I'd hazard, rather than social or moral shame; Clio was very bright at school and they were ambitious for her. But whatever the cause, they've made the girl suffer. Elaine says her bloody father hasn't addressed a direct word to her since the child was born, won't have them eat at his table! How she's stuck it, why she hasn't got away before, I don't know. Maybe you're her first chance. Not that I'm suggesting you take her on as a bloody favour, God forbid, but if you're accepting the Orwell commission you've got a lot on your plate, you can't afford to frig about, you'll need someone to do the chores, and she's at least likely to be a bit grateful. I don't suppose she's a gourmet cook but she'll surely be able to manage the odd fry up for Tim, keep the place a bit clean. I've found her quite competent when she's helped out at the gallery, eager to please, that sort of thing. Elaine's fond of her, she's always been her best friend at the convent, though of course young Clio had to leave a bit early, pregnant girls being not exactly persona grata with the Rev Mum. But they've kept up the friendship. In fact, I did suggest to Elaine that Clio might like to move in with us, company for her when I was away, but she wasn't too keen. She said Clio might feel it was charity.'

Inconvenient, too, when the lovely Elaine wanted to entertain Helen's brother. Perhaps George knew this and was turning a father's blind eye. As long as his beloved daughter was tied up with a middle-aged, married man, George was safe; Elaine wouldn't leave him. Besides, if he did know about the affair he might not want to discourage Henry who was (as Aunt Maud had been so quick to remind me) at the Board of Trade, the Export Licence Division, and a large part of George's business was with New York art dealers. I had no reason to suspect either of them of improper behaviour but George was a man who usually had at least one cautious eye on his own advantage. Take his present concern for Clio. No doubt he was sorry for the girl, but he also had a sound interest in my being able to get on with my work. Ten per cent on my copying fee for Ned's pictures, on top of the larger percentage he would collect when he sold the originals, would add up to a fair sum of money. A bit of a coup for old George, in fact; without Maud's useful 'interference' Ned would presumably have gone to Christie's or Sotheby's.

I said, to Clio, 'This was George's idea, wasn't it? Is this the first time you've looked for a job?'

If things were as bad at home as George had suggested, it seemed to me pretty peculiar. A baby at seventeen obviously narrows the options. But a spirited girl could have found something, surely? Even if it were only a living-in job like the not very arduous one I was offering. And as the law stood, if her father evicted her, the local council would have had to find her accommodation.

She said, 'Having a baby is a job, isn't it? Though, I know *men* don't think so. As a matter of fact, I was waiting till Barnaby was ready for school. He'll be five in January. Do you mean that I ought to have left him at home with my mother?'

She looked at me with sullen distaste as if I had proposed some evil malpractice. Not the girl for me, I decided. I was about to make some moderately jovial disclaimer – I wasn't criticising her, far from it, in fact I endorsed her responsible attitude, so rare nowadays, but perhaps in that case she really should wait until she could see her way a bit clearer – but Barnaby stopped me. He made a sudden, small sound; a soft intake of frightened breath as he pressed close to his mother. And she said, 'Oh, Barnaby, don't be so feeble. You know what I've told you. As long as you're good I won't leave you with Granny.'

The teasing flavour of this response, part comfort, part threat, was unpalatable. The child visibly trembled. Clio said, 'My parents are very negative about Barnaby. They find it hard to relate to an illegitimate grandchild.'

She spoke with comic severity, like a social worker composing a report, but with some dignity, too. Using this solemn jargon to put her cards on the table.

I said, 'George has told me the background. It must have been difficult for you.'

She shrugged narrow shoulders. 'We managed. Barnaby can be good when he wants to be. You'll be good if we come to live here, won't you, Barnaby?'

She gave him a little shake. Again, her amused tone held a faint threat. The child nodded. Still burrowing close to his mother, one small hand clutching a scarlet leg warmer, he regarded me timidly. One dark eye, sliding inwards, squinted towards his nose. His mouth hung slightly open. I said, 'I'm sure he will, he looks like a very good boy to me.'

As soon as I had spoken, I knew that I had committed myself. Barnaby gave me the ghost of a smile, a mere twitch of his lips. I smiled back, I hoped reassuringly. His smile broadened, became a wide, sunny, confident beam. The composed look that had shuttered his face and made him seem older than his young mother was gone. He wasn't a pretty child, with his large, bulging, bony forehead that seemed to squash the rest of his features into too small a space, but smiling so fulsomely, happily, trustingly, he looked eager and open and lovable.

And I was won over. Can it be possible to fall in love, at first sight, with a child? It was gratifying, of course, that a few words of automatic kindness could produce such a startling change in a matter of seconds. And maybe the memory of Tim at that age had something to do with it; a sudden, sweet, painful yearning for a time when he had been young enough for me to gather him up, tuck him under my coat, keep him from harm. No impulse is simple. But what I felt, at that moment, immediately, was an immense, warm rush of sentiment, an overwhelming desire to protect and console this particular, grinning, boss-eyed little boy.

Not the soundest of reasons for employing his mother. But I was desperate to get back to work. To send Clio away would have meant explanations to George, advertising for someone else, telephone calls, letters, interviews; a frustrating tedium that I had as little taste for as I had for holding back the advancing tide of dirt, dust, grubby laundry, unwashed dishes, odd, unpaired socks, stale milk and crumpled old newspapers, that seemed to be engulfing the five floors of my terrace house with the inexorable, impersonal force of some external natural catastrophe; a flood of lava descending upon my doomed domestic arrangements from some distant volcanic eruption. The last straw had been the inexplicable jamming of the catch that released the drawer of the rubbish compactor; the compressed bulk of garbage inside it, egg shells, banana skins, scrapings from plates, fish bones, chicken skeletons, mouldy bread, rotting vegetable parings, had begun to ferment and stink, oozing vile juices like some trapped and dying cave monster.

Clio telephoned the manufacturers of the compactor and

when they told her (as they had already told me) that this model had been discontinued and they were no longer able to service it, she ordered them to come and remove the machine in confident and peremptory tones, promising to call them twice daily until this was done, mentioning health hazards and unwelcome publicity. A truck arrived within the hour and the monster was dismantled and carted away by three large, surly men. To say that I was Clio's slave from that moment would be an absurd overstatement but I was certainly humble with gratitude.

I have said that I was 'desperate' to get to work. It is hard to explain the quality of this desperation, the total, consuming power of the need to get on with the job that has nothing to do with the greatness or littleness of your talent, the importance of the final achievement. Habit comes into it, and the desire for some unifying simplicity; better a single absorbing task than messy odds and ends like rubbish compactors. And money buys time along with a good many other things. I think, when I telephoned Helen to tell her that I had taken on this commission, I had thought, in a hopeful, absurd, childish way, that I might *buy her back*, not so much because of the staggering sums I would earn (part on account, part when the pictures were sold) but because of the flattering *value* they seemed to place upon *me*. An entirely false value, of course, as I told her immediately, part of the whole monstrous concept of art as investment; paintings, not regarded as artefacts to be hung on a wall and looked at for pleasure, but as a safe harbour for money, to be bought by some pension fund perhaps, treated like currency, locked away in a bank vault for safety. Quite a lot of my indignation was genuine. Helen listened. She gasped at the prices George was expecting to get in New York. She giggled. She said, 'Are you frightened?'

Well, fear is always a part of it. You may not be up to it. You may not be worthy. But this is a fruitful fear. It sharpens the tension.

Maud says, the questions she is asked after a lecture are almost always practical. How does she write – with a pen, a pencil, a typewriter, a word processor? How many hours a day, how many words an hour, how long does it take? Never *why*; not what moves her, or drives her. As if her questioners understood, humbly, instinctively, that this central question is a mystery that cannot be answered. Helen asked me which of the pictures I was thinking of starting on first and I told her. She said, 'Can you see how to do it yet?'

Like Maud, I can answer practical questions. I will size the canvas with rabbitskin glue. The colours I will probably be using are white lead, ivory black, Naples yellow, alizarin crimson, burnt umber, burnt sienna, Prussian blue; the brushes, numbers four, five, six and ten round bristles, number six round sables, medium and large flat bristle blenders and half an inch flat oxhair blenders. A palette. A knife. Fingers.

No one is any the wiser.

The longer you do a thing, the less certain you are how you do it. One moment it seems impossible; the next you can see that with a bit of luck you might manage it, or something quite close to it, near enough to begin on and, with a little more luck, start to move in the right direction for long enough to stop thinking about it and simply to do it. It isn't a smooth advance; long, flat stretches and then little jumps and jerks forward that usually come about unexpectedly. Talking to Helen I suddenly remembered that she had a lace collar, an old one, bought at an antiques' fair, off a clothes' stall. The lace had been yellowish, like the lace in the picture, and of a soft, nubbly texture. My eyes and my fingers remembered it.

I said, to Helen, 'Yes, I think I'm beginning to see. It's taking shape, anyway.'

'Good,' she said. 'Then get on with it.'

That brusque injunction rankled rather. Did she really think 'getting on with it' was so easy? Oh, probably. Helen had always been very brisk, very practical. So unlike Clio, whose respect for my work appeared to border on awe. She lowered her voice when she spoke of it. She thought it was 'wonderful' to have an 'artistic vocation' – an attitude I would have tried to discourage if it had not turned out to have so many advantages. She wasn't particularly good at cleaning the house, or only in bursts, bouts of frenzied activity followed by long spells of brooding apathy, but while I was working she guarded my privacy with absolute dedication, answering telephone calls, door bells, dealing with postmen, milkmen, market researchers, children collecting sponsors for charity walks, Jehovah's Witnesses, men who came to read the gas and electricity meters. Helen, of course, had never been at home to protect me from these intruders. Had it ever occurred to her, busy drilling teeth in her surgery, that I might need protection? No, it had not.

Other unfavourable comparisons began to occur to me. Clio owned a few pairs of jeans, a few sweaters, one woollen skirt that she sometimes changed into at supper time; a pathetic, waif's wardrobe that made me see Helen's 'creative' pleasure in her expensive clothes as tiresome, time-wasting; an obsession with 'appearance', a retreat from 'reality'. Oh, how I burned to heap these sanctimonious insults upon her! Vain, self-regarding, unfaithful, cold, heartless Helen! When, for example, had she last sat at my feet in the evening, shown any real interest in *me*, as a separate *person*, not just as a boring old husband; interest in what I might feel, have to say, about politics, art, or even the weather? When I told Clio about my unknown father and his adventures in the wine trade, she was curled up on the rug by my chair, her woollen skirt swirling in a green pool about her, one hand clasping a strong, bony ankle, listening attentively, watching me solemnly. She said, 'I think that's quite dreadful. I mean, it makes a funny story now, but it must have been dreadful for you when you were young. It makes me realise that I've got to be very careful what I tell Barnaby. It must have been dreadfully weird for you to know just that one thing about your father, much worse than knowing nothing at all. It must have freaked you out absolutely. It's amazing, really, that you've grown up so amazingly, well, sort of balanced and wise.'

Her sympathy, though misplaced, was very sweet to me. Helen had never shown any concern for my deprived childhood. Even if I had never expected it from her, a properly loving wife would have offered it, suspecting my claim that I had been happy alone with my mother, never missed not having a father. Indeed, now I thought about it, perhaps Clio's sympathy wasn't so misplaced after all; perhaps, all my life, I had been bravely hiding a deep and shattering grief. It was unlikely – I won't say impossible because the archaeology of the mind is mysterious; who can be certain what lurks in that dark, buried city? What is more probable is that Clio had sensed my unhappiness and, being too young to disbelieve my unctuous lies about the amicable nature of my separation from Helen, had ascribed it to a cause that she, poor child, understood better. (I had not, at this point, ventured to question her about Barnaby's father, or even her own impossible parents, nor, to be honest, had I felt that I wanted to, anticipating a flood of childish and self-righteous grievances. But even if a banal solipsism was the source of her sympathy, I was still grateful for it. She was obviously a sensitive girl. She was kind, and agreeably responsive to kindness; her initial grumpy defensiveness had disappeared very quickly. She seemed eager to please without being deferential. And she was percipient, too. Helen never called me balanced or wise.)

It is clear, I hope, from what I have set down in these pages, what was really happening to me. I have tried to be honest, even about my own folly. All artists or makers – painters, writers, carpenters, builders, bricklayers – live in two worlds, one of work, the other what most people would call their real life. Both are in fact equally real, but although they exist side by side, contiguously, contemporaneously, each is absolutely separate from the other. In my work world, at this time, I was busy and happy. In my other world I was possessed by a fiend, tormented, torn apart, frustrated, bitter and angry. But there is no word in the language strong enough to describe the desperate and demented rage that took hold of my mind and my body when I contemplated what Helen had done to me. It was an illness, a madness, a fever that consumed and crippled me, preventing me from behaving rationally, with proper care and concern for other people.

It may seem bathetic to say that I fell in love in order to get my own back on Helen, but since this is the chief reason for the cringing shame that assails me when I think about Clio, I have to admit it. I deliberately allowed myself to become infatuated with a girl more than twenty years younger than I was, in order to revenge myself on my wife. I made use of Clio, not as a 'sex object', which is the kind of cant term she would use to berate me, but as something much worse: as a weapon in a war that she was not party to, nor even aware of.

I didn't, of course, fully understand this at the time. All I was conscious of, to begin with, was a growing attachment to Clio that was partly sexual, partly paternal, partly grateful because, in a sense, she presented no threat to me. Outside my work, out there in that other world that suddenly appeared to be entirely inhabited by cheerful, glowing, healthy and happy men whose wives were loving and faithful, I felt so low, unsuccessful, such an unwanted and despised reject, that it seemed safer to look for comfort in someone who was even more of a failure in that world than I was. Apparently I wasn't good enough for Helen. A girl like Clio, with no money, no career, no home of her own, an uncaring family and an illegitimate brat, was probably all I deserved. At least she would be too grateful to leave me. And, to be more positive, at least I could do something for her. She had had a rough time; it wouldn't be difficult to make her life a bit easier. That could be a pleasure. I had always wanted a daughter. Although I was repelled (or thought I was) by the pairing of old men with young women that seemed to be going on all around me, telling myself there was something aesthetically distasteful in Henry-and-Elaine, for example, the greying, balding, paunchy man and the fresh and beautiful girl, George-and-Elaine was a quite different matter. That was the kind of relationship I would aim at, establish, with Clio.

Was I deceiving myself? All I can say is that I had no intention of coaxing her into my bed. Which doesn't mean that I hadn't thought about it (I can distinctly remember reflecting that the combined presences of her son and my son in the house were a useful safeguard against any impulses I might have in that direction) or that I denied myself the normal delights of lustful fantasies when she brushed past me in the kitchen or emerged rosy from her bath with only a small towel clasped around her. But that was to be *all*. Look and not touch! And I had the excuse that when I looked it was with a painter's eye. Her running (which to start with I was only aware of as a 'hobby') had made her body exceptionally interesting; thighs fuller and broader than her narrow hips; her torso straight and childlike above strongly muscled legs that were already beginning to show signs of age, roped with blue, prominent veins. I thought that I might paint her naked; half child, half woman. Or in her pale jeans and running shoes against a distant London landscape, an acid green, London sky.

The background to the full-length portrait of the lady with the lace collar was a dramatic country landscape, a lot of dark foliage and a wild, stormy sky shot with light. There were a few sheep, a smocked shepherd boy, and a grandish ruin in the middle ground that looked a little like Castle Acre Priory near Swaffham. The picture had darkened up a bit with age but it had been painted fat over lean, with an increasing amount of oil in each succeeding layer, so there was little cracking or surface deterioration. The canvas had been lightly stained with umber; the darks of eyes, hair and foliage very thinly applied in a transparent brown; the cool tones of the flesh scumbled across the chest and neck; full lights put on with a loaded brush. All that was straightforward. The draperies, the lace, painted with haphazard scratches and marks that only took form from a distance, would be harder to copy with the needed impetuous *dash*. It takes time to make something look natural and easy. I could do it with a little rehearsal, but what had probably taken no more than a day or two would be as many weeks work for me. And my fingers were playing up; knuckles swollen into red, painful knobs, a tedious handicap that I sometimes suffered in winter that had been aggravated by the Siberian conditions of what I had begun to think of as Gulag Orwell. For the three nights I stayed there, I wore gloves in bed.

Even so, my arthritis had worsened. Luckily, I was only taking photographs, measurement, mapping out and squaring up as well as I could with the eldritch Dowager, bundled up in her ski garments, popping in and out of the gallery, keeping a beady eye open to see that I didn't put my grubby labourer's hands or beam compass too close, pretending that she was only reminding me that the pictures were wired to the local police station – one touch, she claimed, and the alarm would blast off! – but contriving to make it clear to me that until proved innocent I was guilty in her view; either a mindless vandal or the front man for a gang of international art kidnappers. I tried to fight back by rather weakly suggesting that I wasn't, myself, absolutely convinced of this particular picture's provenance and that there was a certain amount of unfortunate Victorian 'restoration' and over-painting that was likely to reduce its value even if it were genuine. She received this infantile ploy with a bleak, knowing stare and a remark that I would not have believed anyone could utter had I not heard it. 'Ah, but you're only a *painter*, Mr Er. Not an expert.'

Ned and his burgeoning Polly did their best to protect me, hustling her away when they could, consoling me with reasonable food and good wine and (on Ned's part) guarded apologies. 'The trouble is, she's been reading all that alarmist stuff they keep writing up in the newspapers.' Polly rolled her eyes and hooted with schoolgirlish laughter at this. And when Ned asked if it might be easier for me if the pictures were in George's gallery for the finishing stages, which was where George wanted them eventually anyway, to get as much publicity as he could once the export business was sorted out, proposing to hire Securicor to take them to London, she said, pretty sharpish, 'Perhaps your mother would like to ride shotgun.'

Her speckled eyes glinted with rather more spite than amusement. Though Ned laughed, I thought that he flinched a little. He looked older, and tired. Hag-ridden.

He said, as he helped me pack my clobber in the back of the van, 'My mother doesn't mean to be offensive. She can't really believe that anything she could say could offend anyone. It's a kind of, well, playfulness.'

I said that I hadn't been offended and he seemed relieved. 'Good of you to say so. I suppose one learns tolerance as one grows older. It's a bit hard on Polly. Though she's beginning to stand up for herself.' He sighed. That was a bit hard on *him*! He said, as I started the engine, 'Give my love to Maud, will you?'

It didn't sound like a casual message. He was looking wistful.

Poor old Ned, I thought, on the road, driving home. Trapped between young wife and old mother. A classic warning!

For the first time for months I was feeling pleased with myself, cheerful, expansive, relaxed; a tide of well-being flooding in from a number of sources. Perhaps the spectacle of poor Ned's discomfort had something to do with it. I was satisfied with the ground work I had done on the paintings. The weather was lovely; a cold, sparkling, late February day. The second-hand van I had bought to carry my stepladder and easels on this expedition was humming merrily along; heater working, no sinister mechanical sounds. And, above all, in the last four days I had not once been angry with Helen; the urge to argue, revile her, had miraculously left me. It was almost as if *she* had decided to leave me in peace. I was a free man at last! Not a lonely one, though. My relationship with Clio had defined itself nicely. I was looking forward to going home, seeing her – and, of course, Barnaby, Timothy. My three children, sitting round the table at supper.

Tim wasn't at home. He had been gone for two days. Clio was vague. He had said something about going to stay with a friend.

He had said, 'Tell Dad not to worry.' No, he hadn't said who the friend was. He hadn't left a telephone number. She seemed a bit surprised that I should ask her these questions. A bit scornful. Tim was old enough, surely, to come and go as he pleased? I was torn between the ease of accepting this, and the familiar, nagging anxiety. I said that I didn't want to keep tabs on him, but he hadn't been well. (It seemed unfair to Tim to be more specific; to draw Clio, who was the same generation, into what he might feel was an adult conspiracy against him, reduce him, in her eyes, to childhood.) She shrugged her shoulders. She said, 'If you must know, I think he met a girl at a party.'

I rang Helen – from my bedroom, furtively. She said, 'If Clio says she *thinks* he's with a girl, then he almost certainly *is*. She was just condescending to your middle-aged prurience. You know what they're like, the young. They don't like to give each other away.'

I wanted to tell her that I had stopped being angry with her. But she didn't know that I had been. Not to what extent, anyway. I said, 'Being young doesn't cut you off from the rest of the human race.'

'They think it does, that's what matters. They have different ground rules. You watch out with that Clio, my lad. Don't do anything I wouldn't do.'

There had always been a streak of vulgarity latent in Helen! I refrained from charging her with it, simply answered in the same vein. 'That gives me plenty of scope, doesn't it, darling?'

She giggled – coarsely, I thought. I wondered if she had been drinking. Or if Ted Frobish was with her. Or someone else, a new lover. Of course, it was no longer my business.

I was dismayed to find that my anger was creeping back, heating up again. Perhaps the Spartan chill of the Gulag had only temporarily chilled it. I said, 'If you hear anything from

Tim, perhaps you will be good enough to inform me,' and replaced the receiver.

In spite of Tim's absence and that conversation, I did my best to establish the pleasant family atmosphere I had envisaged during my euphoric journey from Norfolk. I bathed Barnaby, blew soap bubbles for him, dried him, put him to bed, read him *The Tale of Samuel Whiskers* to which he listened with an anxiously solemn expression, watching my eyes and my mouth, as if uncertain what response was required of him. ('Doesn't Mummy read to you?' I had asked, when I first realised that this was a new experience for him, and he had shaken his head, putting on the closed, secret look that made him look elderly.)

Clio didn't play games with him, either. He had three woolly animals, a bear, a monkey, and a fluffy purple hippopotamus called Billy, that were his companions and comforters. He carried them around with him in a green Marks and Spencer plastic bag and I had heard him talking to them when he was alone in his bedroom. He had no other toys, nor seemed much interested in the ones Tim had turfed out of his cupboard and given him, picking up small model cars and trucks and looking at them with a puzzled expression. It wasn't that he was stupid. I had bought him a construction kit that was quite complicated for a child of his age; he had put it together in under five minutes and then sat back on his heels and regarded me with that same baffled look. He had done what I seemed to want him to do, put this object together, what was the point of it? I had said, 'Clever boy,' and at once his face cleared. Obviously the purpose of this curious exercise had been to please *me*.

This evening, I was more cunning. I closed the book and said, 'Do you think Billy liked that story?' He frowned. I said, 'Shall we ask him?' I picked up the animal and whispered into its purple ear. I said, in Billy's voice, holding my nose and producing an adenoidal squeak, 'No, I'd rather have a story about a brave hippopotamus. I don't like stories about silly old cats who get rolled up in pastry.' 'I don't know any stories about hippopotamuses,' I said. 'Then you must be a very stupid old man,' Billy squeaked back.

Barnaby laughed. His face flushed. He squirmed low in the bed, almost disappearing under the duvet. He peered at me over it, holding his breath, dark eyes squinting expectantly. I advanced on a somewhat randomly constructed tale about a purple hippo and a bear and a monkey who lived with a boy whose name I couldn't remember, who spent the day in a green bag and came out at night when everyone in the house was asleep, to have fun and adventures and play with the toys the boy had in his bedroom.

Barnaby said, in an awed voice, 'Is the boy's name Barnaby?'

I said, judiciously, that I wasn't sure yet, but it *might* be, and he wriggled with pleasure. He said, 'Do you think the boy has a Daddy?'

Inspiration deserted me. I muttered, oh, yes, most probably, but this was a story about Billy, the hippo, and that seemed to satisfy him. Or he respected my innocence. He said philosophically (or it may have been drowsily, because his eyelids were drooping), 'I forgot for a minute, hippos don't have Daddies, do they?'

Clio had put on her green skirt and a pair of spectacularly large and ugly glass earrings. There was some glittery stuff round her eyes and lipstick on her full, pouting mouth. The effect of a little girl dressing up for a party was sweetly disarming as was the screwed-up concentration on her face as she served the meal, a pale vegetable stew with a couple of chicken legs in it for my benefit (she wasn't strictly-speaking a vegetarian but she didn't like and rarely ate meat) and a rather more interesting salad with various shades of greenery in it and chunks of white radish that I was fond of but had never been able to find on sale locally. She blushed when I said this. 'I hoped you might like it. I got it last night from one of those funny little Indian shops near King's Cross. I was out for a run and just happened to see it.'

I said, without really thinking, 'Last night? I thought Tim left a couple of days ago.'

'Tim?'

I looked up from my delicious salad. I couldn't understand her apparent total bewilderment. I said patiently, still not really taking it in, perhaps assuming, subconsciously, that she must have made some baby-sitting arrangement with one of the neighbours, 'I meant, who looked after Barnaby?'

'He didn't need anyone. He was in bed.'

'Did he know you'd gone out?'

'He was all right. He was fast asleep. I wouldn't have gone if he hadn't been.'

'He might have woken up. How long were you out for?'

'I don't know. Not much more than an hour. He never does wake once he's gone to sleep. He was quite *safe*. I mean, he couldn't do any harm, either, any damage to anything in the house. I locked his bedroom door.'

'You did *what*?'

Under my astonished stare, her colour slowly rose. Until now she had looked and sounded merely puzzled by my questions – baffled like Barnaby, presented with toys and stories to please some strange, adult whim. When she next spoke it was on an obdurate note. 'You're not being fair! I know how to look after him! I wouldn't leave him if he was sick, or there was anything wrong. But I'd go *mad* if I couldn't get out sometimes and run. It's terribly important for my sense of identity, it sort of holds me *together*. You're as bad as my father! Because of Barnaby, I'm not supposed to have any life of my own, it's a way of punishing me for having him, tying me hand and foot . . .'

I stood up. I said, 'I am not your father, and I have no wish to punish you for anything, so there is no need to rant at me. I'm happy for you to go running as much as you want to if it helps your sense of identity, whatever that means. I don't mind looking after Barnaby if I'm here, or paying for a sitter if I'm not. Just don't leave him alone again, if you please, at least not while you're under my roof. That's a house rule. Right? No more argument.'

I picked up my half empty glass of red wine and the half empty bottle. I said, 'I'm going to watch the nine o'clock news. If you're interested, you're welcome to join me.'

I thought that I had done well; put my point kindly but firmly. But as the day's roll call of disaster flitted across the screen, doubts began to assail me. I had fallen (as always when angry) into priggish pomposity. I should not have lectured her in that elderly way. Responsibility didn't come automatically along with the birth pangs. I should have explained carefully as one might explain to a child. She was so very young. Helen and I had been older by a few years when Tim was born; even so we had not always been exemplary parents. One summer evening we had left him outside a pub, peacefully asleep in his buggy. An old woman (maybe not all that old but she had seemed old to us then) had appeared in the bar, our child in her arms, and screamed abuse at us. 'You should be ashamed, drinking your eyes out, anyone could have made off with your baby.' A comic, ridiculous, embarrassing scene. It embarrassed me now.

Clio came in. She was holding a book like an entrance

ticket. She looked at me timidly. I smiled and she sat on the floor, close to my chair. She watched the end of the news. She murmured, 'There must be something good happening somewhere.' She opened her book, *The Oxford Book of English Verse*. She bent her head over it, her crinkled hair parting to expose her tender, white, immature neck. In that moment she seemed to me the embodiment of doomed, youthful innocence. I combed her stiff hair with my fingers. I said, gently, 'You know, although Barnaby seems quite old to you, and I agree that for his age he is very sensible, he's still only four, and even sensible children get frightened.'

She leaned against me. She said, 'I made you cross talking about my sense of identity, didn't I? You think that sounds crappy. I just don't know how else to put it. It isn't just a physical thing. I feel more *myself* when I run, sort of *whole*. But I won't leave Barnaby again, now I know that it bothers you.'

If not quite what I'd hoped to convey, this seemed good enough to be going on with. And while she was in this compliant mood, there was something else I thought I should know. Barnaby couldn't be diverted indefinitely by the convenient fiction that hippos didn't have fathers.

When I asked her, she stiffened; her neck became rigid under my fingers. I said quickly, 'Look, I know it's none of my business, you don't have to tell me if you don't want to, it would just be useful for me to know what you've told him, so I can say the same thing if he asks me again.'

She said, 'He's never asked me. I don't know why he asked you.'

I thought that she sounded hurt. I said, 'Maybe it's the first time he'd thought of it.' This didn't seem likely. 'Or maybe he guessed that it might upset you. He's sensitive to how people feel.'

He was sensitive to her, certainly. I had seen his eyes follow her. He was a natural spectator; intelligent, watchful and quiet. A bit wary, too, I had sometimes thought, although this seemed an odd word to use of a child with his mother.

She said, 'I don't know.'

'You mean you don't want to tell me?'

'I said, *I don't know*.' She spaced her words sullenly. The back of her neck had flamed crimson.

I felt a sudden spasm of curiosity that was a little like lust. I tried to dismiss it. I had been right not to question her when she first came. I shouldn't have questioned her now. It was hypocrisy to pretend that I had wanted to know for the child's sake. It was just another example of what Helen had called my middle-aged prurience.

I stammered out that I was sorry. She twisted round and looked up at me, her round, child's face implacable, angry, and suddenly I really didn't want to know any longer. But she ignored my awkward protestations, closing her eyes with theatrical patience while I stumbled on about everyone having an absolute right to privacy and being sorry if I had appeared not to respect hers.

She opened her eyes. She said, unemotionally, 'You don't have to go on like that. It's really quite simple. I went on a school summer camp. Some of us got drunk one evening. Three girls, Elaine and me and the other one in our tent, and six boys. None of us thought anything would happen, and it didn't happen to Elaine or the other girl, only to me.' Amazingly – that is, it amazed me – she smiled with an almost impish good humour. 'Just my awful, typical *luck*. I'd not done it before and the other two had, loads of times.'

I felt very old. At my single-sex school, in the fifties, we had often talked about 'orgies' but no one I knew had ever attended one. I said I was sorry. Again. My insistence on apologising seemed to amuse her. 'It's not your fault, is it? And it wasn't really bad luck. The other two were on the pill and I wasn't. I let them think I was because I didn't want to seem stupid. Though I think Elaine must have known. She knew my mother and father.'

'You could have got the pill if you'd wanted to, surely? You didn't need permission from your parents to go to a clinic.'

'They might have found out. I couldn't have risked it.'

'You risked getting pregnant. They might have thought that was worse.'

'No one could talk to them about things like that. If I could have done, I might have been able to get an abortion. I left it too late. I kept hoping. They wanted me to go to university. They'd sent me to this private convent. My father kept on about how much it was costing. I couldn't bear to think what would happen if I told them I was having a baby.'

Particularly when she didn't know which of six boys was the father. I thought – If she were my daughter, I'd have wanted to let fly with a machine gun. I said, 'Are your parents really so difficult?'

She smiled at me kindly. 'It's not their fault, really. They're both very religious. Very strict Methodists. When I was at the convent, I had to do Bible Study on my own instead of going to morning assembly. All the other non-Catholics used to go to assembly but my father was scared I'd be infected by what he called Papish flummery. He only sent me to the convent because there wasn't another school just for girls in our area. He didn't know that we joined up with the boys' school for summer camp. My mother knew, but she didn't tell him. She's a lot younger than he is. My father didn't get married until he was quite old, about forty. He was in the colonial service, in Africa, and when Kenya became independent he came home and went into insurance. He met my mother at some church do or other. She worked in a bank. They're both very boring, conventional people.'

'Most people would say that about their parents. But Elaine said . . . that is, George told me she said . . .'

'Oh, *Elaine*!' She clicked her tongue with dismissive contempt. 'To hear Elaine carry on, you'd think my parents were ogres. Though I suppose that's partly my fault, I did moan a bit sometimes. There was no one else I could talk to, and it was nice of her really to bother, but she made such a fuss. When my father found out I was pregnant he beat me up a bit, cut my mouth. Elaine came to see me and I couldn't hide it, my face was all swollen up, and she went raving on about how I ought to go to the police, as if he had tried to kill me! And when after that he wouldn't talk to me, she thought that was frightful, too, though it was really a whole lot easier than putting up with my mother nagging me all the time, and being so strict about keeping Barnaby quiet. I think she thought that if the neighbours couldn't hear him, they wouldn't know he was there. But that was just *stupid*, not *wicked*.'

It sounded appalling to me. But I didn't want to offend her stoical dignity. I said, cautiously, that it seemed bad enough. She said, with a little shrug, 'I suppose it depends what you're used to. I was used to *them*, wasn't I?' She looked up at me. 'But I'm sorry I said what I did about you. You're not in the least like my father.'

I was glad to hear it. A man who could hit a pregnant child must be a monster! And yet, when I met them later on, when Clio and I were about to be married, I found Elaine's 'ogres' merely drab, rather dull; a faded, anxious-eyed woman who had once been pretty but whose drying blonde skin had withered and browned like a badly kept apple; a ponderous, self-important man whose face, unlike his wife's, had plumped out with age, become fleshy and polished. I had never met anyone who used the possessive pronoun so continuously. 'My' house, 'my' car – walking around 'my' garden, he even said 'my' goldfish pond, without any apparent sense of absurdity. I waited to hear him say 'my' grandson with a simmering rage that was quite illogical because as far as I was concerned the purpose of this visit was to ensure that Barnaby should have at least some minimal contact with his grandparents. That the old man refrained from staking out this particular claim was nothing to do with tact. (Guilt, even of a vestigial kind, was patently out of the question.) It became clear, towards the end of the tour round 'my' garden that he had no intention of admitting any link between himself and his daughter's bastard. He said, with an air of great condescension, 'It's good of you to take on the boy. Not many men would condone that sort of mistake.'

I got the impression that he didn't admire me much for it. I said that Barnaby was a lovely child, gentle and thoughtful and clever, that I felt privileged to be able to take care of him, hoping now, rather perversely, to persuade his grandfather to show some small sign of family feeling. But his big, shiny face remained grave. He said, 'I appreciate your coming here. My wife has been worried. But we won't expect you to come again. You've got enough on your plate with the boy and my daughter. I hope that you don't live to regret it.'

I would have laughed if he had not so obviously meant this sincerely. I said that I was sure Clio and Barnaby and I would be very happy. He nodded as if this reassured him, but before we carried on to the end of the garden to inspect 'my' fruit trees, his eyes, sunk in their firm, pink cushions of flesh, rested on me with a speculative pity that unnerved me a little.

Of course, by the time of that visit (which has not been repeated) I knew more about 'his' daughter. 'My' Clio. Six months further knowledge. During those months she had cut off her hideous, crinkly permanent wave and let her hair grow as I liked it; long, straight and gleaming. She did this to please me. She liked to please me when she could, when it didn't go too much against the grain of her nature. Indeed, to begin with, I think she even tried to be nice to my mother, an effort which, since I didn't understand why she should have to 'try', I didn't perhaps give her enough credit for. But in simpler matters she was flatteringly compliant. Fearless herself, at night in the streets, maintaining that runners were never mugged since they had 'street credibility', she indulged my fears for her, and ran along well-lit, main roads. She respected my ruling about Barnaby. As far as I knew she didn't leave him alone in the house. And it was quite a long time before she hit him hard enough to leave marks on him.

Midway between sleeping and waking, I had thought the child crying was Tim; a time shift of years back to a night when Helen and I had made love rather noisily (drunkenly, after a party) and not heard our small son outside our bedroom door, frightened and whimpering. Then I woke fully and knew that although the room and the bed were the same, the girl beside me was Clio. The guilt I felt briefly was an echo from that earlier occasion. This was not the first time that Clio had shared my bed; we had not woken the child; we had been asleep for hours. Clio showed no sign of stirring now. She lay on her back, very deeply asleep, snoring delicately, hair fanned out on the pillow.

Barnaby wasn't outside the door. He was in the bathroom, trying to rinse out his pyjama bottoms, shivering, sobbing. As soon as he saw me he let out a shriek of fear and squirmed into the small space between the wash basin and the lavatory bowl. He squinted at me and said, 'I'm sorry, I'm sorry . . .'

A yellow bulb of snot hung from each nostril; he had inherited his mother's catarrhal condition. The combination of this unlovely affliction and his absurd, shrinking terror was suddenly irritating. I sat on the edge of the bath, yanked him between my knees, wiped his nose roughly. 'Don't be silly now, little boys often wet their beds, nothing to be sorry for, stop crying, we'll soon have you nice and dry again.'

He was icy cold. His pyjama jacket was soaked up the back. He beat at my hands when I tried to undo the buttons. I said crossly, 'Come on Barnaby, let go, you aren't helping.' He stopped resisting. He gave a deep, resigned sigh and stood still while I stripped off his jacket and the Tee shirt he wore underneath that had a foolish-looking bear in a soldier's uniform stencilled across it.

The bruises on his upper arms were rainbow coloured. He tried to cover them with his little hands, looking at me with bleak despair. He was snuffling drearily; his nose had started to run again. As I scooped him up to wrap him in a towel and sit him on my knee, I saw the scarlet rash on his bottom and thighs. As if she had sat him on a pin cushion. Or beaten him with a stiff bristled hair brush. I kept the towel tight round his neck as I rubbed him dry, jiggling him up and down as I did so, saying in a foolish, bright, nanny's voice, 'That's better, love, isn't it? A bit warmer? Now all we want is some nice, clean pyjamas.'

I carried him into his bedroom, found a pair in a drawer, and left him to put them on while I changed his sheets, carefully keeping my back to him and taking plenty of time, so that by the time I turned round he was finished, buttoned up to the neck, his shame hidden. 'That's a clever boy,' I said, with relief – and realised, with a shock, that he wasn't alone in wanting concealment. He must have recognised this in the same moment; he gave me a shy, conspirator's smile and said, very low and hoarse, 'Don't tell my Mummy.'

I couldn't think what to say. I picked him up, held him close. His arms locked round my neck fiercely. I kissed him and laid him down in his bed. I said, 'I expect she got cross the way we all do sometimes. I'm sure she didn't really mean to hurt you. I expect she was sorry.' He looked at me with a thoughtful frown creasing his high, bony forehead. I said, 'Shall I stay with you? Or do you think you can go to sleep now?'

He whispered, 'You can read me that book about the cat, if you like. Billy said he quite liked it, really.'

He fell asleep in the middle of *Samuel Whiskers*. I tucked Billy under the duvet beside him. I took his wet sheets downstairs and put them into the machine. I emptied the dishwasher. I laid the table for breakfast. I had a bath, shaved and dressed. I cursed myself for a fool. I should have known. Though how could I have done? I had read shocking reports in the newspapers. But the idea that anyone I knew could do such a thing was outside my experience, incomprehensible. And I had never once seen her slap him. I had noticed the odd bruises and grazes once or twice when I had bathed him, but nothing until tonight that could not have been accounted for by an active little boy's natural tumbles. Perhaps, thank God, this was the only time?

At seven o'clock I made tea and took it up to her. She sat up in bed, drinking it, her face damp and rosy with sleep. I said, reluctantly, 'Barnaby woke up last night. He'd wet his bed and I had to strip him off, change him . . .'

'Little beast. I thought he'd stopped that.'

Not a trace of guilt! I said, – 'Clio! What I mean is, I saw the marks on him.'

'Oh, *God!*' She reached out for her spectacles, put them on, glowered at me through them.

'Do you want to tell me what happened?'

She sighed with virtuous exasperation. 'Oh, he needles me sometimes. He can be such a *brat*. You never see that side of him, do you?'

'What did he do? Though whatever it was, it hardly – still, never mind. He must have upset you.'

'Well, you want peace to work, don't you? You don't want him coming up all the time, bothering you. Or rushing about and making a noise. I can't keep my eye on him all the time. And I mustn't lock him in my room. You told me I mustn't.'

'He doesn't bother me. I don't mind a bit of noise. I don't find him a nuisance when I'm working, either.' In fact he had come in several times, settled peaceably in the corner with some poster paints I had given him. But Clio knew this. I said, 'You know he doesn't disturb me. He seems to understand that I'm busy, I don't have to tell him.'

'Oh, of course you don't, he's so *sensitive* isn't he? You're always going on about that. As if *I* wasn't sensitive, as if I didn't have any feelings. You think about him all the time, you don't think of me.'

'On the contrary. I think about both of you.'

She wailed, 'You don't love me.'

'Silly girl. I love *both* of you.' I stopped short. This was the first time I had said this. I went on, rather quickly, 'Perhaps it'll be easier once he's really settled at school. Perhaps he'll be easier. I think he finds it a bit of an ordeal still. All that rough and tumble. He's never really spent any time with other children before . . .'

'There you are, thinking of *him* again! Putting him first! Before me! What you mean is, I'm a bad mother! Well, you're not his father, you've got no right to interfere, if you go on being so horrible, I'll just go away, take him with me, like I did when my *mother* . . .' She caught her breath. This was more than she had meant to say. She watched me warily. She muttered, 'I'm sorry, I'm *sorry*. It's just that I thought, I mean, I really did think, once I'd let you make love to me that I'd come first with you.'

The implications of this sad little speech were fairly horrendous. There were a number of things that I could have said – perhaps ought to have said – in reply to it. But she was looking so scared and so woebegone. I said, 'Of course you're important to me. I'm sorry if you felt you had to make love to me. My memory may be failing, old men forget, but I seem to recall that you weren't exactly unwilling.'

'If you really loved me, then you'd want to marry me, wouldn't you? And you don't. You like having me around, in your bed, not quite as a convenience, but like some sort of *pet*. More useful than a dog or a cat, because I can cook and run errands and answer the door, but all the same not to be taken quite seriously. Silly you call me and it's what you *mean*. I'm a *silly girl* to you, and that's *all*.'

She sniffed miserably. I gave her the box of Kleenex and she blew her nose. 'I didn't mean to hurt him. I didn't know I had until I saw the marks after. I don't know why he didn't *cry*. If he'd cried, he'd have stopped me. I don't know how it happened. It was only once, honestly.'

I didn't know whether I believed this or not. I hoped it was true. I assumed that what she had said about leaving was a pathetic lie. A jealous child's blackmail. I said, 'Look, sweetheart, just don't hit him again. I don't want to go on about it.

I'm your lover, for God's sake, not your doctor, or your social worker.'

She let her glasses slip down the bridge of her nose. She smiled. She said, 'I do love you, you know. Do you love me? You said that you did. I did notice! Did you mean it? Oh, you don't have to answer, I shouldn't ask, really. It's rotten of me to mind because you fuss over Barnaby, really despicable. I really do know that. I try not to mind but I can't help it. Even now when you're absolutely right to stand up for him and be angry, I get this sort of horrible knot twisting and tightening inside me. It's like an illness, a virus or something, that makes me turn spiteful. I don't suppose you know what I'm talking about. But if I was sure that you loved me, I mean really sure that you'd love me whatever I did, I might be cured of it. I know that's too much to ask. I don't like myself very much, so how can I expect you to like me?'

'I seem to manage it somehow.'

She looked at me challengingly. 'You're just saying that, aren't you? I suppose the trouble is, I've got such a poor self-image. But it's horrible to be in the wrong always. Sometimes it seems I always have been. My parents only liked me when I was good. And no one seemed to like me at school very much, I didn't have any real friends except Elaine and she always seemed to like everyone . . .'

She caught her breath in a little sob. 'Oh, I shouldn't go on *complaining*, it'll only turn you against me. I know what you're thinking! That I'm just trying to excuse what I did, trying to make you sorrier for me than you are for Barnaby, and I suppose that is true, in a way, but it isn't the whole truth. I wish I could make you understand, but it seems all I'm doing is making you hate me. And if you are going to hate me, then I'd rather know *now*, and get used to it and stop hoping, and just clear *off*, out of your sight. You wouldn't have to worry about me, I'd get a job somewhere I could take Barnaby, where they needed help badly enough to put us both up. Like a hostel for handicapped children. I think I'd be good at that. I'd know how they felt, you see! I know I'm not qualified, but I could do the cleaning, or help in the kitchen, and go to evening classes at night, and get all the right bits of paper, and perhaps, in the end, if I really worked hard, I'd turn into someone quite *useful*.'

I began to laugh helplessly. She watched me, flushing scarlet, looking about twelve years old, resentful and vulnerable. I said, 'I'm sorry, I shouldn't laugh, but you're such a goose, my own dear, silly goose,' and put my arms round her.

She was absurd. She was touching. If I had made her sound sillier than she was, that is the fault of the medium. The vehicle I am using (the words, the story, picking out moments that stand out in memory, seem to have been crucial) is one that distorts the true picture. In fact she was rarely given to adolescent theatricals. More often than not she was restful; a quiet, soft-footed, gentle-voiced handmaiden.

And she did love me. She needed me to love her. To be loved, to be needed, is a compelling flattery.

Even her jealousy flattered me to begin with.

'If looks could kill I'd have dropped dead at her feet,' Helen said. 'You're not thinking of *marrying* her? That cross, glowering girl?'

We were on our way to pick Tim up from Patsy's flat and take him to buy a suit. Helen had come to fetch me in the car – our car, now her car. And Clio had answered the door.

I said, 'I'm sorry she glowered at you. She's not sure what we're up to.'

'Didn't you tell her?'

'I don't think she altogether believed me.'

I laughed. The idea that Clio should be suspicious of this innocent outing was curiously pleasing. I said, 'You can't expect her to understand why this is important. Why we need to go together to buy Tim a suit, why he wants us to go with him! How can she understand that? He's old enough to buy his own clothes! If he's scared of going into shops on his own, why not ask his girlfriend to go with him? And so on. I couldn't explain. He isn't a child to her. He's the same age as she is.'

'Right enough,' Helen said. 'Young enough to be your daughter. When she's our age, you'll be in your sixties, have you thought of that?'

She sounded disgruntled. I said, 'Why does he want a suit, anyway? Did he tell you?'

'I think Patsy suggested it. Patsy says he ought to try and get a job, and he can't get a job without a suit. It sounded a bit . . . I mean, I do hope she's not putting too much pressure on him. You know what they all say about that. Have you met her?'

'Once. They came for some of his books. A big, busy girl, bags of energy. She did all the talking, smoked like a bonfire, drank a lot of gin. A bit overwhelming.'

'She seems to have taken him over. Taken him on, anyway. I suppose you're pleased about that?'

'Aren't you?'

She sighed.

I said, 'Even if she's not absolutely right for him, it's a chance, isn't it? To have a stab at living some sort of independent life. He obviously wants to try, or he wouldn't have moved in with her. That must have been quite a momentous decision.'

'If he'd made it on his own it would have been. But, as I said,

I've got the feeling that she's just *gathered him up*. In a sort of impulsive, maternal, quite generous way. But she could drop him again just as easily.'

'We can't always protect him.'

She didn't answer. Her profile was suddenly mulish. She was looking very pretty, but quite a lot older. Though she wasn't much older than when I'd last seen her. It was the contrast with Clio. I was ashamed to find myself thinking this. I looked away from her, out of the window. We were driving through a part of north London that I was unfamiliar with; late Victorian villas with coloured fanlights, tidy front gardens, swept pavements, small shopping streets, Kosher butchers. It was Friday and the Orthodox Jews wore big, flat, fur hats and breeches. Then, turning a corner, crossing an unseen frontier, the same houses were suddenly tattier; peeling paintwork, smashed windows. There were rusting motor cars with battered fenders abandoned in the gutters, cheerful black faces, crimped Rasta hair styles. A different world. Another country. I thought I might do a matched pair of paintings to add to my London sequence. I said, 'It's extraordinary how people change the landscape they live in.'

She said, almost viciously, 'You're *bored* with him, aren't you? You've given up on him. It's so *obvious*. It must have been obvious to him, too, why do you think he left home? It's not just this girl, it's the boy, the little boy, like having Timmy back again, when he was small and sweet and sort of full of *hope*. So you can throw Timmy away and start over.'

Her chin crumpled. She said, 'Oh, bloody hell, I don't mean that, even if it were true, I oughtn't to say it. I ought to be glad for you.'

'Christ,' I said. 'That's wonderful, coming from you! Oh, my God! Who threw him away in the first place? You went off . . .'

'I didn't *go off*. You are . . .'

'How is Ted, anyway?'

'Oh, you are wicked! That's really wickedly cruel. I've *told* you what's happened. Do you never listen? Ted's life is just utterly miserable. His wife's out of hospital, they can't do any more for her, one leg is still paralysed, she's not going to get any better, Ted does his level best to look after her . . .'

'I'm sorry, I didn't . . .'

'. . . she's incontinent most of the time and so *angry*. Poor Ted, so penitent, but she'll never let him off the hook, she says, she'll always blame him . . .'

'I'm s . . .'

'. . . and rightly, too, the poor bitch,' she ended, on a queer note of triumph. She glanced at me sideways, face smudged with tears, grimly smiling.

I said, 'I really am sorry about Ted's wife . . . Oh, for God's sake, Helen, keep your eyes on the road, there's no point in us having an accident and ending up in the same . . . oh, for God's sake *stop crying* . . . pull in at the side and let me drive. *Please*.'

She slammed on the brakes; I lurched forward, the strap of the seat belt tightening painfully across my breast bone. She flung herself out of the driving seat and stomped around the front of the car. I got out. I said, 'This poor old car seems to have led a pretty adventurous life since you took it over. Are you practising for the Monte Carlo rally or something? There's that dent in the rear and this . . .'

'I backed into a bollard.'

'You must have been going at about eighty miles an hour. Quite a fair speed in reverse.'

She said, through clenched teeth, 'I really do hate you.'

I sat behind the wheel, adjusted the seat and the mirror. I

fastened my seat belt. I said, 'You nearly did hit that cyclist, you know.'

'I always told you this car had too many blind spots. But you would buy it, you said you wanted a drop head because you liked the sun and the wind, but it was really because you thought it was *dashing* and *young*. You hoped beautiful blondes would leap in when you stopped at traffic lights.'

'If you didn't like it, why did you take it, then? I could have kept it and we could have bought you another one.'

'We couldn't afford a second car at that point, don't you remember? And you said you wanted me to have it.'

'Perhaps I did, in a way. Or maybe I thought you wouldn't accept it.'

'You can have it back if you want it.' She made a funny sound in her throat, half a groan, half a gurgle. 'Henry would be furious if he heard me say that.'

'He thinks you should have taken me to the cleaners?'

'Not altogether. Or not with the reasoning part of him. The reasonable part thinks you've been generous. He understood why you should keep the house, it's your work place. It's the atavistic bit. My *sister*! How dare he treat her like this! That scallywag painter!'

'Maybe he worries about what might happen to him if Joyce should ever . . .'

'No, that's quite separate. Henry lives his life very neatly in boxes. Everything sorted out as he wants it.'

'Joyce might not find his arrangements so tidy.' I didn't want to go on with this. I said, 'I don't need the car now. I've got the van and it's really more useful. More room for my stuff.'

Barnaby liked going out in the van; snuggling down in the back. He said it made him feel 'invisible' and this seemed to please him. I decided that Helen might not find this as touching as I did. I said, without looking at her, 'Before we get to Tim's, hadn't you better clean your face up a bit? He'll guess we've been having a row. You know how that always upsets him.'

'That's always been the most important thing, hasn't it?'

'Not upsetting Tim? Did you want to?'

'Don't be an idiot. You know that's not what I meant. I meant, I *mean*, that for years and years now he's been the only serious thing, that is the only thing we've ever talked about seriously. The rest of the time it was just quarrels or silly jokes. As if there was nothing else of any importance between us.'

Her voice was suddenly flat and calm, without anger; without, indeed, any expression at all. She was gazing straight ahead and her green eyes had a distant, unfocused look, as if she were sitting on a beach, watching the sea. I said, carefully, 'Are you trying to tell me that's why you took up with Ted? Because you could talk to him? What about? About yourself, I suppose, that's what people usually mean. Why didn't you tell me you were feeling cut off? Or whatever you did feel?'

'It wouldn't have made any difference. But that's not why I didn't say anything. I didn't say anything because I didn't know what was wrong. It was only just now, I mean today, in the car, that I suddenly saw. That it, that *he*, I suppose, though it wasn't his fault, had eaten up our lives and left nothing over for us.'

'Perhaps it's the same for all people with children. Or perhaps . . .' I hesitated, watching her profile. I had never seen her sit so still. I said, 'If the other baby had lived, perhaps we wouldn't have concentrated on Tim so much.'

'Maybe. Since she died, we can't know. But it wasn't just having Tim to worry over and plan for that swallowed us up. It was because we let it become an obsession.' She turned and smiled at me, her green eyes washed bright with her tears. She said, 'It's the same thing with Ted and me now. All we talk about is his wife. Our guilt and her misery. Not that we meet all that often. He's found a practice near his home so that he can get back at lunch time and he only comes up occasionally to see a few special patients. We don't – if it interests you – make love any longer. We sit in a pub, or a restaurant, and moan. Ted says that I mustn't blame myself, that his wife is his responsibility, but he wants me to share it with him, all the same, and I do want to share it, feel I should, anyway, but I also feel, all the time, that I'm making things worse for him. He can't have any fun any longer, or not with me, I'm just a gloomy reminder. I don't mean fun in a vulgar and trivial way. I mean that Ted and I have lost what you and I lost, long ago. We can't look outside the grey cloud that hangs over us, all around us. It's not that there *isn't* any light on the horizon, more as if we don't want there to be.'

'You need a break away from Ted, by the sound of it.'

'That's what Henry says. He says . . .'

I had no interest in Henry's opinions. I said, 'I can see how you and Ted must feel trapped. But it wasn't like that for us. Tim is ill, but we love him. And we did have some fun, didn't we? Happiness. Laughter. We could . . .'

She broke in. 'Only like prisoners being out on parole. However much you pretend you are free, you know that the prison is there, that you can't escape it.'

'. . . start again,' was what I had meant to say. What I did say was, 'You're re-writing history.' And then thought, immediately – *making excuses*! Poor, suffering Helen, forced by an unhappy marriage into the arms of another dentist! She had made herself believe this. I said, 'At least we always had hope. Still have. Oh, I know we've despaired often enough, and I know the prognosis. But it's only a label they've pinned on him, psychiatrists don't know everything, there may be a new treatment, some new drug that will suit him, or one he's prepared to take, or he may, on his own, just start to get better. Leaving home may have been the best thing that's happened. Two parents with busy, productive lives, a constant reminder of what he can't do, feeling he's let us down, that we're disappointed. It's no good saying that we understand, that we know how hard it is for him, just to get up in the morning and get himself going. And perhaps even that will be easier for him with Patsy. Presumably they go to bed together, that's something he can do, gives him a role to play. Whatever you say, I think Patsy's good news.'

'You mean she's temporarily taken over the struggle. How long do you expect it to last? I don't suppose she has any idea what she's taken on, do you?'

'You think we should tell her?'

'*No*. No, of course I don't.'

'I know we always agreed that it wasn't fair to him, that we should leave him to make friends without interfering, to find his own level. But perhaps it's different in this case. If she expects too much from him . . .'

'She wouldn't believe us, anyway. She'd think we were just making trouble. Over-anxious parents, terrible, conventional middle-class people trying to crush him into some bourgeois mould . . .'

I said, indignantly, 'I thought it was Patsy who suggested we should buy him this suit? What's that if it isn't . . .'

'Oh, come on, my lad, do give over.' She wrinkled her narrow nose at me. 'Here we are, back on the old treadmill, the same old merry-go-round, soon as we start talking about Tim, what did I tell you? I hope you're not going to carry on in the same way with your sulky young Clio. It's always a fatal thing, men getting married again, carrying along a lot of old luggage with them, building a new nest just like the old one.'

I thanked God that I had not told her about Clio's treatment of Barnaby. How she would crow at the idea of my replacing one sad, threatened child by another! Unfair to think this, of course, but there was enough truth to make me smart in a way that was all too familiar. Helen had always known where to stick the knife in. But she was right about one thing, I told myself righteously. It was too late for us. I said, 'I don't know that I am going to get married. Our divorce is only just through, for God's sake.'

'Oh, it just seemed on the cards.' She fluttered her eyes at me archly and tossed her keys into my lap. 'If you're going to drive, you'll need those. We'd better get going. We'll talk about something else. Some less demanding conversational topic. How's Maud? I haven't seen her lately but she rang to tell me that Ned's had his baby – she didn't mention Polly, of course – and that she's to be godmother. She seemed very chuffed about that. And I saw Maisie last week, we had a jolly lunch in that pub, you know the nice one in the park that we found when she first moved to Bow. She's got a new boyfriend, or rather a very old one, childhood acquaintance, turned up again all of a sudden. She said she hadn't seen you for a week or two and she wondered if you were very busy with Maud's posh friends up in Norfolk. I said that I didn't know because I hadn't seen you either, why didn't she ring you? And she said that she had rung and spoken to Clio but that you hadn't rung back. Since that's been my experience too, I imagine your charming young acolyte tries to protect you.'

I had no idea what she was feeling. Either she was relieved to have spoken her mind, was glad to be rid of me finally, or she was spunkily concealing a measure of sorrow. Whichever it was, a slightly aggressive chirpiness was the tone she had decided upon for the moment. As we turned into the street where our son was living with Patsy and slowed to a crawl, trying to decipher the occasional numbers scrawled on the peeling pillars, looking for Tim's motorbike, parked among the rubbish bins in the derelict gardens, she rapped the back of my hand, sharp, flirtatiously (as if she were an eighteenth-century lady with a fan) and said, 'One thing my lad, whatever you do, marry or not, don't let that girl keep you away from your mother.'

MAISIE

My mother's best friend at school, and later in the munition factory, her inseparable companion when she went to the Saturday night dances at the local Palais, was a fat, stocky girl with a broad, pale, doughy face and incongruously small, doll-like features; snub nose, round eyes, rosebud mouth, artless as a child's drawing. A perfect foil for my mother's slender and perky prettiness and perhaps, in the beginning, that was how the friendship had started; the pairing of a plain girl and a pretty girl having obvious social uses for both. But they remained close. When we were living in Southend, Auntie Dot – 'Auntie', I was taught, was the polite title for older, unrelated females who were friends of the family – was a regular and welcome visitor. She came at week-ends when my mother was always short-handed; a mountainous and laughing lady who rolled up her sleeves on arrival and set to, scrubbing and cleaning, preparing vegetables, and urging my mother to 'let up for a bit, take it easy'. My mother would protest that it was Dot who should be taking it easy, after working all week as she did, cleaning offices in the City. 'Bugger that, Maisie,' Dot would cry, 'you know me, I like to keep busy, I don't come here to have you wait on me!'

The effect, of course, was to make my mother work harder than she might otherwise have done to keep Dot company. By the time Sunday night's traditional cold supper was cleared away, they both seemed exhausted, though in a comfortable way; settling down by the coal fire in the small, basement sitting room, with tea, or sherry and biscuits. Sent to bed after I had drunk my nightcap of warm milk and honey, with cinnamon sprinkled on top of it, I went mutinously, reluctant to be excluded from the warm circle of talk and laughter that seemed to enclose them. 'Just a bit of crack,' my mother said, when she came up to comfort me and kiss me good night. 'No one and nothing you know about, pet, you'd be bored stiff. Besides, Auntie Dot is the only person who knows all about me, we've been friends since we were little girls and there's no one round here I can giggle and be silly with. You don't really mind, do you?'

I pulled a face and she sighed. 'Poor old Auntie Dot needs a bit of company, too,' she said coaxingly, appealing to my better nature. 'Things are a bit hard for her at home and it does her good to get away. So it does us both good. We cheer each other up.'

I didn't mind her cheering Auntie Dot, if she needed it. But my *mother* should not need cheering when she had me for company. I said, piqued, 'Aunt Maud doesn't like her much.'

My mother said tartly, 'Maud picks her own friends. She doesn't pick mine.' And then, biting her lip, watching me closely, 'How do you know she doesn't like Dot, anyway? Has she said so?'

I shook my head. Maud did not have to speak to show disapproval. When Auntie Dot's name had been mentioned she had jutted her chin, pursed her mouth.

'Oh, Maud thinks we should keep grander company than

poor old Dot, I daresay,' my mother said. She paused, chewing her upper lip again, a habit she had when something was worrying her. At last she said, 'Though even Maud could hardly expect me not to stand by the poor soul in this trouble . . .'

She had spoken in a detached, thoughtful way, thinking aloud rather than speaking to me. I said, 'Is Auntie Dot ill?' and she smiled with a bright and obvious effort – as if she had forced herself to come back from some faraway place and bent over to tuck in my bedclothes.

She said, 'Something dreadful has happened, not to her, but to someone she loves, and she's very unhappy. I can't tell you about it because she wouldn't want you to know, and you're not old enough to understand, anyway. I know that's something grown ups always say, but it's true this time, so you'll just have to be good, and try not to ask questions, and help me be kind to her.'

It was a long time before I learned the nature of Auntie Dot's 'trouble', which really was terrible; indeed, in the context of the placid and innocent life my mother and I lived together, almost unbelievable. She had been engaged to be married. Some of the happier evenings she had spent with my mother had passed in eager talk about wedding plans, a bridal dress that would slim her down a bit ('I don't want to look like a white satin sofa,' she had said to my mother) and the number of guests she should ask to the reception. Her husband-to-be was a taxi driver who worked most weekends which was why he had never come to Southend with her. His excuse, anyway. He was, so Auntie Dot said, a quiet man, shy of people and social occasions, a non-smoker and a teetotaller. Not perhaps the ideal mate for Auntie Dot, who was cheerfully gregarious and fond of what she called 'a spot of the demon', but he was the only man who had ever asked her and she was a practical woman, ready to elevate gratitude into love.

He broke off the engagement. He didn't tell her why. He took her to the pictures one evening, drove her home in his taxi to where she lived with her parents, above her father's small grocery shop, and when she got out of the back, didn't move from his seat, simply leaned over, pushed down the window, thanked her for the pictures (she had paid, as she always did, for the tickets) and said that he wouldn't see her again. It was raining. She asked him what he meant and he shrugged his shoulders, staring straight ahead while she begged him to answer her. His silence defeated her. She stood, large and humbled, in the dark, in the rain, juggling with her handbag, her umbrella, struggling to pull off her gloves (women of all ages and classes still wore gloves then) and to get the ring off her finger. At last he did speak. He said, 'You can keep the ring, Dottie, a bit of compensation for the disappointment,' and, as he drove away, lit up his *For Hire* sign.

'That was a really crude thing to do,' my mother said, when she finally told me the story, years afterwards, one evening some time after Eric Major had died. (I can't remember why she told me, only the occasion; a wet, Sunday evening. All the time she was talking I could hear the rain blowing against the window.) I asked her why she thought it was 'crude'. I was always questioning her at that time in what I now see as a censorious and bullying manner, and I was always enraged by what seemed the tranquil inadequacy of her answers. 'Oh, I don't know, dear, it was a bit *commercial*. After he'd just broken her heart!'

'Would it have been better if he had waited until he had turned the corner?' I sneered, contemptuous of this petty example of feminine sentimentality, and she said, 'It would have been more delicate.' She thought for a minute, gazing into the fire. 'It sounds silly, I know. I suppose the reason why Dot let herself get so upset over it was because all the rest was so dreadful, didn't bear thinking about, and so she fixed on that one, silly thing.'

He was a rapist. A murderer. After he had left Dot that night he picked up a woman who had flagged him down outside a public house, drove her to one of the bomb sites that still littered that part of the city, either persuaded or dragged her out of the cab, raped her and strangled her. The body was found the next morning by some children who used the bomb site as a playground; in the afternoon, he walked into a police station and gave himself up. At his trial he was charged with a number of other rapes and attempted rapes. He pleaded guilty to all of them. 'The awful thing is, they all happened while he was engaged to poor Dottie,' my mother said. 'She had no idea that he – I mean, there had been nothing like that between them. Dottie wasn't that sort, nor was he, so she'd thought. A good night kiss and a bit of a cuddle, that was all. She liked him for that. It showed he respected her.'

Her tone of calm reminiscence appalled me.

'Whereas in fact she was driving him mad with unrequited lust?'

'No, dear. I know it sounds ridiculous to you because you think she was so fat and ugly that no man could want her. And, of course, Dot felt terrible. If she'd let him make love to her, she might have saved all those other poor women. But *I* think he was scared of doing it with someone he knew. He'd never had a girlfriend before, never even been out with anyone, so his poor mother said. He was her only son, his father had been killed in the war, and they lived very quietly together, in a council flat in Wapping. She blamed Dot – oh, that was *cruel* – but you can see how she must have felt. Seeing her son in the dock, weeping and shamed, all these horrible things being said, everyone looking at him, how could she bear it? Dot had been good to her, tried to comfort her, you know what a good friend Dot can be, but it was rubbing salt in the wound for the mother. When the judge sentenced him she started screaming at Dot – wicked things, words I can't repeat to you – and they had to carry her out, cursing and fighting. Maud and I thought Dot would faint. We tried to get her to leave the court but she wouldn't, she insisted on staying until he was taken down . . .'

I said, 'It's incredible. I mean, it's incredible that I knew nothing about it.'

'You were only ten. It was that hot summer you had the measles. I had to get Mrs Tomkin in to look after you while I stayed in London with Dot. Only during the week, of course.'

I didn't remember Mrs Tomkin. But I did remember being in bed with measles. I remembered Auntie Dot changing the sheets and making me laugh; a huge, merry woman, sleeves rolled up, dimpled white arms lifting me, smoothing the sheet underneath me. 'Come along tiddler, such a little tiddler, more of a shrimp than a boy, have to put some meat on you, won't we, if you're going to turn into a boy in time for your party!'

I said, 'I remember she came for my birthday.'

'Yes, she did. That was a bit of good luck, as a matter of fact. Your birthday was on the Friday and the trial ended on Thursday. We'd been worried all week in case it dragged on and stopped us getting back to Southend in time to get everything ready.'

'Oh, come on. You don't expect me to believe that?'

'What do you mean, dear?'

'Oh God! Isn't it evident? There you were, you and Dot,

and this man on trial for his *life*, you don't expect me to believe that in the middle of *that* – that great, roaring tragedy – that you and Dot actually thought about . . .'

She interrupted me with unusual asperity. 'It's quite possible, dear, to hold two things in your head at the same time.'

I said, heavily, 'These two particular things were hardly of equal importance.'

'Your birthday was important to you, dear. And it helped Dot to have it to think about. We went out one lunch break and bought a lot of coloured balloons. She'd been in a rare old state all the morning. It was the first time I'd really thought she might break down altogether. But we bought the balloons in a shop just off Ludgate Hill, spent quite a time choosing them, and she said – I remember exactly – *At least your little tiddler has his life to look forward to*. It didn't make anything easier for her, but it steadied her up just enough to hang on through the rest of the awfulness. It wasn't just because she was fond of you, though she was. It was a sort of comfort to her to feel that outside what was happening in that court, other things in the rest of the world were just going on.'

I said, 'It's extraordinary. I mean it's extraordinary the way you talk about it so calmly.'

'It was a long time ago. I don't suppose I was calm at the time. But extraordinary things do happen, you read about them in the newspapers, and some of the people they happen to are quite ordinary. And even though you think to begin with, *this can't be happening to me*, it soon becomes just something you've got to live through, no different from the rest of life, really. And Dot and I, well, we'd been brought up in a rough sort of way. You had to look out for yourself at the factory! And she used to help me behind the bar at home sometimes. You see a lot of life in that sort of pub.'

'Murders could hardly have been an everyday occurrence all the same.'

'People died in the war, didn't they? There was a bomb at the end of our street, killed a whole family, mother and father, three little children, and a couple of lodgers. Arms and legs sticking out of the rubble, bodies dug out in pieces. That's murder, isn't it?'

I sighed patiently. 'It's quite different, Mother. Not like knowing a murderer.'

'Some people must know them, dear. Murderers have mothers. And Dot was going to marry him. I had to stick by her. Maud saw that, even though she didn't like it, my being mixed up with such common people. She wouldn't have minded so much if Dot had been an educated woman. Even if she'd passed her School Certificate and got an office job, instead of just cleaning. Not that it stopped Maud coming to court with us, she was an absolute rock all the time, taking us back and forth in the car and stopping the newspaper men taking their pictures. She actually broke one man's camera! And when it was over she found Dot a job in a hotel up north, somewhere she could start fresh without people jabbering. I don't know what happened to her. She did send me a postcard once, but there was no address on it.'

'Maud must have known where she was if she found the job for her.'

'Well, yes, I suppose so, dear. But I was never much of a letter writer. And I thought, if Dot wants to keep in touch, she'll get in touch, won't she?'

I thought this seemed callous. 'So as far as you were concerned, that was the end of it. You just dropped her like a stone.'

She looked at me with a small frown. 'I think I thought she

might not want to be reminded of all she'd gone through, that a clean break might be better.'

'Sounds like an excuse to me. Laziness. You just can't be bothered to keep up with people. Auntie Dot must have thought you'd washed your hands of her as if she were somehow contaminated. Didn't that ever occur to you? Oh, no, of course it didn't. It's always a case of out of sight out of mind with you, isn't it?'

'I take life as it comes, if that's what you mean, dear,' my mother said gently. 'I'm sorry if it makes you angry. I hold Dot in my heart, I pray for her every night, I haven't forgotten her.'

I daresay I pulled a sour face. Why was I so critical? Maisie's only offence was the natural one of being my mother. 'You love her so much you can't bear her not to be perfect,' was what Helen said. 'Although it's a stage boys go through, you should have grown out of it. But you watch her like a hawk, the tiniest fall from grace and you pounce on her.'

We had known each other three weeks. I hadn't yet asked her to marry me. This was the first time she had met my mother. I said, 'If I'm as vile to her as all that, she shouldn't put up with it.'

'I didn't say you were vile. Just a bit sharpish. A bad habit, my lad. You're not ashamed of her, are you?'

'Don't be an idiot!'

'Then don't behave as if you were. That's what it looks like.'

'Why do you think I might be ashamed of her?'

'She takes things as they come. She's a contented woman. That bothers you. You think it's the mark of a shallow mind. D'you know what I think? What strikes me? You can say that I don't know her, but sometimes, the first time you meet a person, you see some things about them more clearly than you ever do afterwards. I thought, just looking at her, and listening, here's someone to whom something dreadful has happened, who's suffered, come through it, survived. That's what makes her contented. She's not *afraid*. She knows she can take whatever's dished out to her. It gives her – oh, I don't know how to put it. A kind of steady glow.'

I was surprised by this dramatic view of my mother's history, though touched and pleased that Helen should take it. But I said, 'I don't think anything *dreadful* has ever happened to her. There was my father, of course, and whatever happened in France. She won't talk about that. But that hardly qualifies as dreadful, does it? Any more than running a boarding house and bringing me up single handed. She wasn't single handed, anyway. There was always Maud.'

Helen had met Maud in London. She said, 'They're not in the least alike, are they? You'd never guess they were sisters. But I wasn't thinking of your mother's marriages – either of her marriages – but something else, more fundamental, sort of much further *back*.'

Her green eyes were so serious. She was so young. I said, 'Gazing into your crystal ball? I didn't know you had second sight.'

'It was just a feeling I got. A feeling that something had happened to her once, long ago, something hard to face, but she'd faced it, and it had made her wise. Oh, I don't know. Perhaps it's only because I'm in love with you and want to love her because she's your mother, and I was so happy to find that I could, the moment I saw her, that it's made me excited and silly. Do you mind?'

'I like you excited and silly. It makes you even more beautiful. And I'm glad that you liked her. I suppose I was nervous in case you should find her ordinary. That's partly Maud, I suppose. She says Maisie ought to be doing more with her life.'

'Take up pottery classes? Write a novel?'

'Something like that.'

We both laughed. We wrapped arms round each other and walked from my mother's house down to the sea. It was the first day of spring, the end of the winter's bad weather. We were very happy, that bright, distant day.

My mother was still living in Southend then. After Tim was born we took him for seaside holidays; his bucket and spade hung on the mahogany hat stand in the hall, his small sand shoes, soles gritty with crushed fragments of shell, were kept, as mine had always been, in the cupboard beneath. At low tide, in the early morning, my mother took him shrimping; yawning at the bedroom window, I watched them returning, faces rosy from the stinging, salty air, bare legs mottled from the cold sea, savouring the remembered excitement of my own childhood expeditions, the prospect of tiny brown shrimps for breakfast.

They were about the only food Helen fancied the summer she was pregnant with our second child. My mother brought them up to our bedroom with a plate of thin bread and butter and a pot of China tea, fussing over her daughter-in-law, plumping up the pillows, balancing the tray on the firm rise of the baby, laughing when a thrusting hand or foot disturbed the balance, slopped the tea. 'You've got a prize fighter in there,' my mother said.

It was a girl. 'At least you can tell your wife she was perfectly formed,' the midwife said, as if this miracle of eyes and nose and pouting mouth and tiny fingernails might console us for her lack of breath. Helen didn't want to see her daughter. It was my mother who held her lovingly; covered the dead face with kisses; wept. She wept for both of us; I couldn't cry. I said, 'Helen wanted to call her Maisie, after you,' and she shook her head and turned away as if this was too much to bear. She said, still cradling the child, 'At least she's been spared that, poor little lass.'

She had hoped for a girl. When, later that year, after my grandfather's death, we helped my mother to move to London, we found small, smocked, pink-ribboned dresses packed away between the linen in a bottom drawer. I thought it was careless of my mother to leave this sad reminder for Helen to find among the sheets and pillow cases. 'She doesn't think, she never thinks!' I fumed. And Helen said, 'Oh, do stop being sensitive on my behalf. In a way it's worse for her, she minds for you and me as well as for herself. And her father dying, too, a second death, so close. Don't you think how *she* must feel at all?'

I hadn't done. At this time of my life I was quite without curiosity about my mother; about what she did, thought, felt, when I wasn't there. I loved her, but I had grown up, left home; was busy with my work, my wife, my son. She was still young and independent – certainly not yet old enough to be a son's responsibility – and, in fact, I had been irritated by Helen's insistence that we should help her pack up the Southend house. There was some pique involved, perhaps. This was my home as well as hers; had she not thought of that? What about Tim, who would miss his visits to the sea? This sudden move to London to be near her widowed mother seemed an altogether wayward impulse on her part, not properly considered or discussed. She had bought and sold; then rung to tell me she was moving in a week! 'That's the trouble, isn't it?' said Helen. 'She dared to do this *on her own*, without asking you or Maud!'

She sat back, surrounded by the contents of the drawers that she was packing into a camphor-scented chest that had held, when I was young, my winter things; thick socks and sweaters, the grey short-trousered flannel suits that I had worn to go to school in the cold weather. Later it had become a toy box for Tim; woolly animals and games that had belonged to me kept there to amuse him when he came to stay. 'What are you going to do with Arthur?' I asked accusingly, picking up a squashed pink rabbit, bald in places, and with a missing ear.

'It depends on your degree of emotional attachment,' Helen said. 'Sort out what you can't bear to part with, throw the rest away.' She put the baby clothes into the chest and covered them with towels. I couldn't see her face. She said, in a choked and angry voice, 'If you want to help, go and do the pictures. Maisie's worried they'll get damaged, and no wonder. It's like having to pack up the National Gallery! God knows where she's going to put them all. It's tiny, that house she's moving to!'

My mother has a rare collection. She has always been polite about my own pictures, but she prefers the copies of the Old Masters I have given her, that now hang with barely any space between them on the walls of every room, the hall, the stairs, the landing, of her little house in Bow. She likes a nice, rich, glowing sheen; portraits or, at any rate, pictures with people in them. 'Like having a lot of friends about the place,' she says, with an artlessness that is consciously contrived to tease, to hide her pleasure and her pride. Similarly, 'It saves having to decorate, wallpaper is such a terrible price today.' This, said to Maud, and passed on to me as an example of my mother's ignorance and lack of 'taste' was actually part of a standing joke devised by her against her sister, a sly trick, saying what Maud expects her to say.

It was a follow-up to an earlier conversation. 'I'm not clever like you, dear,' I had heard her say to Maud, 'but I *think* that

Bellini is what they call a transcription, not a copy. He did it when he was a student out of a book of sepia prints, photogravures, I think they're called, correct me if I'm wrong. All sorts of famous painters did them. I've not seen it, of course, but he once told me there was a Mantegna in the Louvre with a Degas transcription hanging next to it.' 'You mean a pastiche,' Maud said. My mother frowned and shook her head. 'A transcription is more *serious*, I think. Using the design and style but putting your own *feeling* into it. In this Bellini, you see, there were no colours in the print, so he used the ones he was experimenting with. The colours in the original are different, he took me to see it when it came to London on a travelling exhibition and, to be honest, I was disappointed.' Maud snorted. '*Disappointed*, Maisie? In an original *Bellini*?' My mother smiled. 'Well, dear, all I'm saying is that I liked the one he'd done for me much better. Smaller for one thing, and quite a bit cleaner. I can't see the virtue in dirt myself, can you?' And then, with one of her most innocent smiles, 'I suppose what you are really saying is that the real Bellini is more valuable.'

My mother has several of my student transcriptions and a great many straight copies; a Goya, half a dozen Rembrandts, several Brueghels, and a number of Reynolds and Gainsborough portraits among them, mostly done for practice, but none I am ashamed of, and only a few (I would place quite a hefty bet on this) that, hung in a municipal or commercial gallery as genuine, would not deceive most expert eyes. 'Value is in the eye of the beholder,' she said to Maud serenely – defeating her sister, I think, on that occasion, because although Maud rolled her eyes beseechingly in my direction, she looked plaintively resigned rather than indignant. And, perhaps, uncomfortably wondering if my mother, in her simple and uneducated way, had not touched upon some truth, or statement, about Art that had eluded her. 'Your mother thinks that pictures are just to cover up damp marks and dirty patches,' she grumbled to me in private afterwards. I said, 'That's only what *you* think she thinks,' and laughed.

And that is why, weeks later, Maud was pleased to pass on that remark about the wallpaper. I am sure my mother made it. Maud is an honourable and exact woman. I am equally sure that my mother knew that Maud would tell me and that I would see the joke. Like my mother, I like to tease Maud sometimes although, since she often seems to me the loser in these sisterly affrays, I frequently feel sorry for her, too.

There is, I sense, a resentment on my mother's part (as there is not on Maud's); not deep, or really damaging, but lurking somewhere in the undergrowth of their joint lives. She said, at some point during that fairly horrendous move to Bow (struggling to manhandle unsuitably large pictures up the narrow stair, fitting in cumbersome furniture that had seemed quite reasonably sized in the more spacious Southend house), 'I know Maud's cross with me about this, not telling her beforehand, but I had to do it for Razor Annie's sake. She's gone downhill since Dad died, and you know what Maud is, she'd have her in a Home, or in some kind of retirement bungalow, a box to die in, out of sight and out of mind except for a visit once a month. Whichever it was, she'd be cut off from what Maud calls her common East End friends and that would really kill her, break her heart. But it would have been all hell let loose if I'd let Maudie know I was thinking of coming back to Bow.'

My mother's house is very pretty, in a pretty street of late Georgian cottages, 1810 or thereabouts, that had already been 'discovered' when she moved there; bought up by smart young couples who could not afford Chelsea or even Islington and who have stripped the floors, opened up the dark old basements and put in elaborate, streamlined kitchens, painted their living rooms in pale and neutral colours, hung framed prints, or posters, on their walls. In this conventionally gentrified terrace my mother's house is singular, eccentric; net curtains at the windows and rooms furnished with sentiment rather than regard for overall appearance – this rocking chair came from her parents' sitting room above the pub, this table from Razor Annie's Irish grandmother, these willow pattern cups and saucers once belonged to a great aunt, this Staffordshire shepherdess, cracked and carefully mended, to a childless older cousin, once removed. And, of course, my Old Masters everywhere.

The effect is cluttered, charming; a house to feel at home in. But in spite of all the evidence of moderate urban affluence, the Peugeots and the Renaults in the street, the neatly kept front gardens, the window boxes flowering seasonally with daffodils, pansies and geraniums, it is still a slum to Maud. Although my mother was unfair to her (Maud loved Razor Annie and understood my mother's arguments about moving to be near her) the East End, the *idea* of the East End, fills her with a peculiar horror still.

'It isn't just a snobbish thing,' my mother said, trying, I think, to explain it to herself rather than to me and Helen. 'It's more a kind of fear that it's all chance and luck. One slip, and she'll end up like me, back where she started from! And that would really sink her. Funny, really, when you think of it, Chelsea's not so far, just a few miles across the city. I suppose it's what it cost to get there, all that effort. Oh, well, I suppose she thinks it's worth it, that's what counts. Although sometimes I think I'd like to tell her that she owes a bit of it to me.'

We asked her what she meant. The removal men had gone and we were sitting in the kitchen, among the packing cases. She said things like, 'Oh, that's too old a story.' 'Forget it, I'm just maundering on, you don't want to hear.' Then, coaxed a little, feeling, I suspect, a touch of guilt because she had kept Maud in the dark, 'Well, it was that time I went down to see her in the war.'

She had gone for her sister's sixteenth birthday. Maud was living with the spinster teachers in a small house on the edge of a village; 'quite nice,' my mother said, but a bit higgledy piggledy, books and papers everywhere and not as clean as she (and Maudie, too) were used to. At home you could eat your dinner off Razor Annie's floors. But there were bowls of spring flowers in the bedroom that had been prepared for her, and fresh country eggs, impossible to get in London, for the early evening meal. Afterwards, they sat around a wood fire, Maud in her school uniform, Maisie in her best clothes, bought for the visit; navy costume, matching bag, her highest heels. Usually, it seemed, they all went for a brisk walk after they had eaten, to blow the cobwebs away before Maud settled to her homework, but the headmistress looked at Maisie's feet and shook her head. It would be a pity to spoil those pretty shoes.

If it had not been for her young sister's heavy sigh, Maisie would have accepted this remark as a compliment on her appearance. But obviously the care she had taken to impress was somehow wrong. She glanced at the two teachers (at the two 'old ladies' as she thought them) and was perplexed. She had never owned a pair of such stout brogues; would not have been seen dead in a tweed skirt of such age and bagginess. She could have said that she had had quite enough exercise that day, walking home three miles at dawn after a night shift at the factory to strip wash in the kitchen, put on clean underwear, new blouse, her smart costume, and set off again to cross the city, strap-hanging in the Underground, to catch the train.

Instead she smiled politely and said she didn't feel much like a walk herself, but if they wanted to go they mustn't worry about her being bored. She could listen to the wireless or read a bit more of 'her book'.

The headmistress asked her what she was reading. She said it was a book, called *Anna Karenina*, that Maud had given her last Christmas; she'd been meaning to get around to it for ages but until now she hadn't had the time. She had started it today and read almost two hundred pages, waiting at Paddington, and on the journey (the slow and crowded wartime train), and was enjoying it, although to start with it had seemed a bit off-putting; so long and all those foreign names. 'Russian,' she informed them. 'It's a Russian novel, but a lovely story. Maud knows I like a nice romance.'

Maud sighed again. But her kindly guardians brightened. Up to this moment, although they had been hospitable, greeting her with welcoming smiles, persuading her to have a third boiled egg, more bread and butter, another slice of birthday cake, they had not shown much real interest in Maisie, or not of a kind she understood. They had asked her opinion of the progress of the war, and how she thought the 'spirit of London' had been affected by the Blitz, but nothing personal, like how many bombs had fallen in or near her street, or where she and her family spent the night – in the Tube station, an Anderson shelter, or in their beds? And, except for her unsuitable shoes, they had not appeared to notice how she looked. Now, however, they began to question her about her education. Did she read much? What subjects had she liked at school? Which had she been best at? Had she taken her Matric before she left? Of course, without matriculation, she couldn't go to college. Had she ever thought of evening classes? Puzzled by their sudden eagerness to start with, she had been angry with Maud when she understood it. 'She should have told me Tolstoy was a famous writer. I felt so silly. Not that they laughed at me, those women. They were much too nice. I think they really thought, for a bit, that I was a brand to be snatched from the burning. But of course they saw quite soon that it was much too late for me.'

She told them that she had been bored at school, been glad to leave and get a job, like all the other girls she knew. This was the point at which she should have explained why she had come; not just to see her little sister on her birthday, but to tell her to come home. As far as her parents were concerned, at sixteen Maud had more than finished her education. After she took her Matric in the summer she would be qualified to earn a good living in an office; she could take a typing course at Clark's College in the City; Razor Annie was prepared to pay if that was what Maud wanted. An unnecessary expense in Razor Annie's view, a bit too much butter on the bread, but she knew Maud was ambitious, wouldn't be content unless she had an 'extra bit of paper'. Maisie had assumed that Maud would jump at this, but something about her watchful silence made her cautious. She mentioned Clark's College. A girl she and Maud knew, the butcher's daughter from the neighbouring street, had done a secretarial course there, and 'passed out top'. 'She got into the Civil Service,' Maisie said, expecting Maud to be impressed. Instead, she turned brick red and scowled. 'I don't want to be a *secretary*! At some man's beck and call!'

The teachers, both sensitive and kindly ladies, saw that Maisie was truly mystified, a little hurt. In a harmonious duet, they hastened to explain. The civil service was an excellent career, of course; if you entered at the Clerical Grade, you could always take examinations for the Executive Grade, even if you didn't have your Higher School Certificate. But Maud, who was 'academic', could aim even higher. With a degree, she could apply for the Administrative Grade, and they were hoping that Maud would stay on in the sixth form and take her Oxford Entrance. Before the war she would have had to wait until nineteen, but now there was a special dispensation for girls from grammar schools. She could take the Entrance before her Higher, and if she was accepted, and then got distinctions in the Certificate, she would get a State Scholarship and a County Major, which would, together, cover all her expenses. 'It wouldn't cost your parents anything,' the history teacher said.

The headmistress, slightly shrewder, realising that most of this was double dutch to Maisie, smiled and said, 'Of course, we know that education isn't everything. Your mother and father must be very proud of you, all that you are doing for the War Effort, and I expect they feel that Maud ought to do her bit as well. We all feel that we should play our part. But the important thing is that we each should do what we do best, and when this dreadful war is over the country will need trained minds to help clean up the mess. We can't afford to waste our talents. Maud has great potential, and I'm sure whatever happened she would develop it in one way or another. But as Mr Churchill says, give us the tools and we'll finish the job, and Maud's brain is one of the best tools we've got, that's the way to look at it. What we want is to see it honed and sharpened! Put to fullest use!'

She was flushed and bright-eyed with excitement. Maisie listened patiently to this high-toned harangue, then looked at Maud for help. Maud said bluntly, 'I want to stay at school.'

And later, sobbing, curled up on Maisie's bed in her winceyette pyjamas, 'I'll die if I can't, I really will, I'll *kill* myself.'

*

My mother said, 'I didn't tell my parents that, of course. I just said she was best off where she was. The flying bombs had started, what we called the doodlebugs, and it would have been daft to bring her back. She'd got a nice soft billet with those two old ladies. I had a row with Razor Annie, she thought Maud was lazy, not wanting to earn her living, that sort of thing, getting too big for her boots, Lady Muck, who did she think she was? Well, you can see! My mother, working all the hours God sends, and seeing me work too, while our Maudie took it easy, reading books! She was all for setting off herself, doing what I had been too weak to do, and she'd have gone, if my Dad hadn't stopped her. Mother was really *riled* in a way I hadn't seen before. Maud wanting to better herself in a way *she* hadn't thought of, and turning down Clark's College was a kind of insult.'

I said, remembering my grandfather with amusement and affection, that I wouldn't have thought he was all that keen on education either.

My mother hesitated. 'Well, the thing was, I could always get around my Dad.'

Helen smiled. She said, 'Girls and their fathers!'

Surprisingly, my mother blushed. She picked up her tea cup and peered into it, apparently examining the tea leaves at the bottom. When she spoke her voice was suddenly remote – as if she had removed herself physically and was speaking to us from a great distance. 'Maud was clumsy, always breaking glasses. My father knew she was never likely to be much help in the bar.'

'You persuaded him, anyway,' Helen said. 'I hope that Maud was grateful.'

'She had no cause to be. I wanted her to have her chance. Like I said, it was too late for me.'

She smiled vaguely. Helen said, 'You got married, though. It must have been about that time.'

This closed the conversation. My mother said, 'Maybe so. I can't remember. I have a terrible head for dates, that sort of thing.' She stood up purposefully. 'We'd best be getting on, no more old talk if you want to get home tonight. I want to get those pictures hung.'

'You'd think she'd talk about your father sometimes,' Helen said. 'Not now, perhaps, but when you were a boy. She must have known it mattered to you.'

'It didn't much. Less than you'd think, anyway.'

'You speak French better than most English people. You must have tried quite hard.'

'I don't remember trying. He wasn't a man to be exactly proud of, was he? Not from what Maud told me.'

'I wonder if it's *true* . . .'

'Why shouldn't it be?'

She rubbed at the side of her nose with her forefinger and grinned at me wisely.

I said, 'I think it was a diversion, in a way. She guessed I'd be interested . . .'

Helen said enthusiastically, 'That's exactly right. She's a clever old stick, isn't she? Here is this boy, her nephew, she doesn't want him to start getting ideas about his absent father, go chasing off to look for him or anything that might cause trouble. So she picks her moment, tells him this story, funny enough to intrigue him, but putting him off, too, since absent Dad hardly comes out of it looking very admirable. A smart, diversionary tactic. Not necessarily a true story all the same, or not about the gentleman in question. It sounds a bit apocryphal to me.'

'I don't know. I believed it.'

'Of course you did *then*. You were young enough not to smell a rat! I bet you wouldn't believe her if she told you now. But it was jolly useful to you, all those years you were growing up. A sort of interesting *peg* to hang a father on. A rascal, but a comic one, not bad enough to be ashamed of.'

'I suppose it worked like that. But Maud's not usually so devious.'

'She loves you. She didn't want you to be hurt. Nor Maisie, either. She didn't want you questioning your mother, hurting *her*. So in the tale that she told you Maisie had to disapprove, which is a false note really, when you think about it. She's not so *prim*. There must be something else.'

'If there is, we mustn't ask her. It absolutely isn't any of our business.'

'It's yours, I would have thought.'

'Not really. I'm perfectly happy to leave my father hanging on his peg.'

I had meant to make her laugh. Instead she said, mutinously, 'All right. But what I think is, you're scared, my lad. And not for Maisie's sake – you're not so tender of her feelings usually. I think you're scared of skeletons tumbling out of unexpected cupboards and having to take a good long look at them.'

'What skeletons? What cupboards? Oh, you may be right, it may not all be gospel true . . .'

'You ought to know what *is*.'

'You mean *you* want to know!'

She did laugh then, acknowledging the truth of this, and I kissed her. I called her my 'inquisitive little squirrel'.

She murmured, 'Fair enough. Squirrel won't mention it again, but if you're not exactly *scared*, you're still a bit unwilling, aren't you?'

'Sleeping dog's my name,' I said. 'Just let me lie.'

*

I can't remember when we stopped inventing foolish little love names for each other. Jealousy suggests that it was she who put an end to them; that when she fell in love with Ted these sweet and silly matrimonial intimacies became repugnant to her; at least, embarrassing. But I suspect that it was a habit we fell out of rather earlier. As Tim grew older, more possessive of his mother, she became shy of showing affection to me in his presence. She seemed to think this normal. He was an only child. To touch, to kiss, to use pet names in front of him might make him feel excluded.

All the same, as I recall it, Sleeping Dog and Squirrel had a longish run. Squirrel suited her; my busy, chattering, bright girl. And I do prefer not to poke and pry.

When I finally told my mother about the divorce she said, 'Did you know Helen was so unhappy?' I said I hadn't thought she was. She sighed. She said that she was sorry. She didn't look at me. I waited. She said nothing else. I said, goaded by her silence, 'I thought you loved Helen,' and she sighed again. 'It's your life, dear. Yours and hers. Not mine.'

About my marriage to Clio she was less distressed, and so much less inhibited. 'That girl,' she called her, with an irritable inflexion that I had to admit was justified. To begin with, Clio had made attempts to be agreeable. She had been polite when my mother came to visit. But once she realised that I expected these visits to be frequent (realised, I suppose, that I really loved my mother and was not just being dutiful) she grew resentful, sullen. On the few occasions I had taken her and Barnaby to Bow, she had sat for the most part grumpily silent, boredom personified, glancing every other minute at the clock. My mother had endured this cheerfully enough, tried to include her in our conversation, played Beggar My Neighbour with

Barnaby. I had hoped she had made allowances for Clio's youth, her childish awkwardness. But when I told her we were getting married, she said, '*That girl.*'

I had gone to help her with her heavy shopping, a fortnightly expedition that Helen had initiated after Razor Annie left to go into the Home. (Helen had thought she might be lonely. She had said, 'She's been a lovely ma-in-law to me, but I expect she'd like to have you on your own sometimes, she never says so, but I expect she misses you.') We had put the groceries away; I had carried a tray of tea and sandwiches up from the basement kitchen into my mother's small and crowded living room; she was sitting in Razor Annie's rocking chair. She looked outraged.

'Clio's shy,' I said, placatingly, though perhaps without too much conviction. 'She's clumsy with people. I don't think her parents were exactly sociable . . .'

My mother snorted with something of Maud's disdainful energy – indeed, very briefly looking like her sister, the way she moved her hand in a scornful gesture of rejection, the way she jerked her chin. It was only for a fleeting moment but it solved (or so I thought) a problem for me. The picture I had been working on that morning was of a buxom, titled lady and her younger, much more aristocratic-looking brother. They were as little like each other as were Maud and Maisie, and yet there was a likeness lurking somewhere, a kind of subliminal family resemblance that I couldn't place and that had held me up; I had fiddled with the background, a classic column and some drapery, while I puzzled over it. Now, suddenly, seeing my mother move her hand, her chin, I thought I saw exactly where it lay; not in eyes, or colouring, or feature, but in action; a movement that, in the picture, had been caught and fixed in paint. The Countess and her brother were looking at the painter, had just turned to do so, holding their heads at precisely the same angle, a little high and haughty, as if resentful of the tedious pose this common fellow had demanded. They had been standing there quite long enough, who did he think he was, why didn't he get on with it?

Ned's mother would look like that, I thought, if she was expected to stand for a full-length portrait!

My mother said, 'What's funny? Nothing to smile at, that I can see.'

'No. Sorry. It was something else. I was thinking about something else. I'm sorry about Clio. She's had a hard time and it's made her wary. She'll change. She's very young.'

'Hard time?' my mother said. 'She's a lucky girl, if you want my opinion. Lucky to have been able to keep her baby. It would have been different in my day! As to being young, well, I can see that she might have no time for an old woman like me. But that's not it, is it? That girl wants you to herself. You may not think that matters now, but it'll make trouble for you later on. And it's not *me* that I'm thinking about! I was lucky with Helen all those years, it won't hurt me to take a back seat. What about Tim, though? You've got him to consider. I know you hope he'll be able to stand on his own feet one day, I pray for that, but you can't count on it, can you? And if things go wrong, if he hits another bad patch, you can't expect Helen to carry it on her own. And how will *she* feel? Your Clio? Your son, a grown man, still dependent? And her own boy growing up. Another responsibility for you. A stepson. That isn't easy.'

It was unlike her to be so severe, at least in a conventional way. I said, 'Come *on*, Mum! I thought Eric and I got on all right.'

Her face was blank. Had she heard? Well, of course, she was deaf! I said, 'Your second husband, dear.'

Her colour rose. 'How silly, yes, oh, how *silly*! Do you know, for a minute I – well, never mind . . .'

'Poor Eric. Look, it's all *right* about Tim and Clio. They accept each other. It's a different generation. They have a more relaxed attitude to a lot of things.'

'Like letting other people do the working and the worrying? As far as I can see, my friends around here, that's what it mostly means. Children sponging on their parents, drawing social security, doing sweet fanny adams. I don't mean Tim, you know that. Any fool can see he's sick as I said to Maud the other day when she was carrying on, you know the way she does, saying he ought to sign up for some course or other at the polytechnic, she'd talk to you and offer to arrange it. I said, listen Maud, it isn't any good, as far as Tim's concerned, it's no good making plans ahead. With Tim, I said, you have to take a short view.'

'It's hard for Maud to see that.' I was surprised – and grateful – that my mother did. Though perhaps it was only in opposition to her sister. I had not heard about the polytechnic course. (In what? Woodwork? Philosophy?) Maud knew better than to talk to me about it. But the thought of her, labouring away behind my back, enlisting my mother in the struggle, refusing to give up, filled me with an affectionate sadness. I recognised that this would not have been my response had she been in the room. I said, 'Maud always thinks she can put things right.'

'It's not always an advantage to be clever.' My mother sounded pleased. 'Education isn't the only answer as I've often told her. I never wanted you to go away to school, you know. But she would have it that it was the best thing for you, with me so busy, and in the end she talked me round. You were a happy little boy, but there was your future to be thought of. Tim is a different matter, as I told her.'

I said – suddenly, irrationally angry at the thought of my aunt and my mother using Tim as yet another battleground for them to squabble over, 'I hope he has a future. Do you mean you think he hasn't?'

She frowned at this piece of silly spite. 'Not in Maud's way, dear, passing exams and so on. But I've been thinking a lot about him lately. Since you and Helen – well, that's over now, no going back, but it must have made a difference. I think I see it, anyway. He's quieter. Or quieter in a different way. He holds himself so still. As if something inside him might break if you moved or spoke too loudly.'

I said, 'He's schizophrenic. You know that. I've told you.'

She sat as still as Tim; as if *she* were afraid to speak or move. At last she said, 'I know. Maud knows it, too. It doesn't stop us worrying over what might be best for him. Even if we disagree. The doctors haven't helped him, after all. I didn't mean to hurt you about Helen. You've both done the best you could for him. When I said I saw a difference in him, it may just be that I've noticed something lately that was always there but that I hadn't seen before. I suppose it's watching what's been happening to my mother. Not the same thing, she's old, it's natural she could go that way, but it's trouble in the mind with both of them. It's made me notice more.'

'For God's sake, Tim's not *senile*!'

How could she make this terrible comparison! My whiskery-chinned and toothless grandmother, wandering in her wits, and my beautiful and tortured boy!

'He *knows*,' I said. 'He *suffers*!'

'Do you think she doesn't suffer too? What makes you think she doesn't *know* sometimes? She's still *alive*. A woman like she's been, so proud and strong, not able to remember what's been said two minutes earlier, or where she is, or what she had for dinner? I know how you must feel for Tim. I feel for her in the same way. Seeing her look frightened, or with that sort of listening look I've seen in him – as if she were trying to puzzle out what's going on inside her head.'

Her eyes had filled. I said, 'I know it must be hard. But she's had her life. This is just a short patch at the end of it.'

'It's happening to her now. That's just as painful isn't it? And when you say she's had her life, it isn't much to look back on, all work and worry . . .'

'And Tim's life is so full of possibilities?'

'Don't be unkind! I care about him, you know I do. It's just I see her twice a week, and I hate her being there, stuck in a chair all day, the telly on so loud, and no one there who knows her, what she was like, the person she still is *inside*. The nurses are kind but she's just an old body to be washed and dressed and fed – and sometimes I think I ought to have her back – but then I know I can't, can't manage it, or bear it – and, oh, it breaks my heart . . .'

Her voice broke, as if to underline this sentiment. Her little hands, pressed prayerfully together, were shaking so hard that they were sending shock waves up her arms, making her whole body tremble. I had never seen her so emotional. She was usually so calm, even serene; giving off what Helen all those years ago had called her 'steady glow'. She wasn't emotional about Tim, though! Moaning and groaning over her mother, that poor, daft old bat, and not a tear for him! Her only grandson, for Christ's sake. And then, I thought – how ludicrous! This isn't some weird sort of *competition*! Whose lunatic is worse?

I said, 'I'm sorry about Razor Annie. I ought to visit her more often. So ought Maud. It all falls on you, I know.'

'You're both so busy. Such busy people.' She laughed to show this was not a criticism. 'I don't really mind. I suppose it's partly selfish in a way. I look at her, at all those other poor, dilapidated creatures with their minds in holes, all cobwebby, and I can't help thinking, will *I* come to that?' She shook her head. 'And then I go forgetting Eric – of all people, I'll forget my own head next – and it seems I'm on my way!'

She looked at me, quite merrily, but with a funny little air of slyness combined with satisfaction, as if this had been the sole purpose of her slightly hectic rambling; to find an excuse, or explanation, for her lapse of memory. She said, 'I did love him, he wasn't just a convenience to me, although I think you thought so at one time and I know that Maudie did.'

I laughed. It seemed the only answer. I told her that she needn't worry about her failing mental powers while Maud was still around to charge her batteries. I said that I loved Clio, too; she wasn't a convenience to me, nor I to her. I promised that I would come again next week to see her, and, more vaguely, that I would visit Razor Annie 'soon'. I was sorry that I had to go now, but it was the nanny's day off and I had to pick up Barnaby from school. She refrained from asking why Clio couldn't do this, and why Barnaby needed a nanny when he had a mother, which was just as well since I could hardly tell her why I didn't care to leave my future wife and stepson alone together for more than two hours at a time. She said that she hoped I didn't mind her having 'had her say', and that she hoped Clio and I would be very happy. I said I hoped so too, and kissed her.

This propitiatory interlude made us both feel better. She walked me to the gate and put up her cheek for a final farewell kiss. She looked beyond me, smiling, looking suddenly much younger – the smile, a rising, rosy blush, a certain air of girlish flutter. 'Davey, I wasn't expecting – I don't think you've met my son.'

She put her arm through mine. 'Darling, this is David Prime.'

The name seemed familiar. He was lean and lined and weathered; a short, spry man with a neat and jaunty look. Nautical was the word that came to mind. He said, 'Pleased to meet you. Sorry, Maisie, am I butting in?'

'Silly! Of course not! Anyway, he was just going.' She squeezed my elbow. 'Dave is one of my very oldest friends.'

He smiled at her affectionately. 'Maisie and I go back a long way. Kids together. Lost touch during the war, and then I was away at sea. Merchant Navy. Retired now, of course.'

My mother said, in a delighted voice, 'Such a surprise, after all these years. When I saw him in the supermarket, I thought, that's never *Davey*, but it was!'

'You could have knocked her down with a feather. Always easy to amaze, was Maisie!' Prime winked at me, sharing his masculine amusement. 'Mind you, I'd been on the lookout for her ever since I heard she was around again. My brother kept up with Maudie, always filled me in. If old Doug had known Maisie's address, I'd have called round on the off chance.'

'Maud never told *me* she'd been seeing Doug,' my mother said. 'Oh, she is a funny girl. The Primes lived just across the road from us, you'd have thought she'd know I would be interested.'

I said, 'I think I've met Doug. He and Maud share an allotment.'

'Oh, get away with you!' My mother giggled. 'Your Aunt Maud with an *allotment*! Pull the other one! She doesn't know one end of a spade from another!'

'I don't know about that,' Dave said. 'But she was always keen on exercise. She used to be a swimmer.'

'We used to go swimming, all of us,' my mother said. 'Me and Dave and Maud and Doug.'

'Ah, but Maud was *good*,' Dave said. 'Up and down the pool, always thirty lengths. Not just a splash and a lark like the rest of us. If Maud had stuck at it, she could have trained for the Olympics, like my Else.'

'Dave's wife is Elsie Prime,' my mother told me proudly. 'You know, the Channel swimmer.'

'No reason why he should remember, Maisie. All those years ago!' He said to me, 'My lady wife is suffering the usual fate of swimmers now, I fear. All that muscle gone to blubber. She finds it painful to get about much now. I do the housework and the shopping, which was how I was lucky enough to find your Mum! I recognised her first go! Just as pretty as she always was.'

I looked at my smiling mother, happy to receive these compliments, and saw, behind her lined and pretty face, a younger, smoother one; a ghost, a pentimento of an enchanting girl. And, in the same moment, thought – *that picture*. There was some connection nudging in my mind. I chased it briefly, abandoned it, and said, returning to the immediate puzzle, 'It may not have been Doug. The Mr Prime I saw with Maud had been a postman. I thought that was how they'd met.'

My mother's eyes were dancing. She pinched me – hard enough to make me wince. She said, 'Well, Douglas used to be a postman, dear. But Maud has known him all her life.'

HELEN

Helen rang.

I said, 'Hang on, darling, will you?'

That 'darling' had slipped out. I looked at Barnaby but he was eating his cereal, his eyes half closed, blissfully concentrating on the lovely crunching noise the cornflakes made inside his head. I went to the kitchen door and heard the water pipes thrumming. Clio was still in the shower. I picked up the phone again. I said, 'Okay, if you're quick. Or I could ring you back from a call box.'

Helen said, 'I'm your ex-wife, not your mistress. Oh, this is *ridiculous*.'

'Yes. Not to her, though. She can't handle it. Is it important?'

'Why ask me?'

'I meant, is it important what you've got to say?' Of course it was. Must be. I said, 'Is it Tim?'

She answered with a sob. I said, 'I'll ring back.'

I turned off the coffee pot, lifted Barnaby's egg out of the saucepan, put it in an egg cup, sliced off the top, put it beside him. 'Eat your egg, there's a good boy. I'm going out for a bit. Fiona will be here in ten minutes. If I'm not back, she'll take you to school.'

He said, 'Soldier's legs. You haven't done my soldier's legs.'

I buttered a slice of toast and cut it into strips. 'There. What do you say?'

He beamed through a mouthful of cornflakes. 'Thank you, Daddy. Kiss me goodbye.'

I kissed the top of his head. I took change from the cracked teapot on the dresser, went into the hall. Clio was at the top of the flight of stairs, looking down. She was wearing a towel, a shower cap and her tinted spectacles. She said, 'Where are you going?'

I closed the kitchen door. 'To the newsagent. They didn't deliver *The Times* this morning. Only the *Guardian*.'

'Who was on the telephone?'

'No one. I mean, a wrong number.'

'I heard you *talking*.'

'Silly woman, asking for someone called Muriel. I said, no Muriel here, but she didn't believe me. Maybe she wasn't silly, just deaf.'

'You're a lousy liar.'

'No, Clio. Honestly . . .'

'Why can't the bitch leave us *alone*? She's never given us a chance, has she? It's your fault, you encourage her, she only has to crook her little finger and off you go running. You don't see what a fool she makes of you, and you don't care how I feel.'

'I do care very much. And she's not a bitch, Clio. It's about Tim.'

'Has he turned up?'

'I don't think so, she'd have told me that straight away.'

'Then it's just an excuse to nobble you. I think it's disgusting.'

'Shut up, Clio.'

She pulled off her shower cap and her long hair tumbled

loose. She let the towel slip, exposing one small, pretty breast. She said, with some dignity, 'You don't have to go out. I've got *The Times* in my bedroom. I went down to get some orange juice and brought it back up with me. You can use the phone. I won't listen.'

She turned her back, letting the towel fall completely. She could have been a ninety-year-old hunchback for all the effect her nakedness had on me. I felt bad about this, though less bad than I would have done if I hadn't known that she knew how I felt and meant to reproach me.

She looked at me over her shoulder. Her brief moment of dignity had slipped away with the towel. She said, 'All right, you can tell clever Helen she's won. She's managed to destroy our relationship. Using Timmy to do it.'

'Rubbish. She's frantic with worry.'

'That's what she wants you to think. She knows what a soft fool you are. She doesn't want you back but she can't bear to let go. I wish she'd *die*. I wish *I* was dead. I expect you wish that too!'

I thought – I could hit her. But Barnaby was in the kitchen. And there was a flight of stairs between us. I said, 'You know that's not true. Look, I won't be long. Try and snap out of it in the meantime. This mad game you're playing. That's all it is, you know that, don't you?'

I left the house and trotted down the street to the call box on the main road opposite the police station. It wasn't the nearest but it was less likely to have been vandalised than others in our not very salubrious neighbourhood. Although Clio might not have listened on the extension I couldn't be certain. She usually listened. She even steamed open my letters.

There was a large black lady in the booth. From the way the

glass was steamed up with her breath she had been settled in for some time. I smiled at her politely and to my surprise she put the receiver down almost at once and thrust the door open with her backside. Emerging backwards, clutching about a dozen plastic bags, she said, 'Some people do go on, don't they, my friend's one, nothing better to do since she had that little op, nothing much really it wasn't, but moan, moan, moan, didn't think I'd get away this side of Christmas. I told her, there's a man here wants to ring for an ambulance.' She gave me a lovely grin, sweet as honey, and floated rather than lumbered away, as if the plastic bags, ballooning around her, were buoying her up, like water wings.

Helen answered at once. She must have been waiting by the telephone. She said, 'Oh, thank God. I'm sorry about Clio. But someone rang in the night. Well, this morning. Four o'clock.'

My mouth dried in sympathy.

I knew those night calls. The shrill sound, at first part of a dream, a whistle blown on a playing field, a train going into a tunnel. Waking in darkness to fear; brakes screaming on a wet road, the motorbike in the ditch, the call from the police, from the hospital, from Tim himself, raving or pleading. *Dad come and get me*. Now we each wake alone, fumbling for the switch of the bedside lamp, for the summoning instrument; with dread, with wild, leaping hope . . .

But it hadn't been Tim. The voice was a stranger's. A man's voice, low, pleasant, perhaps slightly drunk (no apology for the lateness of the hour which was, from the party sounds in the background, clearly not late to him), asking if Tim were there, if he could speak to him.

'No, he's not here. Who is it, who's speaking, please?'

'Just a friend.'

He had spoken, Helen said, in a tone of faintly humorous surprise. Just a friend, wanting to speak to his friend, our son, speaking from the world of ordinary life (that bland, sunny country on the far side of a river), in which it is easy to 'get in touch'; all that is needed is an address, a telephone number. The ordinariness of the expectation was somehow embarrassing. To shatter it with the truth would be crude. She had said, 'I'm afraid he's not here.' Using the word 'afraid' in the conventional, social sense, as if it had no other, more terrible, meaning.

She couldn't leave it like that. Any more than I could have done. 'He's missing.' That word, at least, carried its proper burden. A missing person; details on the police computer, age, sex, colour of hair and eyes, other distinguishing features. An appendix scar. A mole under his left armpit. A gold signet ring that had belonged to Helen's grandfather.

'Missing?' Polite incredulity; the rather pedantically clipped, cultured voice placed the speaker as older than most of Tim's friends and acquaintances who speak in a classless voice, or what they consider classless, a deliberately acquired urban twang, a lengthening of vowels, smudging of consonants.

'Two months,' Helen had said.

Silence. The party sounds ceased. No music, no laughter. Was everyone listening? Where *is* this place? Who are these people? Do they know something? Or is there no mystery; the unknown caller has simply closed a door to hear better, speak privately. The connection is fragile. He could put the telephone down.

Helen said, in a bright, even tone, trying not to alarm him, 'When did you see him last? There may be nothing to worry about but we can't help being anxious. I'm afraid' – a short, amused laugh to show this is just a manner of speaking – 'I'm afraid I don't know your name.'

He said – not shiftily, Helen thought, just as if his name could be of no conceivable interest to her – 'I've been away in the States. Just back last week and picking up threads again, you know how it is. I'm sorry to trouble you. Jesus God, I've just looked at my watch. I must have woken you up. I'm most appallingly sorry.'

'It doesn't matter. Really, the time doesn't matter.'

'The trouble is, I'm a bit out of kilter. Jet lag. That's no excuse, of course, for such frightful carelessness. What is an excuse, I suppose, is that I've just been bowled over. Catching up on old chums, a bit of wine flowing. Then I hear this extraordinary rumour.'

'Rumour?'

'Rubbish, of course. It's quite obviously false. I mean, that's his mother? I'm sorry, I mean, you are his mother? The person I'm speaking to?'

'Yes.'

'Then you would know, wouldn't you? He always talked about you with such pride. He was so proud of you. His father too, that goes without saying. He loved you both very much. Both his parents. It was one of the nicest things. So rare nowadays, but so genuine. He was always so genuine.'

Drunk. The throbbing, slurred speech, the thickness in the throat, the sentimentality. 'Blackbird. That's what I called him. Blackbird. Those bright, watching eyes. Oh, Jesus God, I hope I haven't opened old wounds. I mean, if he's really been gone so long. How frightful for you. Believe me, I'm most appallingly sorry. Is it any comfort to say that I loved him too? Nothing more than that, I assure you, nothing that you should worry about. I know that people today have such filthy suspicions. Death to honourable friendship. I loved him like a father, even if I'm not old enough chronologically. You must understand that, the feelings people had for him. If I could, I'd have given him things. The moon on toast, the shirt off my back. You came to fetch him once, you and his father. We were listening to music, you rang the bell, took him off to buy a suit. He came back so pleased, it was lovely to see. What happened to that girl? The one he was living with. I rang the flat yesterday but there was no answer. Oh Jesus, anno domini, I can't remember her name.'

'Patsy. They split. She met someone else.'

'Ah. I thought she'd betray him. I told him so but he was too loyal to listen. At least he's not dead. Thank you, Ma'am. My deepest apologies for disturbing your slumber.'

The pips were going. I had no more coins. I said, '*Helen*, I'm sorry . . .'

We were cut off. I was shaking. I rang the operator and asked for a reverse charge call. She said, 'What is your number, caller?'

I screwed my eyes up. 'Sorry, I can't . . . I haven't got my glasses . . .'

She laughed. 'Hold on, please.'

Silence. Blankness. The receiver was greasy with sweat. Then, 'Go ahead, caller.'

'*Helen*! Who was he?'

'He put the telephone down. You remember the time we bought Tim that suit? This man was in the flat then, that's what he said.'

'People were always in and out.'

Helen said, 'There was an older man around part of the time he was living with Patsy. They used to call him the Butler. Tim met him in the pub and took him home because he'd been chucked out – I don't know where from, somewhere or other. He stayed quite a while, sleeping on the sofa. I know because Tim borrowed some blankets. He used to answer the telephone in that stage butler's voice. He sponged off them for ages. Patsy threw him out in the end.'

'She was good at that.'

'Poor girl. She couldn't cope any longer. Besides, you know Tim. Always bringing home waifs and strays.'

'Someone *he* could look after.'

'I suppose so. This one, this *man*, we don't *know* he's the Butler, how long had he been away? Out of England?'

'He didn't say.'

'You don't seem to have got much out of him, do you?'

No answer. I said, 'Oh, I'm sorry. Horrible for you. Why didn't you ring straight away?'

'At four in the morning? That *would* have pleased Clio!'

My turn to say nothing. There is a telephone by the bed that Helen and I used to share. We would shout at each other, in rage and in fear. 'Why don't you bloody answer it?' 'How can I? It's on your side of the bed.' 'Change places, you're welcome!' 'All *right*!' 'That's a joke. J.O.K.E. Oh, God, I've got to work in the morning!' 'So? I don't work, I suppose?'

This is the cue for Helen to get up, collect the novel she is reading, the glasses she has just acquired and dislikes being seen wearing, her watch, and the apple she always takes to bed with her in case she gets hungry. Clutching these objects to her chest, she stumps past the end of the bed and stands over me, cheeks puffed out and glowing with outrage, or with relief at having found something to be outraged about. Recumbent, in the weaker position, I try on a smile, but she tosses her head like an insolent child, or an angry pony. I fling back the duvet, grab my own collection of night toys; book, radio, ear plugs, handkerchief, digestive tablets. The radio is plugged into a transformer that is plugged into the mains; I drop book, ear plugs, handkerchief and digestive tablets as I crouch to unplug it, remembering as I do so that there is no suitably placed electric point on the left side of the bed, which is why I sleep on the right, because I like to listen to the radio when I can't sleep, nothing to do with wanting or not wanting to answer the telephone. It would be unwise, however, to point this out to her; the energy boiling up inside her, brightening her eyes and flushing her face, needs the outlet of this silly game. If I were to stop playing it she would explode, probably hit me. So I unplug my radio, pick up my things, smile at her charmingly – knowing that this will further enrage her – and stand back like a gentleman so that she can arrange her possessions on my bedside table and get into my side of the bed. She frowns as she does so, disconcerted by my good behaviour, and watches me as I take rather more time to make my arrangements, tugging the lower sheet smooth, putting everything tidy, rolling up the wires around my now useless ear plugs and tucking them neatly into the handle of my short wave transistor. I don't look at her as I adjust the lamp she had turned on when the telephone rang. (It had been a wrong number, which is why we had both got so angry.) I sigh a little as I settle myself, the sigh of the tired and virtuous man, hoping to be allowed to rest finally. We lie side by side, our limbs carefully segregated. Then she says, 'I forgot about the thing for your radio. You won't be able to hear the news in the morning.' 'Oh, never mind, there's quite a lot left of the night. Plenty of time for musical chairs or any other jollity that takes your fancy.' 'Musical beds,' she says dolefully, and begins to cry. I put out an arm and she snuggles up, tears warm on my bare shoulder. 'Try and sleep, love, it'll be all right, he'll be all right.'

When was this particular scene? After he had taken that overdose? Or simply in the early days of the motorbike?

It bothered me that I couldn't remember. Pin down the exact

occasion. There had been so many anxious nights. At least we had been together.

I said, 'If anything like this happens again, anything, any time, ring me at once.'

She said, doubtfully, 'I don't want to upset Clio. I don't want to make things difficult. For either of you.'

'If you rang in the night she wouldn't hear. She sleeps like the dead.' Why not say that Clio slept in the spare room? Loyalty? Pride? I said, 'Why did he ring you and not me? Who gave him your number?'

'I can't tell you that, can I? I should have been quicker off the mark. Got his name. What confused me, I think, just before the phone rang, I'd been dreaming. Tim had rung the surgery bell and I'd gone down, and seen him through the glass of the door, not his face, just his head, the shape of his shoulders. He was wearing that red-leather jacket and he had his crash helmet on. But of course it wasn't the surgery bell. It was the telephone ringing . . .'

I thought – the telephone is a terrible instrument. I should be able to put my arms round her. I said, 'Maybe that's a good omen.' I heard my voice, falsely jocular.

In response, hers was glacial. 'I'll try and think of it that way. You've given up on him, haven't you?'

'You know that's not true.'

'Oh, I don't *blame* you! Thirty thousand young adult males disappear every year. The people they leave behind go on living. You're making a better job of it than I am, that's all.'

'Do you think I don't dream about him? I see him just about everywhere, every time I see a young man on a motorbike . . . Oh, God, *Helen*! This is the most awful bloody mess, if we hadn't . . .'

She groaned. 'Don't be *pathetic*! At least you've got someone, there's someone to share it with. I know *that*'s my fault, my fault absolutely, but you needn't rub it in, moaning, getting moral *credit* for suffering.'

She sounded a great deal more cheerful. Bawling me out had always had a healthy effect on her. (After a good row, as after sex, she always fell sweetly asleep, like a baby.)

She said, 'There's no point, is there? You can't keep at fever pitch all the time. You've got your work, I've got mine. I don't know why he went, where he's gone, why he didn't tell anyone. It's not like him. I know there was that time he went off to Brighton but he was with Mike, and he thought that Mike's mother knew. But maybe it's something like that, he's told someone, thought they'd tell us, maybe he's written a letter and it's got lost . . .'

'Or he's forgotten to post it.' This was more likely, but still unconvincing. I said, 'Maybe we should ask Patsy. I know she hasn't heard from him, but she may know where the Butler is. If it was him, on the telephone, he may have heard something . . .'

'Only this stupid rumour . . .' Her voice faded, then came back robustly, 'Look, my lad, if Tim was dead, I would *know*. In my *guts*. That's the thing to hang on to. You hang on to it, too.'

'Yes. I'll try . . .'

'I think I'll tell the police all the same. That this is the story that's going about, that a friend of his told me. It might give them a bit of a prod. They've got him on their computer, but that's a fat lot of good, as I tell them, if no one ever bothers to look at it. Henry says the trouble is they're not really interested. Young men have their reasons for leaving home, it's not a crime. Henry says we ought to try the Salvation Army.'

'Bugger Henry! Why must he always . . .'

'Think of something *we* haven't thought of? He's trying to help. He says the Army have a good record on this sort of thing.

You never give him any credit! He really is worried, and sorry for us. He thinks how *he*'d feel if it was one of his children. And he says it's made him re-think his own situation. What a mess it might be if Joyce should ever find out about Elaine. Though maybe he was moving towards the end of that, anyway. Running out of steam.'

'You mean, he's decided to put a stop to his little junket? Because our son has . . .'

'Don't sound so incredulous! It isn't so simple, nothing ever is. It's just brought Henry up short, that's all, made him *think*. That everything you do has its consequences, like throwing a stone in a pond and the ripples . . .'

I said, 'I am delighted that Henry has made up his mind to face up to his family responsibilities. I hope he doesn't take it out on Joyce. But if he's making a connection between our divorce and Tim's disappearance, then I think it's pretty outrageous. Unfair to you. It's certainly not a connection I've made. I don't blame you.'

She giggled. 'Pompous! Henry doesn't blame me, either. Or you, for that matter. He says that mad people – sorry, what he actually said was *neurotic* – have to live with the mess and muddle other people make of their lives just like anyone else. It's just that it's made him think rather more clearly about his own mess and muddle. Is that so wicked?'

'And you call *me* pompous! No, of course it's not *wicked*. What fascinates me about your dear brother is the way he turns everything to his own personal *use*. Even other people's misfortunes. It's quite a talent, even an art, you might say. The house next door catches fire, the first thing Henry would do is increase his insurance.'

'He would call the fire brigade. Rescue the cat. Oh, you've always been mean to him!'

'You've been fairly sharp yourself! Eye on the main chance. Calculating Henry. Always the first to arrive at any official party, the last to leave, hanging about, making sure of a word with all the right people, the Chairman, the Minister. The traditional method of advancement for the mediocrities was what you once called it.'

She said, 'He's my brother!'

'So that entitles you to be rude about him?'

'No. I'm entitled to criticise him because I love him. If you did, if you were even remotely fond of him, you could say what you liked. Within reason. And just now, if you want to know, I'm regretting every nasty name I've ever called him. He's being *wonderful* to me. Really *kind* and *considerate*. He's the only person I can turn to, knowing he'll help if he possibly can and that he won't try to trip me up, start some silly quarrel . . . I should have rung him, not you . . .'

I said, 'Don't cry. Darling Helen, don't cry . . .'

But she had put the telephone down.

I saw Barnaby from the other side of the road; Mrs Lodge (Fiona Lodge, expensive, middle-aged daily nanny) holding his hand, instructing him, I was glad to see, in his road drill; look left, right, left again. His face was tense with his eagerness to perform this important duty correctly, his absurdly large satchel dangling from one small, hunched shoulder, his legs white and spindly beneath his new, scarlet blazer, his new, grey, uniform shorts. He looked up and saw me and at once one foot was over the edge of the kerb, hand jerked free, wildly waving. Sensible Fiona Lodge (money well spent!) caught him by the back of his blazer, yanked him back as the Post Office van, driven by a grinning lunatic, swerved round the corner. I thought, *white legs, the boy falling out of the sky*, and ran across the pedestrian crossing, heart in mouth, reassuringly smiling.

He said, reproachfully, 'You shouldn't run over the road, it isn't safe, Daddy.'

'Daddy knows that,' Fiona Lodge said. 'Naughty Daddy.'

She smiled at me archly, baring exceptionally even and ugly false teeth. I smiled back, forgiving the archness, the teeth, because she had saved him. 'Yes,' I said, 'naughty Daddy. I'm sorry, darling.'

Fiona Lodge said, 'He didn't want to go to school till he'd seen you.'

He tugged at her hand. He said, 'My Daddy calls me darling because he loves me.' And beamed at me proudly.

Adults smile to conceal anxiety, fear. Or simply out of moral fatigue. I smiled appeasingly at Clio (dressed and eating her muesli breakfast) as I told her why Helen had telephoned. She smiled back with nervous contrition. She said she hoped Helen didn't know she'd been 'silly'. I forced myself to smile understandingly, tenderly. Helen must have guessed, obviously; otherwise I would hardly have rung her back from a call box. 'You could have said that the line was bad, that you couldn't hear properly.' Her wistful tone was deliberately childish. I laughed and it seemed to ease her constraint. She pushed her glasses up on her nose and smiled, still with caution, but a little more naturally.

She said, 'I suppose I feel threatened. She's stronger than I am. I don't mean just prettier, I can cope with that. It's her being unhappy that beats me.'

I pretended not to understand. 'She's hardly chosen to be!'

'There you are! That's what I mean! You jump in at once to defend her. Even though I wasn't attacking her, you treat me as if I were some sort of *enemy*. I know it's awful for her. But she's not the only person it's awful for.'

'She's his mother.'

'You're his father! It's awful for you. It's even quite awful for me. I was the last person who saw him. I didn't do anything wrong, or say anything, but I know you think that I must have done. You've kept on and on, *asking*. You want to be able to blame me. If I hadn't been here, if you hadn't married me . . .'

'It's myself that I blame.'

'So you push *me* away? I'm on your side, but you don't want me to be, you don't want me near you, you don't want to make love to me . . .'

'Can't,' I said. 'I'm sorry. You shouldn't have married an old man.'

She hesitated – wondering, perhaps, if I might be speaking the truth, that it was normal for impotence to overtake a man in his forties? Then said, resentfully, 'You just can't bear to touch me. You only married me because of Barnaby, and because you were miserable. Now you want to be alone in your misery.'

There was enough truth in this to depress me. I said, to divert us both, 'If I've questioned you about Tim, about that last afternoon, it's only because I keep hoping for something, some sort of clue, something he said that didn't seem odd to you at the time, not worth remembering.'

'Like what? I've tried to tell you everything. It was all so *ordinary*. I made him some coffee. He went up to his room and stayed there a bit, he came down with some books and I found him a plastic bag because the one he had was torn. I asked him if he wanted to stay for supper, and he said he might, if you came home soon, but you didn't, you were later than you'd said you'd be. He hung around for a bit and then said he'd better be going. But I've told you all that.'

'I know. I'm sorry.'

'I did think, I wondered if he was still upset about Patsy, but he didn't seem upset, just a bit quiet, a bit quieter even than usual.'

'A good quiet or a bad quiet?'

How could I expect her to know the difference?

'Not *bad*. Just as if he was trying to work something out. That's not quite it. As if he thought he ought to make up his mind about something and didn't really want to, not yet.' She looked at me accusingly. 'I know what you're going to say. If I thought there was something wrong, why didn't I ask him? I didn't think he wanted that kind of hassle. He's had enough of that, where is he staying, where is he going, as if he couldn't look after himself. Enough *spies* in his life!'

I hoped he hadn't felt that. 'So he just said goodbye?'

'He said, *Look after Dad for me*.' She flushed. 'I wasn't going to tell you that. You don't want me to look after you.'

She got up suddenly and rather clumsily, banging her hip on the corner of the table. She took her bowl to the dishwasher. I watched her while she put in the powder, closed the door, turned the switch. She seemed to be concentrating on this simple activity. A little girl playing house.

I wondered if there was anything else she had omitted to tell me. I said, 'You do look after me. I don't deserve it.'

She stayed where she was, looking out of the window. The dishwasher had started its cycle; something clattered inside it; water thumped in and the clattering stopped. I got up reluctantly and put my hand on her shoulder. She turned to me with a faint moan and buried her face in my chest, locking her arms round my waist. I braced myself against the expected physical shrinking, but it didn't come. I felt nothing. At least that was a lesser kind of betrayal. I said, 'I don't mean to hurt you.'

She murmured, against my chest, 'If it isn't Tim. If you're fed up with me because of Barnaby, I really will try to look after him better. We don't need a nanny. If you'd tell her to go, then I'd know that you trusted me, even if you can't love me.'

'But I do love you,' I said. 'Silly one.' I pushed her away and put my hands either side of her face. 'You don't really want to get rid of Fiona?'

'You mean you don't want to. You don't want to risk leaving me alone with him.'

'It would be silly to get rid of her just to prove something. There's a lot of things you can do that you couldn't do if you had to look after him all the time. You wouldn't be so free to go to the Health Club for one thing. Nor so free to help me! And when George puts the pictures on show, he'll want an extra pair of hands at the gallery.'

Her round, upturned face, framed by my fingers, was sullen. 'What you're still saying is, you don't trust me.'

I didn't want to answer that, so I kissed her. She had very full, moist lips. Like rotten fruit – the image came into my mind, unbidden, unwanted. I kissed the tip of her nose and pushed her gently away. She said, 'It'll be all right, won't it? You do love me a little?'

'Do you really think that I don't?'

Her forehead creased. 'No. It's just – oh, you *know*.'

I felt very tired. I said, 'It's nothing you've done, or haven't done. It's a straight physical thing.' Inspiration seized me. 'It happens sometimes, off and on, when I'm working. As if I needed to channel my energy, what there is of it. And I don't seem to have too much to spare at the moment.'

I widened my eyes with rueful amusement. She said solemnly, suddenly dismayingly humble, 'I'm sorry, I didn't think. I should have thought, shouldn't I? I don't know, of course, I'm not a creative person, but I suppose it's something like the last stretch when you're running, like having to gather up all you've got, to push yourself to the absolute limit.'

I nodded gravely. 'Maybe. I don't know. I'm not exactly athletic.'

She said eagerly, 'If I could help, I think I'd feel better. Not so useless, anyway. Though I suppose that's a bit selfish, too. What I really mean is, I want to be with you. But I could read to you while you worked. Not if it annoyed you. I'd stop whenever you wanted . . .'

All I wanted just then, a fever of need, was to climb the stairs to the top of the house and the peace of my work room. I would have agreed to almost anything to achieve it.

'Bloody women!' George said.

I had thought Elaine was ill when I arrived at the gallery. Silent, unsmiling, white-faced, she had barely acknowledged me. She had given George a bad time all weekend, it seemed; angry outbursts of tears for no obvious reason, slamming doors, sulking. 'Tragedy queening,' George called it. 'Some man, I imagine. Christ, I could break his bloody neck. Not that she's told me and I don't ask, you know. Though I suppose she might have told Clio?' I shook my head, shrugged my shoulders. 'Oh, well,' he said, resigned. 'I suppose she'll get over it. He can't have been exactly suitable, or she'd have produced him. Not that I'm all that anxious to lose her to some stalwart young stud. Although there were moments, these last forty-eight hours, when I'd have been happy to hand her over to just about anyone. Any passing street cleaner. Dear God! It's the first time I've found myself missing Lily, found myself thinking, that girl needs a mother! I tell you, my friend, you're bloody lucky not to have daughters.'

Elaine was not the main target for his chauvinist fury. The pictures, brought down from Norfolk that morning, had been crated, on Ned's mother's insistence, by a local carpenter. George said, 'I wanted to send my man, you know, but this stupid bitch – Lord knows what she thought I was up to, some fearful skulduggery, or just trying to do her down, charge her extra. All that bloody fuss with Securicor, and she goes and hires this bodger for the sake of a few quid.'

Although without packing or padding, five of the crates were good enough; no harm done to the pictures except a few chips off the frames. The sixth crate had been made a fraction too small; the picture forced in, actually breaking the top and one side of the frame, and fastened down with two-inch nails that had scratched the surface of the painting in a couple of places. Unfortunately for George's emotional temperature, this was the first crate he had opened. 'I thought I was going to have a stroke. Blood pressure going up through the roof as I opened the others. That's something I don't want to go through again, enough for one lifetime. Thank Christ it's just this one. Recoverable. Though one of those nails could have gone through the canvas. Dear God, when I think of it! Hell on earth! Half a million quid, or whatever . . .'

'I think it's a copy,' I said.

His jaw dropped. This is not a cliché. His mouth fell open as if a hinge had suddenly broken. '*What*? Which . . .'

'The one you've got on the easel.'

He swivelled round and marched smartly up to it. I knew there would be no more swearing and bluster. After a longish silence he said, 'Who are you thinking of? Zoffany? Hayman?'

I said, 'If you were a used-car dealer you'd at least know the difference between a Ford and a Cadillac. No. It isn't contemporary. Quite a lot later, a couple of hundred years. I'd say, nineteen-fifties.' He turned and looked at me; dark eyes sharp as pins in his smooth-skinned, oval face, his bald pate glossy under the light, his short arms sticking out at an odd and somehow despairing angle from his short, egg-shaped body. He looked like a child's drawing of Humpty Dumpty. I said, 'Of course, it's just my opinion.'

He gave a short, high-pitched squeak of exasperation. 'Don't be a fool.'

'It's the idiom. Now I see it, of course, there are other things. It's a bit blandly painted. But there was something about the woman's face that bothered me all along. I thought it was a family resemblance with the brother, not much of one, the kind of thing you only catch now and then. But then I wasn't sure of that, either. I couldn't tell from the transparencies and the photographs, not to be certain. Now I think what I'd spotted was something different.'

Humpty Dumpty looked baleful. I thought, I am putting this badly. I had thought I had caught a rare flash of likeness between my aunt and my mother but my interest in this small discovery had obscured what had really seized my attention. The sudden look of scorn on my mother's face had reminded me, not of Maud, but the Duchess.

I said, 'It's that Egyptian look women had in the fifties. Long eyes curved up a bit at the corners. Elizabeth Taylor. My mother's older, but I can show you photographs, if you like, the same look, the same period.'

He said, thoughtfully, 'I agree, you'd expect more surface deterioration. More cracking and blistering. A good many of his things were restored in his lifetime. But the provenance is good. Well, better than most. It isn't part of the original collection. Orwell's father bought it in the fifties, from Cattleman in New York. Cattleman got it from Dubois, in Paris . . .'

'That doesn't . . .'

'Hang on a minute. There's something else. There was actually some sort of doubt when it arrived in the States. I don't remember the details, exactly, but Dubois had set a low value on it and the American Customs got suspicious and thought he was pulling a fast one to avoid import duty. There was a lot of that sort of thing going on then, as you know. I forget what Cattleman's arguments were, I never knew him, only that he had a pretty sound reputation, but the upshot was, Customs brought up their big guns, decided the picture was genuine and fined Cattleman, oh, I don't know, some exemplary sum, a fairly punishing number of dollars, anyway, which he presumably wouldn't have paid if he'd thought it was fake.'

I said, 'Oh, come on, George, don't be innocent. Look at it another way. Cattleman pays his fine, gets the picture, a receipt for his money, a document setting out why he had paid it. As good an authentication as any dealer might hope for. All he needed was a customer who had faith in the judgement of the New York Customs.'

George sighed.

I said, 'It's an old trick. There was that "Titus" – about the same time, perhaps a bit earlier. That man in Florence who commissioned a copy, got the painter to cover the signature with tempora, add his own, and then wrote anonymously to say he suspected that this picture was being smuggled in. All the customs had to do was clean off the copyist's signature – and behold, an Old Master! The Florentine's chum in New York got fined fifteen thousand dollars, and well worth it, I daresay he thought, as he trotted off to the auction.'

'Ah,' George said. 'But that was a Rembrandt!'

He looked pleased with himself, as if he had produced some clinching argument.

'Worth more, you mean? Worth the risk? I don't know Dubois or Cattleman, before my time as well as yours, but there are sliding scales, what's worth how much and to whom, and maybe they were less grand as cheats go, or less greedy. Or maybe they'd heard the Titus story and thought they'd try it on, too.'

Suddenly I thought – with some hilarity – of my father. I said, exhilarated, 'Look, no one could have accused Cattleman of fraud, whatever he did. All he had to do was pay up or not, accept what Customs said, or disagree with them, in which case they could have impounded the picture, or sent it back to France. I don't know what they do in these cases. But there was no evidence, was there, of any kind of conspiracy? With Dubois, I mean.'

George shook his head. He was looking more solidly egg-shaped than ever, and very glum.

I said, 'So Cattleman was in the clear either way.'

'Technically, if that's how you want to look at it. So are we. This picture will go to the States with the documentation from the US Customs as part of its history. I happen to think that documentation is entirely correct.' He smiled suddenly. 'The daft thing might be, from your point of view, that this is the only picture National Heritage are being sticky about. The National Gallery is buying the Gainsborough and I thought that part of the deal was that they wouldn't quibble about the export licences for the others. It's time they raised the limit, actually, eight thousand is ludicrous nowadays, for referral. It's not been refused, mind, still in the pipeline I gather, but such a fine example is the kind of signal I'm getting. As you say, such unusually good condition.'

I said, 'I agree. Very comic.'

'It doesn't worry you, though?'

'You know what I think. As long as it's not locked up in some basement or bank vault. I don't care if it's an original or a copy as long as it's worth looking at. And this is a very good copy.'

George said, very flatly, not looking at me, 'You can't prove it, can you?'

I decided to put him out of his misery. 'No one can. You can have it examined, X-rayed, stick pins in it, analyse the pigments, all those games. All you have in the end is someone's opinion.'

He said, rather more cheerfully, 'And yours has to be a bit tentative, doesn't it? After all, this is only the second or third time you've had a good look at it. And you've always had a bee in your bonnet about fashions in faces.'

'It's one of the clues I find useful, yes. But I'm only a painter, as your friend Hermione Orwell would say.'

He giggled. 'Did she really say that? Cor, stone the crows! What a bloody cheek!'

I was reminded how much I liked him. George had always respected the workman. The primary producer. I said, 'On the other hand, if you were to drop a delicate hint in a suitable quarter that there might be a tiny doubt, not on your part, perish the thought, nor a proper, expert opinion. Just the tiniest of frowns on the brow of a workaday painter.'

He said, with alarm, 'Dear God, it would have to be bloody delicate.'

'That's up to you. That's your province, isn't it? Creating the right thoughts in the client's mind. But I wouldn't think it would be very difficult. Those people don't like to get egg on their faces.'

I thought – Elaine would have been a good emissary. A word casually dropped into the pillow talk. A pity that Henry had chosen this particular moment to discover his scruples. Very risible.

George said, 'What are you grinning for?'

'Nothing. Just the whole scene. Or, if you like, just this painting. It's a good piece of work, you know it, I know it. But it's not what we talk about, is it?'

He said, irritably, 'What we're talking about is your bread and butter as well as mine. And I'm not flogging pictures to widows and orphans, exactly. No one is going to be scraping up their last pitiful pennies. I think it's genuine. There's a bit of Correggio about it and that's right for its date. Alleged date. What do you want me to do?'

'Get a new crate made to put it in and don't charge the Dowager. And let's look at the others.'

He gave one of his little squeals, more amused this time than exasperated. 'Can you manage to keep your artistic conscience under wraps while we do it?'

We put the pictures up in turn on one easel and my copies on another beside them. Neither of us spoke while we did this. I found I was sweating. From time to time, George glanced at me, raised his eyebrows, nodded briefly. This taciturn display was not meant to punish me. Whatever reservations George might have about the artistic conscience, he was tender about artistic sensibilities. Nearly two years' work. He would think about that. At last he said, in a shyly affected drawl, 'Not half bad . . .' And then, more easily, 'If you're as pleased as I am, then you'll be celebrating.'

The relief was enormous. I said, 'Oh, I'm a sedulous ape. There's a bit more work, obviously. I'd like to dampen up here and there to bring up the background colour, make sure I've matched it. I didn't dare do that sort of thing in Norfolk, the Dowager would have thrown a fit. And I wasn't sure about the girl in *Harvesters*. The pentimento round the head. It looks as if he started to paint a bonnet. I couldn't tell from the transparencies.'

He said, in an abstracted tone, 'It looks fine to me. I shouldn't have said that about celebrating. Bloody clumsy. I take it you haven't heard anything?'

'All the police say is that he's on the computer. I don't think they're exactly exerting themselves.'

'Too busy tearing about in their panda cars. Whatever happened to Constable Plod? I'm bloody *sorry*. Bloody hell for you!'

'You get used to anything. It's a kind of limbo.' A tunnel of darkness; a dark hole in a mountain; Tim vanishing into it; a dwindling shadow. I laughed to disguise the sudden constriction of anguish that tightened my throat. 'Work helps, as always. I try to think of him as having joined the Foreign Legion.'

'Tim? That's an imaginative leap, isn't it? More likely, some kind of commune.' He put my *Harvesters* up on one easel, the original on the other. He stepped back. He said, '*Very* nice.'

'I think I got the greens right. I had to be a bit cautious. He gets his effects with such a simple build-up, not more than two layers of paint in this one. You can even see the grey ground here and there. So you can't be heavy handed or you muck it up. That's why I've been a bit spare. It's my second go, actually. I wasn't free enough, first time round.'

He nodded slowly, not really interested, I thought, though politely trying to be. He said, 'Apparently the first wife had *Harvesters* cleaned at the Hamilton Kerr. Bit of luck. Her mother-in-law would probably have got her charlady to go over it with a scrubbing brush. I think this is the one we'll put on show, get your copy framed to match. That's the one you'd like, isn't it? You haven't put your mark on it yet, have you? I don't mean your signature.'

He gave me a quick, wicked grin. This was something he had never mentioned before. My sly, private pleasure. He said, 'I thought there was something missing.'

'Do you mind?'

'Why should it bother me? Gives you a bit of fun, the toiler's revenge, doesn't interfere with my profit, and it'll make a nice subject for the art critics fifty years on. Mind you, they'll have to be a bit sharper eyed than most of those around at the moment. How long is it going to take you to finish?'

'Ten days. Two weeks.'

'Two weeks, then. I'll get the framer in to measure up, notices sent out, invitations, and so on. Clear the shop, I thought, just the two *Harvesters* at one end. I'd like to show them all but the bloody insurance is crippling. I've had to turn the place into Fort Knox as it is. Guard on all night, new locks, Christ knows what they'd ask if we had them all out of the stock room together.' He huffed and puffed a bit, inflating his shiny, plump cheeks, miming a despair that was partly a joke, partly genuine. 'I shan't be sorry when it's over, I tell you. Not that I'm not grateful to your good Aunt Maud for putting me in the way of it, don't think that. It's just that it's out of my league a bit. I like a quiet life. Maybe it's Elaine that's hyped me up, really. Of course I'm sorry for the girl but it's been the last straw. I suppose I knew there was someone, she always checked timing when I was going away, when I'd be back, and so on, and, Dear God, why shouldn't she have a lover? She's not a child, no reason why she should tell me, none of my bloody *business*.'

He was smarting painfully, all the same. He had been so smugly in love with his adoring and beautiful daughter. Had he fallen out of love with her now? Or was he simply castigating himself for his folly? I had never seen him so agitated. He said, with a whistling sigh, 'It's all that wild and windy emotion concentrated on *themselves* that I can't stand in young women. Well, in all women, come to that. Though they get a bit less gusty as they get older.'

I said, 'That's not been my experience.'

'No? Well you ought to know.' He shook his head, looking sheepish. 'I'd forgotten Clio was the same age for the moment. Putting my bloody foot in it once again!'

'It's hormones, that's what they'll tell you,' I said. 'I'm sorry about Elaine. It was probably some married man who didn't want his wife to know, which would explain why Elaine didn't tell you. And now he's given the poor lass the push. She's probably well rid of him. But I daresay the process was painful.'

This seemed to be all I could decently say. I turned my attention to the two *Harvesters*. In the original picture the girl in the foreground wore a broad-brimmed black hat; there was a buff-coloured bonnet still faintly visible behind it. I wondered why the painter had changed his mind; perhaps he had thought that the hat made a bolder statement, gave the figure more prominence, an added dignity to this farm labourer's wife, or perhaps older daughter, taking a rest from the wearisome business of tossing sheaves of corn up to the cart behind her, to look out at the world with a calm, interested, direct gaze. She had wide-set, hazel eyes and a blunt-featured, soft prettiness, but it was her expression that had attracted me.

I said, 'She looks as if she wouldn't put up with that sort of nonsense. Or nonsense of any kind.'

George laughed. 'That girl? No. Very sure of herself, isn't she? Very confident without being pushy or getting above herself. Quite *modern* in a way. You've caught that look exactly.'

That was all he had noticed.

I wasn't surprised. People see what they expect to see. I had sharpened the features a little, narrowed the chin and the nose, deepened the green tint in the hazel eyes. But although it was Helen who looked out at me from my picture, George still saw a peasant girl with loose, reddish curls, tumbling over her bare neck and kerchief.

George is not unpercipient. Perhaps it was the fact that they both had the same straight, level look that had deceived him. The harvester, painted in the year of the French Revolution, and the dentist painted nearly two hundred years later, shared the same air of confidence, of unchallenging boldness, as if they both knew where they stood, morally, socially.

I had puzzled over this likeness. It may have been simply accident; similar personalities. Or they had both been born into settled societies. A far cry from eighteenth-century Suffolk to the commuter's town in Surrey where Helen had been brought up, but the assumptions of continuity, of the improbability of change, may have been much the same.

Certainly, Helen's parents, when I first met them, appeared to believe that now the war (which had briefly interfered with their comfort) was over, life would reassume its accustomed and agreeable rhythms. Helen's father was a solicitor; her mother had a private income left to her by a godfather. Between them they paid for a large (and hideous) mock Tudor house, a maid, a gardener, regular continental holidays, subscriptions to the golf club, the upkeep of the tennis court and the swimming pool. They made donations to various respectable charities and to the Conservative Party. As far as they were concerned, this was not only life as it should be but life as it *was*; if anyone had told them that other people lived differently, they would have agreed that this might be so, but since these other people could be no one they knew it was hardly relevant. I had expected them to object to our marriage, and, indeed, Helen said they had been shocked when she told them she was going to marry 'a painter'. Their relief when they found that she didn't mean a house painter and decorator smoothed our passage thereafter; long enough, anyway, for them to accept a son-in-law who was not quite what they'd hoped for – a lawyer, a doctor, or even an estate agent or another dentist would have been preferable – with politeness if not enthusiasm.

Their social horizons were too limited for them to be snobbish in any sophisticated way. Their recreations were confined to golf and bridge; the books in their house were for display only, a uniform edition of Dickens, Who's Who, the Concise Oxford Dictionary; and they had no pictures other than enlarged and tinted photographs of Helen and Henry at different stages of growth. As a result they couldn't place me in any context with which they were familiar. A novelist, a poet, a sculptor, or (for slightly different reasons) a senior diplomat or a university professor, would have presented the same kind of difficulty.

Naturally, the appearance of my immediate family at the wedding confused them further. Though they made a gallant effort to conceal it, they were obviously puzzled by the difference between my aunt's and my mother's vowel sounds, and more noticeably alarmed by my grandmother and grandfather, even though my grandfather kept his teeth in, and Razor Annie, under Maud's vigilant eye, restricted her alcohol intake and toned down her coarse cackle. At the end of a very long speech extolling his daughter's many successes, on the tennis court, in her ballet class, at the expensive private school he had sent her to, and predicting further huge success for her in her 'chosen profession', my father-in-law expressed his regret that he had not had the opportunity to 'meet the groom's family before the wedding'. He managed to convey both an apology for having introduced these unsuitable guests to his friends and relations, and a heartfelt reassurance that he, for one, never wished to see them again.

Nor did he. Except when Tim was born, when they and my mother appeared at the same time at the hospital, my parents-in-law kept themselves to themselves in their leafy outer suburb. I didn't dislike them, nor, I think, did they dislike me; in fact, I became quite fond of my mother-in-law who displayed, on occasion, an unexpectedly theatrical imagination. She rarely came to London – 'so noisy and dirty and crowded'. When we bought our house in the inner city and she came to visit us, she always arrived in a state of excited exhaustion like a nervous traveller in some foreign and dangerous country, full of dramatic tales of her adventurous journey; trains stopping for hours between stations in the Underground, buses that broke down or turned out, by some stroke of malevolent fate, to be going in the wrong direction, strange men, drunk or importunate, who had accosted her, taxi drivers who insisted on taking her an unnecessarily long way around and whom she had courageously refused to tip even though she had been afraid they might respond violently. 'It's amazing I got here,' she would say, bravely smiling. 'Still, never mind, I'm here now, that's the important thing, isn't it?'

My father-in-law was less engaging. He was agreeable enough on his home ground, when we visited the Tudor mansion in Surrey. But he disliked London even more than his wife, refusing to drive in the city, and when he came with her, although less perturbed by the perils of public transport than she was, the discomforts he had endured tanked up his indignation so that he entered the house on a great gust of anger, eager to vent his unattractive opinions about black immigration, dirty streets, the idleness of the working classes and the folly of a Welfare State that provided an easy living for scroungers. Once Tim was born these fulminating energies were concentrated on his grandson's education. When we told him that we planned to send him to the local primary school, he was incredulous. 'In this sort of area? Might as well throw him on the scrap heap and be done with it.' And, with a twist of his own peculiar logic, 'If he was a girl it might be a bit different, but it's important that a boy should mix with the right sort of people.'

'Ossified,' Helen said. 'Fixed. A bit scared too, I suppose, everything changing so fast, they don't like it. Why should they? They liked the world as it was, as they think it still ought to be, everything in its proper place, tidy and comfortable. Very bourgeois and dull, I suppose you would call it.'

Excusing them, wanting me to like them as she (so much more easily, being more open and loving than I was, by nature) liked my aunt and my mother, she was also explaining herself. She was nothing like her parents, not as timidly conventional as her mother, nor as belligerently conventional as her father. But their rigidity had given her a solid frame to develop within. She had always known where she was with them, how they would respond, react, what they would say and do, and by the time she was old enough to dismiss this predictability as 'dull and bourgeois' she had benefited from the ordered sense of security that it had given her. She didn't need to 'rebel' – she was safely grown, her own woman. She had shed their beliefs but kept the confidence with which she had seen that they held them. If they had such a firm right to their opinions, she had the same right to hers. It had made her independent, direct, and, where her own feelings and behaviour were concerned, more or less fearless.

*

'What rubbish you talk,' Helen says, in my mind. 'You do get yourself in a twist when you try to *think*, don't you? Okay, so my parents were a bit stupid and boring. They brought me up in the suburbs. I had tennis lessons and piano lessons and ballet classes. My father always fetched me from parties, and my mother was proud because I was the head girl of my school. I belonged to the Girl Guides. What's all that got to do with you and me *now*? You're just making use of it to *prove* something, aren't you?'

Well, perhaps. But all I was consciously trying to do when I started what Helen so rudely refers to as 'thinking', was simply to copy a picture of a girl helping with the harvest on a Suffolk farm. And I cannot copy a portrait (or copy one to my own satisfaction) unless I can understand, or to some extent feel myself into, the person in front of me. Most painters will paint something of themselves into a portrait; their own eyes, the set of their lips. If you have a receding jaw line, it is difficult to allow a more determined jaw line to your sitter! I try to avoid that kind of vain compulsion when I am copying; it seems to betray the original painter. But I need, all the same, to see something I can get a hold of. It isn't anything tangible; not feature, or colouring, youth or age. Even the most familiar face, even your own, is more than the shape of a nose, the tilt of a head. (This is why people are often surprised by their own photographs; that glossy, fixed image is not how they see themselves, not their true self that is constantly shifting and changing.) Painting a face, you can get every line right, light and shade, form and marking – and still something is missing! 'Spirit' or 'soul', perhaps, but those words carry too sentimental a burden nowadays, for most people. Expression? Character? A bit flat and dull for all the shades of meaning I am fumbling after.

Recognition is better. The excitement of *seeing* and *knowing*, at once, instantly . . .

There is a kind of magic at work here that is hard to pin down. The best I can do is to say that if I had caught that long dead farmer's daughter 'exactly' – George's kind word, not mine – it was only because I thought I had seen Helen in her, in her straight level look. And it was that 'look' George had noticed. Not a 'likeness', but a shout in my mind that said *Helen* to me.

When Helen came, I was working on the picture in George's stock room; a long, narrow, low-ceilinged attic with a window in the sloping roof. The attic was badly insulated and very cold. My hands were playing up; my fingers aching from holding the brushes. Helen said, 'Shall I rub them for you? God, you must *freeze* up here. Doesn't George have an electric fire you can plug in somewhere?'

She had cancelled her appointments for the morning and 'dropped in' to see me. It was just after one o'clock. Elaine had gone to meet Clio at her Health Club for lunch. George had let Helen in and chatted to her for a while before he locked up the shop and followed his daughter. Now Helen sat on the framers' trestle table that I had pushed against the wall to make room to move round the easels. She was wearing knee-length leather boots and a dark blue, full-skirted coat with gilt fastenings that looked vaguely naval; her face, framed by its high-standing collar, was pinched and pale.

I said, 'I think there may be a fan heater somewhere, behind the crates probably, but I don't want to stop and look for it in case my joints seize up altogether. You'd better not try to look either. You'll get that lovely coat filthy. It's new, isn't it? Have you been on a shopping spree?'

She pulled a wry face. I said, 'Don't look so guilty. It's not my business any longer how you spend your money. Never was, really, you earned it, after all. And you look very nice. Are the boots new as well?'

She made a low, angry, growling sound. I said, 'If you'd like coffee, I think Elaine's got a kettle and a jar of Instant down in the office.'

'I don't want any coffee. I'm interrupting the great work. I'm sorry.'

'You don't sound it!' What she sounded was miserable. There was nothing I could do about it. But there should have been. I should have been able to help her. We should be helping each other. I said, 'I'm sorry. If I wasn't so busy . . .'

She muttered, 'It's just that I felt, oh, so awful this morning. It's so cold. It was so cold in the night. And the wind and the rain . . .'

I said, 'I expect he's found somewhere warm and dry. He could always look after himself physically. He . . .'

'And so I go out and buy myself new boots, a new coat, a kind of stupid *diversion*. The depressing thing is, it worked in a way, made me feel more human, just for an hour or so.'

'That's better than nothing. Would you like to go out to lunch?'

'Oh, God I'm not *hungry*. And you don't want . . .'

'We could go to a pub. That wouldn't take so long. Whisky would warm you up.'

She shook her head. Then got off the table. Her green eyes were like chips of glass. She said, with a sudden, involuntary shiver, 'I'm all right. Well, as all right as you are, I suppose. It's the waiting. Not *knowing*. Well, you know that, too. Have you nearly finished the pictures? George sent me an invitation to this junket he's having. I suppose it would be better if I didn't come. I don't know that I want to come, either. Though it seems a stupid thing to be fussing about one way or the other.'

I said, 'Try not to bat about. The only thing is to go on doing what there is to do. What has to be done. Hang on if you possibly can. Well, there isn't any alternative. No point in being morbid. They'll find him. Or he'll turn up . . .'

'Do you believe that?'

'Absolutely.'

She looked at me. I looked back at her. I had put my brushes and palette down. I held out my hands. She took off her gloves and held my fingers in hers, massaging, pulling them. Her hands are large for a woman; bony and competent. I said, 'You're hurting me.'

'Sorry. Your knuckles are very swollen. It might help if you soaked them. Hot salt water.' She let go my hands and tucked her own under her armpits, hugging herself. 'I wish we could have got him to go back to that doctor.'

Which one? There had been so many. None of them had been able to help him. Or he had not let them. He had pretended he was keeping his appointments, lied to us, thrown his pills away. I said, 'There's no point in going over and over. You know we did try.'

'And that's all that mattered? That we tried?'

'No. What matters is that we failed. Or have failed up to now. When he comes back we'll have to try again. Until then all we can do is to wait. We can't make any plans. It will depend on him, how he is, what's been happening to him.'

She said, 'When he comes back.' She spoke with no particular intonation. And then, with a visible determined, bright effort, 'I suppose now I'm here you might as well show me what you've been up to.'

She looked at the paintings. She didn't recognise herself. She said that I must have worked very hard. Although I thought this was meant to be praise, I was stung. I said, 'Is that all?'

She shrugged her shoulders, very deliberately. 'They seem all right to me. What else can I say? You wouldn't presume to say whether I'd made a good or bad set of false teeth. And I wouldn't ask you. Or expect you to know.'

'I'd know if you'd made them for me!'

She didn't smile. She was stiff with resentment. Or disappointment. 'You never wanted my opinion. Ever.'

'That isn't true.'

'Oh, you used to *ask*. But only to put me down. Whatever I said was bound to be wrong. If I'd said you were a genius, you'd have jeered at me.'

'I expect I'd have thought you were making fun of me.'

'There you are!'

She did smile now, in a mock regretful but satisfied fashion. I thought – my old sparring partner! And found myself suddenly aching with loss.

At least we could try to be friendly. But I had nothing to offer her. To placate her, amuse her, I told her that the only picture that had not yet got its export licence was one that I suspected might not be genuine. I said, 'George thinks I'm wrong, of course. Well, I may be. It's just that the story behind it sounded familiar.'

I told her the *Titus* story. She listened, watching me gravely. I said, longing for some response from her, 'There is something immensely pleasing to a certain type of mind in discovering some foolproof piece of hokum. It's just the sort of thing my father might have got up to.'

She said, 'You ought to give up on that, don't you think?' Her expression remained grave, but her eyes had a faint, smiling malice.

She had been to see my grandmother. Razor Annie had smiled at her without recognition. 'I know your face, dear, but my memory's terrible for names nowadays.' Helen had sat beside her, held her hand. She had taken photographs with her, as we always did, of my mother and me, Maud and Timothy. She found my grandmother's spectacles. 'Your daughters, darling. Your grandson.' On Razor Annie's good days, photographs helped her to connect a few scattered fragments of memory, a small victory that usually pleased her. Today seemed a bad day; she regarded the pictures with a puzzled air, then grew agitated. Helen was about to remove them and substitute the small presents she had brought with her, a lace handkerchief, peppermint creams, a miniature bottle of brandy, when the old woman's eyes suddenly lit in the way they still did occasionally, as if a dusty electric light had been switched on in a long-empty room. 'Oh, *him*,' she had said, stabbing my picture with a thin, crippled finger, 'I know *him* all right.' 'Your grandson,' Helen had prompted and Razor Annie's eyes had grown brighter still. 'D'you think I don't know, you daft ha'porth?' 'What about his father?' Helen had asked, seizing on this moment of clarity, and the old eyes had flashed anger. 'Who said anything about him? I didn't, did I?' And then, retreating, fretfully whining, 'Who are you, anyway, you meddling girl.'

Helen waited.

I said, 'Is that all? For God's sake, she's *senile*.'

'That's not an absolute condition.'

'No. At least she sent you about your business. I don't understand what you're trying to *do*! You don't care who my father was, do you? Any more than I do. Oh, I might have done once, if I hadn't been given this acceptable myth, but I don't any longer. Don't tell me you're interested in the truth for its own sake. Who are you trying to hurt? Me, or my mother?'

'It's not that. You know I wouldn't want to hurt Maisie. Or

you, either, or not about this, you know that really. It's just, I can't seem to get *through* to you . . .'

She had gone very white; a greenish tinge, as if the colour had leaked from her eyes to her skin. She gabbled, 'I can't bear it, the way that you lie to yourself. Most of us lie to ourselves some of the time but you lie to yourself all of the time. About me, about your poor mother – you even lie to yourself about Tim, that's what I really can't stand . . .'

She didn't look in the least like the Suffolk farm girl. She was lost and bewildered and vulnerable.

She was in my arms. She moaned, into my shoulder, 'Henry says, if he's dead, it's the end of a tragedy, not the beginning, that's how we must look at it; oh, he's probably right, oh, I know he's right, but I can't, I really can't *bear* it. I don't mean I can't bear it for me. I can't bear it for *him* . . .'

This was what she had come to say. Had needed to share with me. Had been gathering her courage to tell me while she went shopping. And I had rebuffed her.

I held her and rocked her. I murmured, 'Hush, hush, my love. My poor baby.' I thought – Damn and blast Henry, why did he have to? Why bloody well *now* when I'm frantic to finish? And – This is a terrible moment, all I should be thinking of is my son and his mother. Worse still – at least, it seemed to me worse – at the same time I was responding to the familiar, soft warmth of my weeping ex-wife pressed against me, calculating, wondering if there was anywhere we could do it, rejecting the unsteady trestle table, the floor covered with shavings, considering the expensive new coat. There wasn't time, anyway. I shifted my arm cautiously, raised my wrist behind Helen's back and looked at my watch. Elaine would be back in ten, fifteen minutes; Clio probably with her; George had said something about asking her if she could help get things ready, help Elaine clear the shop. Had he meant today? Oh God, why hadn't I *listened*?

I loosened my arms and removed myself just a little, conscious of my erection. Helen stepped back – either understanding, or misinterpreting this delicacy as another rebuff. She said, with a shuddering sigh, 'Oh, we've been such fools, my lad, haven't we?' She smiled at me, damply and ruefully and accepted the slightly grubby handkerchief that I offered her. She blew her nose, pulled a face. She said, '*Yuck*, smells of turps, well, you always did, didn't you?' And, with another smile, still a bit shaky but with an impish gleam to it, 'I always did find it erotic. Pity I didn't cancel my afternoon surgery too, isn't it?'

I shall never understand Helen. Perhaps I am too close to her. Perhaps you never understand anyone. I suppose it is common to be aware that your own mind is full of shadowy confusions, contradictory impulses, irrational (or inconveniently physical) urges, and still assume that other people swim in a clear pool of certainties, mean exactly what they say, want from you no more than they seem to be asking. There is daily life to be lived, work to be done, other people to think of, bills to pay. Time is too short. Always.

I said to Helen that afternoon, 'Are you sure you're all right?' And, as I had expected (meaning 'hoped' in this context), she nodded briskly, handed back my smelly rag of a handkerchief, opened her purse and (with merciful speed) put on fresh lipstick.

What she thought and felt as she left I can't tell you. What I felt was relief that she had gone before Clio appeared but this scurvy consideration, together with the shame and guilt that went with it, was a minor matter beside the new discovery that had suddenly seized my mind, taken it over. I had told myself that I had seen a reflection of Helen in the original harvesting girl, when in fact it had been the *other way round*! Oh, there was a connection between them, a kind of affinity. But I had made use of it to fix Helen in my mind as a gritty and independent personality about whom I did not have to worry because she was capable of looking after herself.

Perhaps she was. Perhaps she is. That is beside the point, really. As is the order in which you see each aspect of what is before you. All artists work crabwise, selectively; take what they want from their friends and relations, what they need at that moment, and leave what they don't. What matters is the interpretation, the execution: the painting, the poem, the novel. But it saddened me suddenly to see how I had used this curious, intuitive, often muddled process, to *thin Helen down*, diminish, dismiss her. (Even my thumbnail sketch of her parents, though true in its detail, is slanted towards this effect, over-simplified. Who would guess from it that her father was a dab hand at tapestry? Or that her mother, when she got Hodgkin's Disease, would die with tremendous, quiet courage and dignity?)

What was depressing me, I suppose, was the limits of art. A glimpse here, a glimpse there, a flash of blue water beneath the shifting ice floe, truth slipping away through the cracks. And, of course, my own failure. I cannot bear pain in people I love. The portrait of Tim, for example, the one that I painted for my mother's birthday, is not a bad likeness, if a bit derivative technically. My mother likes it. Or says that she likes it. But there is no *life* in it. There was a light about him that came from his pain. Although I could see the light, I couldn't bear the pain behind it, and so I couldn't paint it.

In the same way, I cannot bear to see his mother's suffering, see her as vulnerable. So I choose to see her as brave, direct, eager and strong. In my visual memory I see her walking towards the door of George's stock room that afternoon, shoulders back, head held high. Jaunty and gallant.

COLOPHON

Maud had parked her Porsche on a double-yellow line outside the gallery. 'Just keep an eye on it, will you, my duck?' she said to the woman security officer on the door. 'The wardens will have gone home by now but you can't trust the police in this area not to get up to mischief.' And, to me, not troubling to lower her rich, booming voice, 'You'd think that these people would dress to look a bit less conspicuous, wouldn't you? That white blouse and dark skirt! Like someone from the KGB. And she's so obviously *lurking*!'

Ned smiled an apology at the officer. Hand under Maud's elbow, he steered her away from the door. 'Intentional, don't you think? Meant as a warning that there are probably others, unobtrusively mingling.'

This seemed to amuse him. I said, 'It seems a bit overdone. But there's quite a crowd. I suppose . . .'

Maud said, 'I'm sorry we're late. The Council meeting dragged on. And the traffic is fearful. I drove as fast as I could . . .'

'Wrong way down a one-way street, two red lights,' Ned said feelingly.

He was craning his neck. I said, 'Your mother's here somewhere, Ned. I gather Polly's not coming. I'm sorry.'

'She couldn't really leave the baby. Not when the poor little chap's teething.' Maud answered for Ned. It sounded almost as if this had been her decision.

If it had been, Ned appeared happy about it. Suited him, probably; wife and child in the country; his dear old chum, his Egeria, in the city. It suited Maud, certainly; she looked in contented high spirits as she surveyed the room. She said, on a clear note of satisfaction, 'George has done you proud, hasn't he? Hung a lot of your pictures. Pushed the boat out.'

This was Maud's kind of party. Critics, diarists, gossip columnists, all the newspaper freeloaders; television presenters; representatives from the Arts Council, the British Council and, now Maud and Ned had arrived, from the Royal Society of Art and Literature; one or two peers, a few politicians. Maud hesitated briefly on the brink of this sea of delights, and then sailed in, Ned in tow (attached as by an invisible hawser), towards the ex-Minister for the Arts who was holding court at the far end of the gallery, his broad, solid back to the two *Harvesters*. As she weighed anchor beside him she glanced back at me.

I avoided her eye. I was looking for Clio.

She had said, looking at the guest list, 'I didn't know George was asking so many people. There won't be room for them to look at the pictures.' And Elaine had laughed at her. 'They don't come for *that*, you innocent child, they just come to talk to each other, get themselves noticed, advance their own careers, and swill as much booze as they can down their greedy gullets.'

This was before the party began. The security team had

checked the window locks, including the skylight upstairs, and were making tea in George's office. George and I had finished crating four of the pictures that were to be shipped to New York tomorrow (the Gainsborough had already gone to the National Gallery) and brought down the two *Harvesters*. Now we were setting them up on the easels.

Clio and Elaine had not looked at them yet. The waiters who were to serve the wine had not yet arrived. In the meantime, the girls were taking the glasses out of their cardboard boxes and arranging them on the table. There had been some discussion about how many were needed. Which was why Clio had picked up the guest list.

Two beautiful and busy girls in a long, empty room; Elaine in a red shift that clung to her breasts and her buttocks; Clio in a much more demure dress of plum-coloured velvet, with a cameo brooch pinned to its high neck. Elaine had helped her to choose the dress. I had given her the brooch this morning and she had worn it all day on her sweater, now on the dress. She kept touching it as if she were afraid she might lose it. She said, 'If you're right about all these people, Elaine, then I think it's disgustingly *rude*. But if they don't look at the pictures this evening, it'll be more because they're frightened of making fools of themselves. In case they can't tell which is which.'

George said, 'That's right, young Clio, you tell 'em. I bet you'll know, won't you?' And, to me, 'She's got a bloody good eye, you know. Come on a treat, hasn't she?'

It was then that I had felt the first, dull thud of apprehension; a real, physical twinge, behind my breast bone. About an hour had passed since. It seemed very much longer. I had seen Clio several times after the guests started arriving, and been pleased to see that she was moving among them with more assurance than I had expected, not fiddling with her brooch or pushing her glasses up on her nose all that often or, at least, not too nervously. I had thought – I am only feeling the natural anxiety one would feel for a child (or a much younger wife) on what was for her a new and alarming social occasion. I had caught her eye a couple of times; once when she was listening to Maud's 'very intelligent man on the *Guardian*', and once when she was getting a glass of Perrier water, carrying it carefully through the crush for the benefit of a reformed alcoholic who occasionally wrote for *Encounter*. Both times she smiled at me, chirpily, proudly. *Look how well I am managing*. But the last time I'd seen her was about twenty minutes ago.

She had been right in her estimate of how George's guests would react to the two pictures. No one had asked me which was the original, which the copy; most people had either eyed me a bit shiftily or pretended not to have noticed me. There had been a few open guessing games. The *Guardian* man had got it right; the *Encounter* man, wrong. One or two subtle souls had looked at my townscapes and then at the two *Harvesters* and nodded sagely. But the majority had regarded the pictures in a respectful silence and turned to the talk and the wine. The fact that the ex-Minister had stationed his considerable bulk in front of the easels had made it easier to avoid looking at what was on them.

I told myself that I wanted to find Clio to tell her how right she had been; how splendid it was that she had put it so straightly and simply; how much it had made me love her.

But I couldn't find her.

It is a disadvantage to be a short man at a party. You meet other short men in the street, on the buses, but at this kind of stand-up-and-shout celebration they are all about eight foot tall. A gap opened in front of me and I saw Elaine on the far side of the room, pinned against the wall by the long, ape-like arm of an extraordinarily elongated and willowy and very young man. She was smiling up at him in an animated and youthfully happy way; quite different from her usual sultry and sexy expression. Perhaps that was reserved for older men; Daddy, and Daddy's friends, middle-aged lovers. Picked someone her own age for once, I thought, as I plunged into the wall of backs in front of me. By the time I had squirmed my sweaty way through, she had gone.

Still no sign of Clio. Just about everyone else – most of the rest of my life, it seemed suddenly – was on stage here; appearing and disappearing in brief glimpses, vignettes, as the scrum surged and eddied. Over the shoulder of a woman in a man's pin-striped suit who had just accosted me as if she knew me (as indeed I knew her, even though at this precise moment I was unable to remember her name, what she did, or where I had met her before) I could see Elaine again, still with her young man, each of them with a full glass of champagne, apparently toasting each other. George's tonsured head bobbed up for a moment; a gleaming, pink egg against someone's dark jacket. Maud was merrily lecturing a pair of newspaper editors who seemed to be listening with flattering attention.

My mother, rather surprisingly, was deep in conversation with Ned's mother, the Dowager. They were the only two women in the room wearing hats. Hermione Orwell's venerable tweed was stuck about with feathers, presumably from some game bird or other. My mother's equally ancient (though with more than one owner in its long history) was a romantic Cavalier hat with a high brim and a white plume that looked a little threadbare in places. Perhaps it was their headgear that had brought them together. I wondered what they were talking about; if either of them had 'placed' the other's accent. It was entirely possible, I thought, that the Dowager might think my mother was foreign.

The woman in the city gent's suit was talking about the Otto Dix exhibition she had just seen in Munich. I caught the words 'pitiless realism'. Over her shoulder, I smiled at my mother, who had looked up and seen me looking at her. She lifted her glass to me, and the Dowager, her attention caught by this gesture, winked at me flirtatiously. My mother mouthed something, her white plume dipping and swaying as she nodded at someone behind me. I turned, and saw Helen.

I thought – Drowning men are supposed to see their lives flash in front of their eyes.

Helen was smiling at the woman who had been telling me what she thought about Otto Dix. I said, 'Hallo, darling, do you know . . .?' Helen waited, but only a second. She said, '*Ismelda*! How lovely to see you.' She leaned forward and kissed the air by the woman's cheek. Her own face had darkened with suppressed laughter.

Ismelda? Hardly a common name. But I was no wiser. I smiled ingratiatingly. Helen said, 'We're just going, actually. We only dropped in for a minute. It all seems to be very successful.'

She had a man with her. For a hallucinatory flash I thought he was Ted. He had the same open air, boyish look. But he was only a Ted look-alike. Though not Australian. He had a slow, pleasant, slightly plummy drawl. East Coast American? He said, 'She wanted to wish you luck. Although of course she doesn't exactly feel up to a party. Well, you understand that, of course.'

He stood beside her protectively. A proprietor, I thought. A natural owner. Very tall, very masculine. Utterly reliable – and with a thick head of hair. I suppose she must have introduced us. I know we shook hands because I remember being conscious that my fingers were unpleasantly sticky. I said – God knows why, the drink talking, probably – 'Look after her.'

During this exchange, Ismelda had produced a long, thin, black cigar and fitted it into an ebony holder. She hadn't lit it. She had a face like a cat; something about the nose and the eyes. She watched Helen go. She said, 'I haven't seen your wife for a long time. In fact, I can't quite remember . . .'

'Helen,' I said. 'Only she isn't . . .'

'Oh, I know her *name*. It's just when and where!' She shook her head, laughing. She was wearing large, gold hoop earrings that didn't quite go with the rest of her gear. 'Don't *tell* me,' she said, 'it'll come back to me in a minute.'

'You need another drink,' I said, and took her empty glass from her.

Clio must be somewhere. Had she seen Helen? Perhaps she was hiding. I patrolled the room, a glass in each hand. The party was thinning out rapidly. George, standing by the door, was shaking hands vigorously. He was looking pleased with himself. Maud was circling the room like a royal personage making her gracious farewells. She was wearing a fussily feminine blouse; above its foaming torrent of lace, her short neck was patchily red from the heat and the wine. Ned was shepherding his mother, my mother, a solicitous hand under each arm. Of course, he and Maud were taking them both out to dinner. The two mothers-in-law. Was that how they would see themselves? Surely Maud was not going to force them into the uncomfortable back seat of her Porsche? Perhaps Ned had ordered a taxi.

The Dowager fluttered her mauve eyelids at me. 'Such *fun*. Your mother and I have been getting on famously.'

My mother smiled at me happily. A cheerful, respectable, charming middle-aged lady. I wondered how she had been entertaining the Dowager. Which lurid option? The tale of Aunt Dot and her rapist lover? Or how Razor Annie, when she grew senile, had chased her round the house with a carving knife?

I said, smiling back at her, 'You look beautiful, darling. That's a very fine hat.'

'Give my love to Clio,' she said as I kissed her. 'Say goodbye for me.'

I filled Ismelda's glass and my own. I couldn't see her, so I emptied both, fairly quickly. The waiters were clearing up, swilling dregs into a plastic bucket; I grabbed a couple of bottles that were still almost full and carried them into the office for safety. Elaine and her willowy young man were embracing behind the door. He was holding her chastely, hands on her shoulder blades; lower down, her red shift clung to the sweet, rounded curves of her bottom.

I put one of the bottles on the desk and retreated. The waiters were leaving. George was locking the door. I said, 'That was a good party.'

'Well, you cast your bread on the waters. We may have sold four of your pictures. We'll know tomorrow. Two possibles, one probable, and one certain. That woman . . .' He clicked his fingers, conjuring her name out of the air. 'Ismelda. Ismelda something . . .'

'I talked to her. She . . .'

'Grant,' he said. 'Ismelda Grant. Dear God, terrible the way names slip away. She buys for a couple of pension funds. Advises, anyway.' He chuckled. 'Nice to know you're becoming an asset. Is there anything left in that bottle?'

The waiters had removed the glasses. I filled mine (or it may have been Ismelda's) and gave it to him. He said, 'Thanks very much. Are the girls about?'

'Elaine is. I haven't seen Clio . . .'

'She did her stuff, didn't she? Been a great help this last week or so, I hope we haven't put too much on her. Quite an ordeal for her, I fancy, this evening. I wondered . . .'

I said, 'Did the export licence come through?'

'Yes. Didn't I tell you? Bloody lucky. What I was going to say was, I wondered, Elaine's off to Rome in a fortnight's time, would Clio like to go with her? Bit of a thank you for all her hard work and she might enjoy it, a bit of a jolly, a bit educational. Elaine's got to do a bit of work, see a few people, but that might interest Clio, too. D'you understand this new legislation? I bloody don't. A new twist just about every day. A bloody *picture frame* got a notification last month at the antiques fair in Florence!'

This was George's way of relaxing after this kind of working party. He rambled on, getting more and more heated about the Italian heritage laws that had proliferated lately. Works of art that were 'of national interest' had to be given a notification by the *Belle Arti* authorities, and, once notified, could not be exported (or exhibited, or even sent to a restorer) without their permission. As a result, prices were tumbling. The absurdity of this situation, according to George, was that a lot of the pressure for notification came from rich collectors who wanted to be certain that what they were buying was genuine. 'Too busy making and keeping their money to learn how to spend it themselves,' George grumbled. 'But they're just cutting off their noses to spite their faces. It's so bloody stupid. Notification ruins the re-sale value, ruins the trade, who the hell benefits?'

'The collectors, if they buy their stuff cheaper.'

'Only if they want to keep it.'

'At one time that was why people bought pictures. Because they liked them and wanted to keep them. That was why old Orwell bought his, originally. That's how it should be. You know what I think.'

'It's the *principle*,' George said indignantly. 'The freedom of the market!'

'Sacred,' I said. 'Absolutely. George, I really must . . .'

'Clio asked me to give you this,' Elaine said. The young man was behind her. They were both smiling dreamily. She gave me Clio's blue canvas running bag. The velvet dress was inside it.

It had been raining. Cars swished on wet roads, gutters tinkled, the air was soft and still heavy with moisture. I wound down the window of the van and drove slowly. I had had too much to drink. And I was looking for Clio.

As I had looked these past weeks, was still looking, hope against hope, against reason, for Tim. Along the Embankment, under old railway arches, in the city graveyards, in Soho . . .

Once you start looking, the army of the lost multiplies. Every turn holds them, each derelict for a heart-stopping moment familiar, but then, immediately, shadowy, nameless; huddled in doorways, raking through dustbins, shuffling down side streets; bundles of old clothes stretched out on benches, on tomb stones, over the warm air of gratings. I thought – I would make a bonfire of Rembrandts to warm them. If I had the option. And, what will happen to him if I die? If Helen dies? *When* we die? This is the abiding fear. No future for him. Or, at least, *this* is his future; cold city pavements, dark alleys.

It didn't bear thinking of. But I thought, all the same.

*

I caught Clio up on the Pentonville Road. She was running out of the shadow of St Pancras into the lights of King's Cross, skirting a group of skinheads playing football with an old can in the paved precinct. She was running well, easily, with no sign of exhaustion; loping freely and gracefully.

I slowed in the gutter behind her. The tyres of the van thumped the kerb. I called, 'Clio!'

She glanced over her shoulder, stopped briefly, running on the spot, and then turned and bolted, speeding up, sprinting. I blew my horn and she shook her head without changing pace. I shot a red light and slowed again, crawling along. Level with her, I stuck my head out of the window. 'Clio. Don't be silly. Get in.'

She stopped. I was barely moving. She crashed her hand down on the roof of the van. A fearsome, metallic explosion. My ears seemed to be bursting. I shouted, 'For Christ's sake . . .'

'*Leave me alone*.'

I laughed. I opened the door. 'Come *on*, silly girl. You've run miles. Long enough.'

I was out of the van. The ground lurched beneath me. I staggered and caught at her arm. A little way up the hill three people, a man and two women, were walking towards us. I said, still laughing foolishly, 'Darling, don't make a scene.' I was tugging her sweater; her arm felt like iron beneath it. She wrenched free with an angry gasp. Then said, in a loud and desperate voice, 'Stop it, oh, *please*, just stop chasing after me.' It wasn't until she had gone, racing away up towards the Angel junction, that I realised my behaviour could have been misinterpreted.

The man was much bigger than I was. He shoved me in the chest, winding me, slamming me back against the side of the van. I slithered down. My jacket caught on the inside door handle and I felt it tear. One of the women said, 'Dirty bugger.'

I struggled to my feet and the man hit me; not all that hard, but I was off balance. This time I fell back into the van, sitting, more or less, on the floor. I said, 'For God's sake, look, this is ridiculous. That was my *wife*.'

'That's likely, isn't it?' the man said.

One of the women sniggered. 'Tell us another.'

They were standing over me, ringing me, but the man had stepped back a little. I decided that he didn't intend to hit me again. All the same, I stood up fairly cautiously, trying to look harmless, submissive. I said, 'I'm sorry, I know what it must have looked like . . .' I looked up the hill. But Clio had vanished.

The man said, 'Plenty of tarts round King's Cross, but she wasn't one, see? Just a kid, jogging.'

'She's not a kid. She's . . .'

'Oh, we heard you the first time. I'm not stopping to argue.'

I thought – I ought to be grateful to this excellent citizen. Haven't I always been frightened for Clio, running through the city at night? If I argue, insist on my innocence, he might be discouraged another time. Pass by on the other side.

He said, 'You leave decent girls alone, right? No more kerb crawling.'

I bowed my head meekly.

All the same, as I drove off the main road into a side street and stopped the car, I was seething. Damn that good Samaritan. Damn Clio! Surely she must have realised what was happening? Oh, probably not; she had flown up the hill, winged with anger because I had slighted her. I had been a fool not to have realised that unlike George (or Helen herself) Clio would have been quick to see what I'd done. Jealousy sharpens the eyes and, as

George had said, Clio's were sharp, anyway. I ought to have known she was bound to notice; prepared her, tried to explain. Of course, I had been busy, preoccupied. She would not accept that excuse. And why should she? She had tried so hard to support me, to overcome her shyness at the party, talking and listening to strangers, smiling, wearing her pretty dress, and this was her reward! Helen's face looking out at her. A public statement that I was still obsessed with my first wife. A public humiliation for Clio. She would have thought it deliberate.

Well, perhaps I could put it right. I had not meant to wound her. I should go home, abase myself, comfort her, make a joke of the foolish predicament she had left me in. I might even turn the tables a little by injecting an element of wry reproach into this little comedy. There was the rent in the jacket of my best suit. And no doubt a bruise or two, here and there . . .

But I was so tired. Or as George would say, so *bloody* tired. How often did he use that commonplace adjective correctly? How often did anyone? Bloody toothbrush. Bloody handkerchief. Bloody nose. I chanted these words aloud. What other suitable nouns could there be? My mind seemed to have come to a stop.

Tim had once tried to cut his wrists with a razor blade. He had just been discharged from hospital. Blood in the bathroom; a trail of spots on the landing carpet. He had sat on his bed, shamefaced, weakly smiling. Apologising. Not because he had frightened us, but because of his failure to finish the job he had so bravely started. Like me, he cannot bear pain.

I wanted to throw back my head and howl like a wolf. No one to hear in this empty street. I groaned and beat my head on the steering wheel.

The street wasn't empty. I hadn't heard the Panda car, nor seen its lights. The policeman had one hand on the roof of the van. 'You all right, sir?' His face, peering in, was close to mine. I tried to hold my drunkard's breath. I remembered someone telling me that the thing to do was to get out of the car. Apparently this was placatory; an act of submission. Like a puppy rolling over and exposing its belly.

The policeman had already opened the door. He said, 'Bit of trouble, back there on the Pentonville Road, wasn't there?'

'Oh, just ridiculous! A stupid misunderstanding.' I rolled my eyes, shook my head, attempting to convey an impression of helpless amusement. 'I was trying to pick my wife up. She runs. I mean, she's a runner. She was jogging home. I thought she'd had enough. I thought she was tired. She didn't agree with me. We had a bit of an argument. And of course it looked . . .'

He said, dubiously, 'I don't know about that. But you hit the kerb a couple of times, swerved out wide when you turned the corner. The cyclist came off his bike. Lucky no one was coming. No other vehicle.'

'I didn't see a cyclist!' I was righteously indignant. Bloody police! Too busy harassing innocent motorists to look for my missing son! Oh, no doubt it was easier! I said, 'If I had seen a cyclist, I'd have stopped. Naturally.'

He said, 'We observed the incident. There were two officers in the patrol car.'

I got out of the van. The Panda car was a few yards away, yellow lights winking. Another policeman was walking towards us. He was carrying something. I said, 'Is the cyclist hurt? Have you called an ambulance? I suppose you want my insurance, my licence?'

He said, 'If you would just blow in the bag, sir.'

I got home (on foot, the van hauled away to a car pound) just after midnight. Except for the histrionically barking dog that belonged to the basement flat in number twenty-two, the street was sleeping and quiet; closed down for the night. I thought – Who am I to complain about drunks?

Tim was sitting on the doorstep. His pale face gleamed like a white flower. He said, 'What's happened, Dad? You look terrible.'

'Nothing. Nothing that matters. Oh, Tim. Oh, God, *Tim*.'

I wanted to hit him. Shake him until his teeth rattled. I wanted to embrace him, hold him, never let go. I was angry, and jubilant. I said, 'Tim, how could you? Oh, God. Oh, thank God.'

Tears were running down his face. He stood up and flung himself at me. We hung on to each other and swayed together in an awkward dance. He felt so thin, a bundle of bones, his breath reeked, his clothes stank.

He started to cough. I let him go and he doubled up, his whole body jumping and jerking with each paroxysm. I said, automatically, 'You ought to stop smoking,' and he gave a wild hoot of laughter. I said, 'Forgive me, that was stupid. How long have you been here? Your mother . . .'

He coughed a bit more, hawked and spat. He wiped his mouth with his sleeve. He said, 'Sorry. Disgusting. I've had a bit of a cold. I've seen Mum. We tried to ring you but the line was busy, so I just came. The house was dark and I couldn't see the van. So I waited.'

I had opened the door. There was no light in the hall. I went down the stairs to the kitchen. The fluorescent tube flickered and buzzed when I turned it on. The telephone receiver was dangling loose against the wall. I said, 'Clio sometimes leaves the phone off the hook when she goes to bed. But you've got a key. Or you could have rung the bell.'

He came slowly into the kitchen. 'I didn't want to scare Barnaby. And I gave my key to Clio.'

She hadn't told me. Why hadn't she told me?

I said, 'In any case you shouldn't have sat out there on the step, not with that dreadful cough, catch your death in this weather.'

'Maybe that's what I hoped.'

He said this with one of his 'silly' smiles. Sly, or shy; half wanting, half not wanting, to be taken seriously. I said, 'I was stuck at the police station. I got picked up for excess alcohol. I could have been there all night. You should have stayed with Mum. I could have waited till morning. Just another night. It's been long enough, for Christ's sake!'

'Oh, Dad,' he said. 'Don't go *on*.'

A familiar, agonised cry. And he looked agonised. He was a dirty grey colour; there was hardly any flesh on his face; his cheeks were sucked in, his jaw jutted. He fished a squashed pack of cigarettes out of the pocket of his filthy red leather jacket. I grabbed a box of matches from beside the stove and lit his cigarette before he could get out his lighter. He smiled his gratitude, not for this gesture, but for the reason behind it. He inhaled deeply and started coughing again. When he could speak, he said, 'I couldn't stay with Mum. She's got someone there.' He glanced at me, hesitating. 'A *friend*,' he said, delicately. 'And she was angry anyway. Bawled me out.'

'You understand why, I hope?'

'Yes, Dad, I suppose so.' Eyes downcast. Very humble.

'Good. Well, forget that for a minute. I don't know that we've got any fatted calves in the cupboard, but you look as if you ought to eat something. And you could do with a bath.'

He said, 'I smell bad because my body is rotting.'

He spoke flatly and calmly; stating a fact that he believed absolutely.

No point in telling him it wasn't true. I had learned that

much. I said, as casually as I could, 'A bath won't do any harm, all the same. For my sake, if not yours. Fiona is in your room, she's staying the night because we weren't sure how late we'd be home this evening. You'll have to share my bed with me. So a bath, if you please.'

He trailed up the stairs after me; stripped off his clothes while I ran the bath and shook in pine essence. I tried not to look at his body, not because he appeared to be modest, or even self-conscious, but because it tore at my heart to see the ravages it had suffered. His buttocks and thighs were like an old man's; shrunken and withered. He sank under the green, scented water with a grunt of what I hoped might be pleasure, and then, as I began to gather his clothes, shot up with a look of alarm. I said, 'Okay, I'm only going to put them in the washing machine.' An incinerator would be a better place for them. He said, with real terror, 'Oh, no, Dad. *Please.*' I thought, what a fool I am! My son comes back, returns from the dead, and all I can think to do is put him in a bath, take his things away. I said, 'All right, I'll leave them. Only they do pong a bit. I'll find you something to sleep in.'

I don't wear pyjamas in bed in the ordinary way but I have a couple of pairs Helen bought for me years ago when we used to spend the odd weekend with her parents who would have been shocked by a son-in-law who slept naked. I found them after a bit of a search, crumpled up in a drawer, and got a clean towel out of the linen cupboard. The door of Barnaby's room, next to mine, stood ajar. Only the top of his head was visible under the duvet. His night light was on; I closed the door gently. There was no sound from the floor above, where Fiona and Clio were sleeping. I took the towel and pyjamas to the bathroom. He was sitting up, washing his hair. The green water was the colour of a muddy pond, thick and murky. I said, 'Rinse your head under the tap, not in the bath, there's a good boy.' I despised myself for speaking in this nannyish tone. I said, 'I'll get something to eat. I'm hungry, if you're not.'

I put eggs on to boil and rang Helen. A machine answered me. She was 'not available'. At the end of the recorded message and before the bleep I thought I heard a faint chuckle. A ghost of a laugh. Was that meant for me? I spoke to the machine in a light, amused tone. 'He's here, safe. Well, I suppose you knew that. Sleep well, my darling.'

I buttered toast, spread it thinly with Marmite the way that he liked it and poured a pint of milk into a beer mug. When I got upstairs he was in bed. His face was still grey, but a lighter shade, almost transparent. His dark hair clung to his scalp like wet seaweed. His eyes burned in his face. He shook his head at the eggs, drank some of the milk, ate half a slice of the Marmite toast. He reached for his red leather jacket on the floor by the bed and took out his cigarettes. I gave him a saucer. I said, 'I couldn't find an ashtray. Clio's put them all away somewhere.'

'Do you mind, Dad?'

I shook my head. He smoked, leaning back on the pillows, watching me warily. The tendons in his neck stood out, thick and knotted.

I said, 'No questions. You talk when you want to talk. Otherwise not. I'm tired. I expect you are. Do you think you can sleep? I might be able to find you a pill. Or some whisky.'

He shuddered as if I had offered him hemlock. I said, 'I'm going to clean my teeth. I'll be back in a minute.'

I cleaned the bath, mopped the floor. I thought, in this world I am a useful domestic animal, a provider, a father; that's all; I can't control anything; put anything right. I am only in charge when I work, in my other world. If he could paint – or write, or throw pots, make a table – could he extract order out of his chaos?

He was sleeping. Or seemed to be sleeping. I turned off the light by the bed, got in beside him. I thought, I shall never sleep.

He was weeping; little, stifled snorts and sobs. I looked at the illuminated dial of my watch. It was four o'clock. He was sitting on the floor, huddled up, jacket over his shoulders, head on his knees. The saucer beside him was overflowing with stubs. I got out of bed and knelt beside him. He said, coughing, 'Sorry, Dad. Sorry I woke you. I'm not used to beds.'

I said, 'You know we looked for you. Everyone. Mum and me. Aunt Maud. The police. Even Uncle Henry. How did you manage? You didn't have any money. I put money into your bank account. You didn't touch it.'

'I left my cheque book behind. I thought, if I left that, and my keys, then you'd know. I didn't mean to come back.'

I said, 'I think I'd like a cigarette.'

He shook one out of the packet and offered it. He took one himself. In the brief flare from his lighter his face was an assembly of pale geometric shapes. A La Tour painting. He said, 'Don't start smoking, Dad. It really is *bad* for you.'

'You should know.'

He laughed softly. 'Don't do what I do, do what I say.'

We smoked in silence. He finished his cigarette and lit another from the butt. He said, 'I thought, there are only two things to do. I could get my head together, get a job on an oil rig or something, amaze you. I got a lift on a lorry, halfway to Scotland. But I couldn't make it. I thought, I'd die on the hills, just get cold and die. Or in a wood somewhere, and the leaves would cover me. But then I thought, some poor kid might find me. I stole things out of fields. Cabbages. A farmer let me stay in his barn. I tried to help on the farm for a bit but my bones gave out. Started crumbling.'

He stubbed out his cigarette. He put his head on my shoulder. He said, 'Oh, Dad, I can't live, I can't die.'

'Don't tell your mother that.' I put my arms round him. I said, 'Come back to bed, darling.'

It was twenty minutes past eight when I woke again. He rolled over and muttered as I got out of bed, but settled at once. He felt hot; his hair was damp with sweat; he smelt of sweat and tobacco. I picked up my clothes and went into the bathroom. I ran a bath. When I had shaved, I got into it. My head ached. I had a confused sense of myself as a juggler, trying to keep a lot of coloured balls in the air. I should inform the police that my son had come home. I must speak to Helen. Tim had a fever. I must try to persuade him to see a doctor. I must find him clean clothes. I had to go to the car pound and redeem the van. I ought to speak to my solicitor and ask him to find out when I would have to go to court. Presumably I would lose my licence. In the meantime, while I was still on the road, I must go to the gallery and pick up the copies. I had told Ned that I would take them to Norfolk some time in the next couple of weeks. I had thought I might take Barnaby out of school for a couple of days, spend a night with Joyce. Now there was Tim to think of. And, of course, Clio . . .

I was too tired to face up to all this. Like Tim last night, I sank under the water.

Barnaby came in. He was wearing a black patch over his lazy eye. He said, 'Daddy, d'you know what? My *brother*'s come back, he's in your bed, I looked in and saw him. I went to tell Mummy but she's gone to work. She was a bit cross this morning. Fiona told me to clean my teeth. I've got to go to school in a minute. She says I've got to wear my patch. Do I have to?'

I thought – How children cope with life! One step at a time! I sat up in the bath and soaped myself vigorously. I said, 'Don't you like your patch? I think it makes you look like a bold, wicked pirate.'

I waited until Fiona came back. She had been a nurse, she understood about Tim; she would take his temperature, call the doctor if she thought it necessary, cook him breakfast, get him to ring his mother. Helen had been incoherent with joy when I spoke to her. It puzzled me that I felt so leaden. One son was safe, sleeping; the other had been persuaded to wear his black patch to school.

It took several dreary hours to get to the car pound, pick up the van, drive to the gallery. Since I would have to park on a yellow line, I rang George from the pound to give him an approximate time, tell him about Tim, ask him to tell Clio. I had been curt; put the receiver down on his astonished, ebullient quacking. When I arrived he was standing outside the shop. 'Dear God,' he said, 'you shouldn't have bothered, there was no hurry, I've got the others off my back, that's the main thing. The carrier was here earlier than I'd expected, first thing this morning. That was a fearful kerfuffle. But a relief all the same. Oh, it's bloody wonderful about Tim. Well, we knew he'd turn up sooner or later. What a night to choose, though. Clio hasn't stopped crying.'

There was a traffic warden patrolling the opposite pavement. Elaine stood by the van while we loaded the pictures. I had brought blankets to protect them. George said, 'Do you think the Dowager wants her crate back? If she does, you can tell her I'll send it cash on delivery. Give Helen my love.' There were tears in his eyes. He took out a huge, orange handkerchief and blew his nose. He said, 'You must feel bloody marvellous.'

I felt like a zombie. I had kissed Clio but I hadn't looked at her. While we loaded the van, she had got into the passenger seat. She was wearing a thick fisherman's sweater, jeans and running shoes. She said, as I started the engine, 'I wouldn't come with you but I ran all the way here this morning and I'm too tired to run back.'

This was too childish to be worth answering. I put my hand on her knee and she picked it up and held it briefly; then returned it to me like an unwelcome present. She said, looking out of the window, 'I'm terribly sorry.'

'Sorry?'

'I mean, I'm terribly glad about Tim, of course I am, you know that.'

'But?'

Her voice was nasal, husky with tears. 'Why didn't you *tell* me?'

'You were asleep last night when I got home and found him. He was sitting on the front step. He gave his keys to you when he left, apparently. Why didn't you tell me *that*?'

She said, defensively, 'You didn't ask! And I thought it would worry you. I thought you needed to get on with your work. But that's nothing to do with your not telling me he'd come back. If you didn't want to wake me up, you could have left a note on the kitchen table. I felt such a fool.'

'I assumed I'd see you this morning. I didn't know you'd go chasing off. Or that I wouldn't wake up until after you'd gone.'

'You could have rung me at the gallery. You knew I'd be there. Instead of leaving it for so long and then asking *George* to tell me. You should have told me *yourself*.'

'If you weren't so determined to feel aggrieved, you'd realise how silly you're being. I haven't rung my mother yet. Or Maud, either. And I came to the gallery as soon as I could, largely because of you. The pictures didn't matter. George could have kept them a day or two longer. He's not that short of space.'

'I expect you've spoken to Helen.'

'Yes. Very briefly, this morning. Tim went there last night and she tried to ring us, but you'd left the phone off the hook. I might have woken you, all the same, if you hadn't been behaving so stupidly.'

'Is that why you didn't tell me? To *punish* me?'

'You thought up a pretty smart punishment for me, as it turned out. Running off the way you did on the Pentonville Road. I got picked up by the police in the end. But I can't blame you for that, altogether.'

She said, 'I couldn't help it. I was so angry.'

'Because of the painting? I suppose I understand why. Though it seems a bit trivial and you ought to have known it. You claim to be interested in my work. This was just one of the tricks of the trade, making use of a resemblance, no deep-seated, psychological meaning.'

She said, in a small voice, 'I suppose I did know that, really.'

Her sudden meekness encouraged me. 'It's one of the ways I put my personal mark on a copy. The girl reminded me of Helen. A bit foxy. A bit cold.' I was only very mildly ashamed of this shameful deviousness. I added, 'A sort of signature.'

'Like writing *Pizzaria* very small on that Canaletto your mother's got?'

'There you are! George is right, you don't miss much, do you?'

She said, 'Please don't. Please don't flatter me. I can't bear it. After all that I've done . . .'

She sounded desperate now. Horrified. I said, 'Come on pet, it wasn't as dreadful as that. You were in a temper and I was drunk. That will have boring consequences but the cause was only partly your fault. You can make up for it by learning to drive, once I'm a convicted criminal!'

It struck me that I was feeling very much better. Maybe it was just that my hangover was lifting. Or the relief of Tim's reappearance had finally worked its way through to me. But the recognition that I had been half quarrelling with her in much the same way that I had always quarrelled with Helen had something to do with it. As if we were both adults, enjoying a verbal spat. Or adults playing at being children. Whichever it was, we were on the same *level*. I was not patronising her. This might be a good sign, or a bad sign. It was a change anyway.

We had stopped at a traffic light. She. was looking at me with an odd, veiled expression. Shocked? Bewildered? I put my hand on her knee again and this time she lifted it and held it to her cheek. I said, 'Look, this is a bit of a stormy time. But nothing that can't be sorted out, I promise you.' I didn't know how hard this promise would be to keep.

I didn't know for six days. She was unusually quiet, somewhat withdrawn, but this seemed to me understandable. Tim's return occupied us all. He was sick, if not dangerously so; both lungs were congested, and he was weak from lack of food and generally exhausted. He slept a good deal and when he was awake lay in front of the television. To be physically ill was something he could accept, and, indeed, retreated into, precluding any discussion of his mental state. He took his antibiotics without complaining that they were poisoning him, checked his own temperature, ate the small, frequent meals that the doctor advised and Clio prepared for him. She was gentle with him, thoughtful and protective. Helen came, and my mother, and Maud. Clio monitored these visits tactfully, producing coffee, tea, drinks, at regular intervals; leaving Helen and my mother alone with Tim for as long as she thought he could bear; staying in the room when Maud was there, fielding the questions my aunt thought it her duty to put, answering them for him with such sweet, sisterly concern that Maud could not be offended. She kissed my aunt and my mother when they arrived and departed; she was gravely polite to Helen.

I was proud of her. I thought she had grown up at last.

After breakfast on the seventh day, I went up to my work room. I hadn't looked at the copies since I had taken them out of the van, lugged them up the stairs. I was fairly sure there was nothing more to be done, I had finished the detailed work in the stock room with the originals in front of me, but I wanted to look at them with a fresh eye, assess them in a different way, not merely as imitations, as copies. This is always the test for me. Do they stand up on their own? Is there independent life in them?

On the whole, I was pleased. I am never quite satisfied; there is always temptation to be resisted; the urge not to leave well alone. I thought that I might re-work the right hand of the Suffolk Countess. There was something stiff about two of the fingers. They may have been stiff in the original, but I was not tied by that now, no reason why I should not improve on it. And I was agreeably surprised by my first copy of *Harvesters*. I had abandoned it as a rehearsal, but now I looked at it again it had more ease about it, more freedom, than I had remembered. That is often the case with a dry run. It was leaning against the wall. I removed the blanket from the second copy and put it on the easel. I looked at both pictures. I felt as if someone had hit me very hard on the head with a hammer.

Clio was in the doorway. Perhaps she had been there all the time, watching me. But she spoke breathlessly as if she had just run up the stairs, 'It's my fault, oh, it's my fault . . .'

I said, 'How the hell did it happen? Oh, for God's sake, don't start crying. This is *serious*.'

She was gulping and gasping. I said, 'Don't throw a fit, that won't mend anything. Take your time.'

She wailed, 'Oh, you'll *hate* me.'

'Stop that. Stop thinking about yourself, silly girl. That isn't important. How on earth . . .'

'The carrier people came early. George took them up to the stock room to get the other pictures. They were all ready. It was only this one that hadn't been crated. It was still in the shop, with your copy. They were both still on the easels. George had brought the crate down. He left the other man, the carpenter, to pack up the *Harvesters*.'

'And he packed the wrong one? For God's sake, George must have told him!'

She said, with sudden anger, 'They look alike, don't they? Except for that one thing. What you pretend is a signature. I didn't do anything.'

'George left you in charge, though?'

She was silent. I said, 'You mean you stood by, let this happen? Oh, God, it's incredible!'

'Elaine had been looking at them. I couldn't bear it. I thought she'd see what you'd done and laugh at me. You don't know Elaine, she can be really bitchy. And I was so miserable. I thought you must hate me. You hadn't come down to breakfast. I thought you were skulking upstairs, waiting until I'd gone. I didn't know about Tim. You hadn't told me.'

And I'd thought she'd grown up! I said, 'So this was your revenge, was it? You said to this man, this poor, innocent carpenter, something like, not *that* one, the *other*?'

'No, I didn't. I just didn't *stop* him.'

I didn't believe her. I said, 'George will kill you.' And thought – More to the point, this will ruin George!

She said, 'I'll tell him. If he wants to kill me, he can. I hope that he does, then the whole horrible thing will be over, I'll be glad to be dead and out of this nightmare, in fact, if he doesn't kill me, I'll kill *myself* . . .'

I crossed the room in two strides, closed the door that she had left slightly open, swung on my heel and hit her hard, on one cheek, then the other. I said, 'Don't you dare talk about suicide, you foul child, with that sad, sick boy downstairs, suffering.' I took her by the shoulders and shook her. She let her head roll submissively forward. She collapsed against me. When I lifted her chin to look into her face, her eyes were half closed; slits of light gleaming. She whispered, 'What can I do?'

I held her more gently. She hung limp from my hands. I felt a monster. A wife batterer. I walked her backwards, half dragging her, and sat her on the stool; the same stool on which she had sat, reading poetry. I said, 'Be still. Let me think.'

I thought – No one will believe this. There is no way that it can be made credible. Except, perhaps, to a psychiatrist; a specialist in deranged adolescents. It will mean the end of George's career as an honest dealer. Not that he was Simon pure. He had been ready enough to ignore my doubts about the Duchess.

Clio's forehead was pressed into my stomach. She said, in a stifled voice, 'It was all so quick. I was paralysed. I thought George would *know*. After all, the picture was still there, on the easel. I kept thinking, as soon as he notices, he'll do something, it isn't too late, he'll ring the carrier firm and they'll stop them somehow before they get to the airport. But he didn't notice. He might have done if you hadn't rung about Tim. Once you'd done that, nothing else seemed to matter.'

And perhaps nothing else did.

I said, 'Okay, okay, I see that. But, Clio, that was a *week* ago!'

The auction had been the day before yesterday. George had telephoned. Prices had been astronomical, in my view; much as expected in George's. A bit over his estimate for two of the pictures; a fraction less for the other three. Or maybe it was the other way round. In this fuddled moment I couldn't remember; all I was certain of, because it had amused me, was that the Suffolk Duchess had done (or 'performed' as George put it, in his singular jargon) the best of the lot. If he'd known about *Harvesters* only two days ago, he could have withdrawn it. Explanations, excuses, would have been embarrassing, hardly good for his reputation, but still not disastrous . . .

Clio looked up. Her cheeks were marked by my fingers. 'I couldn't,' she said. 'I just *couldn't*. I thought, perhaps I was wrong, perhaps it was just something I'd *wanted* to happen, just a sort of horrible dream . . . then, when you didn't look, didn't notice, I *prayed* . . . if I was good, nice to everyone, it would be all right somehow . . .'

I said, 'George could go to prison for fraud.'

Her glasses were misted. She took them off. She rubbed them with the tail of her shirt. She said, bleakly, hopelessly, 'Perhaps no one will notice . . .'

Obviously no one had so far. Five pictures had arrived in New York, expectations created by a lot of fuss and publicity; no reason for anyone to suspect that one of them (well, two of them, if you included the Duchess, but that was just my opinion) might not be all it was cracked up to be. And it was in no one's interest to be suspicious now the transactions were over. Unless. Unless. There is always the worst case to consider.

I found myself laughing. She put her glasses back on and frowned at me. I said, 'Oh, Clio, Clio, what have you done?'

Her brow slowly cleared. Presumably, if I was laughing, there was nothing so terrible. She was a child, still.

She said, eventually, pouting a little, not certain yet, testing the water, 'I did think, once or twice, *this is so stupid.* Why pay so much for that one, and not for yours? If they can't tell the difference?'

I said, 'That's too long an argument to go into, just at the moment.'

I used not to dream. Or, since we are told everyone dreams, I had never remembered on waking. Now I am plagued with, or visited by (sometimes it troubles me more than others), a continuing, or serial, dream.

There is a large, heavy-framed canvas in front of me; a vast, complex, changing landscape. Sometimes there is a bit of Claude about it, with poetic lighting effects, a mass of trees on one side, a smaller mass on the other; small buildings in the middle distance, a farm, or some cottages, and some small figures, the drama of their lives absorbed into the larger drama of Nature; in the far distance, a gleam of water, sun or moon shimmering on it. These are the calmer nights. More often, as I approach this picture (which appears to be hanging in a handsome, well-lit, but quite empty gallery), it is busier, more inhabited, more rapidly changing. There is always a city, with towers; a mountain, or one stark, jagged rock; a rushing, wild sky. The distant gleam has become a lake, or an inland sea, either dark and turbulent, or flat and steely with storm light. There has been a shipwreck; sometimes a masted boat on its side, sodden sails heavy and dragging; sometimes a pedal boat, unmanned and drifting. Something has happened but no one else in the picture takes notice; men are cutting corn, quarrelling, making love to their women; children are playing. At some point in this dream I am in the water (which is, by this time, black and heaving) trying to swim to the rescue of someone I can see is in trouble, not impossibly far away, but I am tired and their need is urgent. Occasionally it is Clio who is drowning, or Helen, but it is more often Barnaby, wearing his black patch and his school uniform, throwing up his arms, gasping and calling me. And always, invariably, as I strive to reach my small stepson, I see a white, flailing arm, somewhere to the side of me, on the extreme edge of my vision. Tim is fighting to keep afloat, he knows I will come for him when I can; he knows I have to rescue whoever it is I am making for and so he doesn't cry out; he struggles in silence, and I try to keep an eye on him, knowing, as I force myself onwards, away from him, that one day there won't be enough time, or I won't have enough energy, and the sea will have claimed him.

In the meantime, for the moment, he is still within distant reach. He keeps his pain to himself; bears it silently, gallantly. He watches television, he does the crossword, he walks to the corner shop to buy cigarettes. He bathes when someone reminds him. He plays Snap and Old Maid and Junior Scrabble with Barnaby. He visits his mother, whom I visit too, rather more frequently than I would wish Clio to know, but since George has begun to employ her on a regular basis, and sends her abroad on occasion, I can organise my opportunities rather more easily. George has great faith in Clio's judgement. He doesn't know how nearly she brought him down; nor how I have saved him from shame and disgrace, if not worse. If any suspicious busybody should cast a cold eye on my *Harvesters* (hanging in the Museum of European Art in Philadelphia) and decide to look into its provenance, visit the Orwell Collection, he will find a similar copy (dirtied up a bit, apparently earlier) and unless he is in the business of making trouble, in which case he will have a hard time of it against the army of 'experts' the Museum will rustle up to refute him, that will be that. A copy of a copy. Well, everyone has been made to look silly; everyone will want to keep quiet about it. And my mother is unlikely to boast about the very fine Stubbs that hangs in the spare bedroom of her house in Bow because she is only moderately pleased with it. She says it is a lovely picture of course, but to her mind not quite up to my usual.